Vicky,
I hop
enjoy
Christa Cha

The Sleepless Nanny

CHRISTA CHARTER

ONE

I wake with a start when the bottle drops from my hand and shatters on the nursery floor. I had fallen asleep in the rocking chair feeding Miranda her bottle. Miranda starts wailing and I panic when I see that it is already 20 minutes after noon. Jake gets out of school at 12:30 and I have to wrestle the baby into the Snugli, grab the stroller and diaper bag, and get to the preschool. From point A to point B isn't very far, but because of the crooked little streets in the West Village, I have to cross about 8 or 9 intersections.

I get to the school as quickly as possible, dragging all the paraphernalia along and trying not to jostle the baby awake. Of course, the elevator is out of order, and I have to climb the stairs. Four flights of stairs carrying thirty pounds of stuff is no picnic on a good day, and a good day this is not. I still feel a bit dazed from my unscheduled nap. If I could just get some sleep at night...

I sound like an asthmatic by the time I reach the preschool. I try to catch my breath while waiting to be buzzed in the door. Thinking I'll find Jake sitting all alone with his lunch box and a sulky look, I'm surprised to find all the usuals waiting - as usual - for class to let out. There are three or four mothers, but mostly nannies: black and Irish for the most part, and one American girl besides myself. I know them all, at least to say hello, which I do as I squeeze through the crammed hallway. I perch on the edge of a table to take some of the weight off my back. Miranda's not yet three months old, but she already weighs fifteen pounds.

1

Fiona says hello and comes over to sit next to me. At 26, she is the oldest of the young nannies I know. The little girl she takes care of is in Jake's class.

"Going to tumbling today?" she asks. Jake and Katy have a toddler tumbling class after school on Tuesdays. "Yep. For once it's not raining. I don't know why it always seems to rain on the days we have to haul our asses all the way downtown."

Fiona smiles, a little uncomfortable by my use of the A-word in front of mothers. It seems to me that the Irish girls have a little more respect for their employers than the rest of us. It may be the way they are raised, but then again, that green card situation might figure in, too.

Judy, one of the mothers, looks over and flashes a tight little smile. I hate her. Her son, Raymond, is the most obnoxious child I have ever known. Thankfully, Jake calls him "that bad kid" so I don't have to endure any playdates with them.

Judy now shoves her way through the crowd, and nearly trips over the diaper bag at my feet. She glares at me, then turns to Fiona with a phony smile.

"Fi-*oh*-na," she cries. "When are we going to get together? Raymond so wants to play with Katy. She's all he ever talks about at home. I might even say he's smitten!" She tosses her head and lets fly a fake giggle. She pulls Fiona aside to confer about a playdate. "Yes, well," she says, "it's got to be Wednesday, because Raymond has music Tuesdays and Thursdays and Art Appreciation on Fridays." She taps her left temple with a scarlet fingernail, thinking. "No," she mutters, "it can't be Monday. We're spending a long weekend in the country."

Fiona, who has been watching this display without any visible sign of disgust says, "Oh, I am sorry. Katy has ballet every other Wednesday." This is a lie. She truly looks sorry, too.

Judy runs a hand through her bobbed orange hairdo and pulls out her filofax. She starts flipping pages frantically and chewing her lips. "Every *other* Wednesday? Then you should be free next week! Right?"

Fiona shoots me a look of distress. I shake my head: don't you dare. Wednesdays are reserved for our play group, to which Raymond and his beast-mother are not invited, and in fact are not to even know of, since Judy could probably finagle her way in through my boss, or Fiona's. Thankfully, Judy discovers that precious Raymond has an IQ evaluation set for that day, so they make tentative plans for two weeks from Monday.

Raymond is not smitten with Katy. He hates everyone except his mother, whom he calls Judy. She thinks it's precocious. The only reason Judy is so desperate for this playdate, is that Katy's mother is Anne Bouchet, the high -profile editor of a fashion magazine who occasionally appears on television.

By the time the negotiations are complete, and Judy has returned to the cluster of mothers triumphantly waving her filofax, the classroom door has opened and a wave of three-year-olds spill out into the hallway, craning to see their mother or nanny in the crowd. That's one thing I love about kids. They go to school every morning, and still every afternoon they are so surprised and delighted that someone has come to pick them up.

Jake throws his arms open and runs towards me. Grabbing me around the legs, he plants a kiss on my kneecap. This is about as affectionate as he gets. Kisses on the face are very rare, and quite an honor.

"Where's Miranda?" he asks. Only he says it *Miwanda*.

"Right here, silly," I say. He grins as I crouch down so he can see his sister. The arrival of a baby was so sudden for him he worries that she may vanish just as abruptly. All that can be seen of Miss Miranda is the top of her head, which is round, warm, and quite bald. I can see her soft spot pulsing gently.

Jake sees it too, and points. "There's where you don't touch," he says very seriously.

"That's right. But you can give her a kiss." He declines, shaking his head. "You know what?" I tell him, "We have tumbling today!" He gasps and claps his hands. "And," I say, raising my eyebrows, "What comes after tumbling? On the way home?"

"Chocolate milk!"

"Right!" A couple of lingering mothers frown at this. I ignore them. Bitches. "Let's get your stuff together now. We don't want to be late. Should I help with your coat, or do you want to do it yourself?" This I learned very early: give him two choices, both of which get the coat on him. Fiona has gotten Katy buttoned up and they are edging for the door. After zipping up Jake, and adding a lunch box and finger-painting to my load, we head out, trying to catch up to Fiona.

The stairs are like an obstacle course. All the kids are screwing around: hopping down the stairs, yelling 'slow poke' at each other or sitting down every few steps to 'rest'. Jake has visions of chocolate milk in his head, and I get him down the stairs with little trouble.

We meet up with Fiona and Katy on the sidewalk. They look like they could be mother and daughter, with their dark hair and light green eyes. When I tell this to Fiona she groans and says she's never having kids of her own. She's had enough of other people's to last her a lifetime. She's been a nanny ever since coming to New York from Ireland five years ago.

Fiona buckles Katy into her stroller for the ride down to Murray street. It's a long way, but we figure we need the exercise. Katy sits with her little hands folded in her lap and patiently waits to be pushed to her class. I wonder if it's just her inborn temperament, or if she already knows that she's rich and privileged.

I go to open Jake's stroller and discover that I've left it upstairs. Miranda has started stirring, and if I don't get moving soon, she'll wake up and want to eat. I decide not to go back.

"Let's just go," I say. "Jake can walk." Jake's lower lip puts in an appearance, and I push it back in with my finger. "Don't worry, pal, you can make it. You're a big boy now. A big brother!" The magic words. We set off down Varick Street. Jake gives it the old college try for about half a block before he starts drooping and saying, "I'm lazy. I can't do it!" He grimaces, and looks longingly at Katy's stroller. He is so melodramatic, it's a struggle not to laugh at him sometimes. Fiona is looking at her watch.

I lift Jake up onto my shoulders and start walking again. We must look like a human totem pole with Jake's little head above mine, and then Miranda strapped to my chest. By the time we get to Canal Street, my back is screaming, and my knees are about to give out. We take the train the rest of the way.

The tumbling class takes place in a loft on Murray Street. The instructor is a little bitch named Jill. She has a thick blonde braid down to her butt, and a vast assortment of shiny Spandex garments. She's about four foot eight and maybe 90 pounds, max. She's one of those small people who are not only unintimidated by the larger population, but instead make the rest of us feel huge and awkward, like big, lumbering water buffalo. She is incredibly, inexplicably rude, barking out orders with a voice like heavy machinery. Hence, our secret nickname for her: Drill. For some unknown reason, the kids seem to love her. I can only assume that she takes on an entirely different personality once the classroom doors have shut. Visitors are not welcome in the sacred tumbling chamber. I think she's brainwashing them in there. And all for the economical price of eighty bucks a lesson. Call me crazy, but no three-year-old kid I've ever met needs to be taught how to jump and roll around and act like an animal.

The kids have been removed of their street shoes and sent off with Drill, who slams the door behind her with an evil look at all of us in the hallway. Fiona rolls her eyes. At the far end of the hall, the elevator doors open, and Amy rushes out with a twin on either side of her. Her cheeks are flushed, and she race-walks towards us, removing the twins' coats as she goes. Just before the door, she lifts first one girl, then the other, tearing their shoes off and setting them on their feet again before they know what has happened.

Though neither Fiona nor I are inclined to say anything, Amy waves her arm and says, "I know, I know!" Turning away, she squares her shoulders before throwing open the door and pushing the twins ahead of her into the classroom. I catch a few notes of Raffi before the door slams shut. Fiona and I look at each other and shrug. We are used to this sort of thing with Amy. She never stops. The only time I've ever seen her still is when she is passed out drunk. Even in her sleep she thrashes, as if the dream state for her is characterized by Rapid *Body* Movement. She herself has never gotten used to it. She is always late, always hurrying, and perpetually in a panic.

When Amy emerges again, the three of us -- four, counting Miranda -- decide to sit in the coffee shop around the corner to wait for the kids to get out. It is fairly crowded, but we manage to grab a booth in the back. Amy and Fiona sit on one side, and let me have plenty of room for Miranda. We order a round of Diet Cokes and I remove Miranda from her trappings and pop a bottle in her mouth before she can get too worked up.

Fiona closes her eyes and drinks through her straw slowly, her cheeks collapsing in. She leans back, sated by her caffeine fix, her eyes at half-mast. Amy simultaneously tosses back great gulps of her drink, twists Fiona's straw wrapper, looks wildly around at the other patrons, and picks at an infected ear-hole, her seventh in the left ear alone. All this while she wiggles in her seat, as if there is an incredible dance tune playing that only she can hear, and she just can't help herself.

I laugh to myself. I still have trouble seeing how she ever got herself a nanny gig. She's very good with the girls, but if I were a mother I would have severe reservations about leaving the fruit of my womb with Amy. It's not only her hyperactivity that would give me pause, but the way she looks would scare the hell out of me. Her skin is of a waxy pallor that I thought only existed in vampire movies. She has inch-long hair dyed black and stiffened with some sort of muck that makes her look like she woke up in the morning and sat down for a few stimulating moments in the electric chair before breakfast. Besides her vast array of earrings, (seven in the left lobe and nine in the right) she also has one tiny glittering diamond stud in her left nostril.

The night I met her, at some painful meet-and-greet put together by our au pair agency, I had been prepared to hate her just because she was laughing so loudly and vibrating around the room like some kind of lunatic. She also smoked those little black cigarettes which smell oh-so-much-fouler than the standard variety. But then she had shivered over to where I stood, stupidly, by the stereo, and pronounced, "I love your hair!" I had been so surprised by this, that I pulled a strand of it in front of my face for examination. "Mine's curly, too," she said, with a look of sorrow. All of us so afflicted have an instant bond, and commiserate about the taming of the 'do. I looked at her near-bald status skeptically. She saw this, and leaned closer to explain.

"One day I got a hairbrush stuck in it, and after about an hour and a half of trying to get it out, I was so pissed off I just cut it out and then shaved my head. After that my boyfriend dumped me."

Not really knowing what sort of reply a story like that demanded, I said, "What a dick."

She laughed and we had talked for an hour more, all the while downing vodka tonics. The nanny party had been interesting, to say the least. Approximately twenty girls between the ages of eighteen and twenty-two drank, smoked, and bitched about their jobs. We were gathered in an apartment on the Upper West Side. Jenny, our hostess, had a private apartment as part of her deal. Her "family" lived two floors above.

Amy and I stayed at the party until the estrogen content in the room had reached dangerous levels, and I thought that if I heard one more high-pitched, hysterical giggle, or dumbfounded "Oh my God!" I would be forced to do something rash.

Amy and I caught a cab downtown and wandered the streets around Thompkins Square Park, wondering what it was we smelled. We ended up discovering a dive bar called the Rail, which was so disgustingly dark and vile, sold alcohol so cheap, and best of all didn't ask for ID that we had made it our home away from home.

I met Amy there once or twice a week, sometimes more, depending on my workload and mood. You had to be in a certain spirit to be with Amy. She was exhausting, as if to keep up her perpetual motion, she had to drain the energy of her companions. We both had to work late two or three times a week, but rarely later than midnight, which left the best hours of the night. I think the thing that really clinched my friendship with Amy was that she, like me, was an insomniac. Sometimes, if neither one of us could sleep, we'd meet at the Rail, and when that closed at 4, we'd find a coffee shop and buy The Post, reading and drinking Diet Coke until it was time to go to work.

I look across the table at Amy, who sees me musing at her, and says, "What?"

"Nothing. I was thinking about the night we met at Jenny's party." I put Miranda over my shoulder and alternately pat and rub circles on her back, working the bubbles out.

"*That* bitch," Amy says, gearing up for a tirade. "I just heard a great story about her." She sits back and waits.

"Well? Are you going to tell me?"

"Will you come out tonight?" Blackmail.

"Okay, don't tell me. It can't be that good, or I would have heard it already." I shrug. I can't go out with her tonight.

"Well, if you're going to be a hag, okay I'll tell you. But let me say this, Michelle, you're getting to be a real pain in the ass lately. If you don't get out of the house more often people will start to think you like your job."

"I do like my job," I say quietly, looking at Miranda who gurgles happily.

"Spare me the Mary Poppins routine. Can I just tell you, please?" Not waiting for an answer she goes on," I got a call last night from a new arrival. Susan, from Montana or someplace. Calls up with the usual spiel," Here she adopts a high, timid tone. " 'Hi, I got your number from Barb at the au pair agency. I just got here, my name is Susan...blah blah blah' I always get this shit. Like every couple weeks or so. I would have to be first on that damn list."

Here I burst in: "Hello?! Can we get to the point here?"

"Okay, after fifteen minutes of the old job comparison: how old are your kids, how big is your room bullshit, she asks me if I know Jenny Hunter. It seems that Montana Sue had just gotten off the phone with her. Jenny told her that they could get together for coffee sometime to meet. Then she said, 'And if I like you, we can go out.' Can you fucking believe it? Jenny Hunter is conducting interviews to be her friend!"

Fiona cracks up at this. "Who *is* this girl?" she asks.

Amy and I look at each other, at a loss to explain the Jenny phenomenon.

Fiona looks bewildered by we American girls, as usual. She is quiet, and sometimes seems disapproving, and I wonder if she likes to hang out with us. But one time, not wanting to bother her, we failed to invite her to an outing, and she was very hurt. Apparently she does enjoy our company, but sometimes it's hard to tell.

Besides her often unamused attitude, she is the driving force behind our playgroup. Well, maybe "driving" is the wrong word.

She is more the bonding element that holds us all together. Whenever people start to get lazy and drift off, and miss meetings, she'll set them straight. She is the Wendy to our Lost Boys. To hear her tell it, though, she was once the most lost of the boys. When she first came to this country she worked for a family in Westchester County. She was here illegally, and so was pretty much at their mercy. They were forever using the stick and carrot method with her, the carrot being a green card, for which they promised endlessly to sponsor her, and the stick being deportment. Fiona can not go back to Ireland. She is the oldest of six children in her family. Not only are there no jobs to be had in Ireland, but no room for her at home.

This first family that she worked for used to treat her like shit. Of course they felt no guilt in doing so because, after all, she was lucky to be in The Land of the Free and to have any job at all. The Winslows had three ill-mannered children, the youngest of which she had to share a room with. Bunk beds, no less. Mrs. Winslow did not work, but required an au pair to free her up for sunbathing, tennis, shopping, and luncheons. Fiona not only cared for the triumvirate of brats, but did all the housework. The Winslows in their wisdom had dismissed the cleaning lady on hiring Fiona. Why pay two women when you could get one poor Irish girl to do it all for half the price? Fiona worked 15 hours a day, seven days a week. Once, when her favorite brother had been in New York for a few days, the Winslows would not allow her to have even an evening off. And people think the days of indentured servitude are over.

Fiona had finally extracted herself from that job by feigning a death in the family. Instead of going back to Ireland, as she had told the Winslows, she had come to the city and answered an ad in the *Irish Echo*. Since that time, she has worked for three different families. She has impeccable references and commands twice the salary that the rest of us do. But she's been a kid-wrangler for five years now. She deserves it.

Fiona looks at her watch for the hundredth time in an hour and pronounces that it is time to pick up the kids. Amy and I don't argue that we need to finish our drinks, but obediently pack up our things and follow her out.

Once outside, I feel a cold blast of wind in my face. I'm surprised by the coming winter. It seems like just a few weeks ago I had been resigned to the heat and the smells of New York in the summer. I wrap my light jacket around Miranda in the Snugli. I hope that Jake will be warm enough on the way home.

As we walk back to tumbling class, Amy tells us the entire plots of all the sit-coms she has watched the night before. Then she begins complaining about the fact that she hasn't been out lately, not even to the Rail, and looks pointedly at me.

"So, Michelle, what time are we leaving tonight?" she says, thinking she's sly.

"Leaving?" I play dumb.

"You are coming out tonight in exchange for the information on Jenny," she informs me. By the way she's flipping her head from side to side and jangling her multitude of earrings, I can tell she's gearing up for a fight.

"Amy, I have to baby-sit tonight," I lie. "I told you that this morning."

"When?" She looks suspicious.

"On the phone. Weren't you *listening?*" This is a fairly cheap shot, since we are always accusing Amy of not listening to anyone, and being absent-minded.

"Oh, right." She nods vigorously. "I thought that was tomorrow night?"

"It's both," I say, in a flash of genius. "Both of them are working really hard this week. Some big deadline."

"That sucks," says Amy, grimacing, more for her social life than my long hours, I think.

This is a subject Fiona can relate to. "I have to baby-sit four nights this week. It's the magazine's double issue this month. I get Katy up in the morning and put her to bed at night. She won't see her mother until Saturday afternoon, probably." She shakes her head. "It's really sad. Sometimes I think Katy will forget she even has a mother. And with her father away lecturing at medical conferences all the time, she only sees him two or three times a month!"

"Why the hell did they even *have* a kid?" I say.

Fiona has obviously thought this one out, because she says simply, "So that people will tell them what a beautiful daughter they have."

By this time we are in the elevator on our way up to Drill's loft. Miranda has started squirming and whimpering, impatient at being confined so long. "Shhh," I tell her, and kiss the top of her head, "We'll be home soon."

When the kids are released from class all flushed and wound-up, but sleepy, we get the shoes and coats back on and head for home. With three nannies and five children, we are a force to be reckoned with on the sidewalk. Some people choose to duck into doorways until we pass, and others back up against parked cars.

Jake is singing softly under his breath, and first the twins and Katy pick it up, then the rest of us come in on E-I-E-I-O. Amy sings loudly and with realistic animal sounds and gestures. Fiona, rather embarrassed, moves her mouth, but it's debatable as to whether any sound is coming out. When we get through all the farm animals, we do the jungle animals, and when we've exhausted those we sing that Old Mac Donald had a Jake, Katy, Carmen and Camille. Then of course, Old Mac Donald had a Miranda with a "Waah, Waah!" here, there, and everywhere. Miranda joins in unhappily on her verse.

We three go our separate ways at Bleeker Street, and I take the kids home.

By the time we get to Bank Street, I can barely get the key into the lock, I'm so exhausted and cold. We go in through the downstairs door. We live in a brownstone built at least a hundred years ago. I get both kids, myself, and all the equipment through the series of three doors, and drop everything in the entryway. My back is killing me. I take Miranda out of the Snugli and collapse into the big green armchair in the playroom. I want to close my eyes and sleep here and now, but Jake and Miranda are both whining for their dinner.

With an enormous amount of effort, I haul myself out of the chair and drag into the kitchen. It's almost completely dark outside now, and the kitchen is gloomy. I turn on all the lights and the radio. I warm Miranda's bottle and make two grilled cheese sandwiches, my specialty. Thankfully, Jake never gets tired of grilled cheese. Frankly, neither do I.

As I finally sit down to eat with one hand while I feed Miranda in my lap, it dawns on me that I have completely forgotten about the chocolate milk I promised Jake. I pray that he doesn't remember, because at this time of day, it would be a major problem. One that wouldn't be solved until I'd gotten us all bundled up again to go to the newsstand on the corner for some damn chocolate milk. In my attempt to avoid that, I pour about an inch of my Diet Coke into his dinosaur cup, and then fill the rest with water. When I give him this concoction, his eyes light up and he drinks slowly, closing his eyes in mock ecstasy. He wouldn't mention the chocolate milk now for anything, Coke being much higher on the list of desirable beverages. I hope that the minuscule amount of caffeine he's getting doesn't keep him up a minute later than usual. Miranda is beginning to drift off into her evening nap - she doesn't truly go down for the night until eight or so - when Debra comes in, bringing a blast of cold air with her.

"Hello, hello!" she calls out from the entryway.

"Mommy!" Jake runs for her.

"Hi, sweetie," I hear her say. "Oh, honey, Mommy can't pick you up just yet. Let me go upstairs and change first."

Her high heels clatter on the tile as she makes her way to the kitchen trying to extract herself from Jake's knee-embrace. "Jake honey, *please*."

She comes around the corner into the kitchen. "Hello, Michelle. How did it go today?" She glances up at me once, as she sorts through the mail.

"Great. Jake went to tumbling and he made this great finger-painting of a..." I trail off, seeing that she's not listening to me.

"And how's my little peanut?" she croons, taking the baby from my arms. "How much did she eat today?" she asks, finally looking me full in the face. I try to think quickly, adding ounces and the number of bottles of formula. Every day we go through this, and I never know exactly how much she's had.

"Well, she's had...let's see... three, no, four bottles."

"Six or eight ounces?"

"Um, I think six. No, maybe eight." Shit, I can't remember.

"Okay, whatever," she says, and sighs. She hoists Miranda up onto her shoulder and heads to the fridge for a drink. She steadies Miranda by her diaper when she opens the soda can. "What's this?" she says, looking at Miranda's big, swollen diaper. Uh-oh, I think. I try to remember when I last changed her. It could only be before I left the house to pick Jake up from school. *Shit!*

"She's absolutely *soaked*, Michelle! When was the last time you changed her diaper?" She looks at me like she's found Miranda covered in blood instead of with a wet diaper.

"I changed her while Jake was tumbling," I lie. "She was dry practically all day. She must have been saving it up." Debra gives me a look like: *not likely*, and heads upstairs, taking the baby with her.

I take Jake into the playroom and get him set up with some Legos before going to clean up the mess from dinner. As I'm loading the dishwasher, the intercom buzzes, and Debra's voice fills the kitchen. "Michelle!"

"Yeah?" I holler. What now?

"Did you get a chance to do the baby's laundry?" She knows damn well I didn't. She's probably up there in the nursery staring at the full hamper right now.

"Uh, no. Sorry. I'll do it first thing tomorrow."

"Please. And also you need to pick up our dry cleaning. The tickets are in the drawer down there."

"Okay, Debra. Sorry about that laundry thing. And the diaper too. Sorry." Sorry I'm in your house. Sorry I don't know what I'm doing. Sorry I annoy you.

"Oh, it's fine," she says half-heartedly, and then the kitchen is quiet again until the phone rings. I pick it up and it's my friend Joanne from home.

She is calling from her dorm room at the University of Washington -- the room I would have shared with her, had I not opted to drop out of college after freshman year and move to New York. Joanne tells me about the latest doings on campus, her classes, and all the fun I'm missing out on. She complains about her new roommate, the one who's not me, and who she was stuck with through the process known as "roommate roulette". She wants to know what's new with me, and I tell her the innocuous stuff. She knows I can't talk when Debra's around. I get off the phone when I hear Debra's tread on the stairs. I like the fact that the stairs squeak, it gives me plenty of warning. I tell Joanne I'll call her later. I can call again when the house is asleep, and thanks to that handy time difference, she'll still be up.

I join Jake in the playroom, and by the time Debra makes the ground floor, I have constructed a tower of Legos to rival the Chrysler building, and Jake is laughing happily. We switch kids, and she takes Jake upstairs for his bath. I read "Cinderella" to Miranda, worrying more of the damaging effects it may have on her love life than the uselessness of reading to an infant.

As we sit in the big green armchair the words I'm saying grow less and less distinct and I can feel myself start to drift off for the second time today. Miranda, on the other hand, shows no signs of going to sleep anytime soon. Actually, it's just about time for her evening fit. I consult my watch. Seven o' clock. I've been on duty for twelve hours.

Debra calls downstairs over the intercom for me to come up and say goodnight to Jake. His room is on the fourth floor, so I throw Miranda over my shoulder and start the momentous climb. I pass Debra on the third-floor landing and hand off the baby.

I enter Jake's darkened room upstairs, wishing I could crawl in beside him and go to sleep. His mom has gotten him bathed, jammied and tucked in. Although she gets on my nerves at times, I have to say there are a lot worse bosses than Debra. At least she's involved with her kids, and takes responsibility for them beyond the task of hiring a nanny. When I think of the set-up Fiona has, I feel lucky to be in this situation. And this time with Jake may be my favorite part of the day. Despite being tired and oftentimes cranky, sitting in the half-light with Jake usually calms me and recharges me for the rest of the evening. I can hear Miranda's wailing all the way up here, and guess I'll be needing that second wind tonight.

I sit on the edge of Jake's bed in the darkness, the way my mother used to sit on mine. Most nights I read a story (or two) but occasionally we'll talk quietly or sing a song together. Jake smells of Ninja Turtle bubble bath, and his blond curls are still slightly damp at the temples. When I've finished the story it's an effort to get up and leave. Jake gives me a kiss on the thumb (the only acceptable alternative to the kneecap) and says to me, as he has every night since I arrived three months ago, "Don't ever go away, okay?"

"I'm not going anywhere tonight," I say, as is my habit, "I'll see you in the morning."

I make my way to the kitchen, Miranda's screams, and Debra's pleading becoming louder with every step I take. When Debra spots me she says, "Oh, thank God. Here take her, she's driving me crazy!" So I take Miranda and bounce her up and down, walking the circle from the kitchen, through the playroom, past my room, through the entryway and back into the kitchen through the other door. We call it "doing laps." As I take my turn with the colic queen, Debra throws a frozen dinner in the microwave. When the dinner is done I get myself another Diet Coke and sit down just to be sociable. I hold the baby while she eats. It's not what you could call a relaxed dinner, and doesn't lend itself to conversation, but since we don't have all that much to talk about besides the kids and my own shortcomings, I really don't miss the chatter.

At last, Miranda starts to settle down and want her bottle. Thankfully she is in her mother's arms when this happens. It must be hard to watch your child with someone else, but you'd think after three years, she'd have gotten over being jealous. I am the Goldmans' fourth nanny. The last one disappeared after only a week and a half. When they went to wake her up for work in the morning they found her room empty. Two weeks later they got a postcard from her asking for her last week's salary. This incident, I have to assume, is the reason for Jake's concern about me leaving.

Since Miranda seems on the verge of sleep, Debra takes her upstairs to her crib. I most likely won't see Debra again tonight. She pretty much sequesters herself in her room after dinner and the kids are taken care of. She goes to sleep fairly early. Miranda still gets up once during the night, but Debra takes care of that. The nursery is right next to their bedroom on the third floor. Thankfully, they also deal with Jake in the middle of the night should there be any nightmares or bed-wetting to contend with.

I clear off the table and load the dishwasher. I don't start the machine though, since the noise covers the squeaking of the stairs. I wipe down the countertops and sweep the floor, killing time. When the kitchen is finished I head for the shower.

I never have time to shower in the morning, and I don't like to compete for hot water, so I shower before bed. It also gives me a chance to wrestle my hair into submission while it's still wet. If I sleep with it in a damp braid, there's a chance it may be somewhat cooperative when I wake up.

I take a long time in the shower, shampooing twice, shaving my legs, and enjoying the hot water. When I step out of the little laundry room that doubles as my bathroom, I am struck by how cold the tile feels on my bare feet. It truly is getting to be winter. It seems so strange not to be in school.

I pad across the chilly tile and through the playroom to my bedroom. I have to admit, I have the best room of all the nannies I know. I'd rather have this one little room with bars on the windows than Jenny Hunter's high-rise apartment of her own. I have a twin bed, dresser, rocking chair, lamp, and TV. The walls above the dark wainscoting are a pale, creamy yellow, that in combination with the bright white of the ceiling and molding makes my mouth water. I don't know what it reminds me of, but it must be something edible. Sometimes when I can't sleep, but don't have the energy to get out of bed, I turn on the lamp and just stare up at the walls and ceiling trying to remember what that something is.

In my room I dry off and throw the damp towel over the back of the rocking chair, where about four others of it's kind lie mildewing. My carpet is covered in clothing and cassette cases. When I feel extra ambitious, I collect all the cases and match them to the tapes they go with. I haven't been that ambitious in quite a while though, and I walk gingerly through my self-made obstacle course. I put on a big T-shirt, cut-off sweat pants, and big floppy gym socks, then go out to the playroom to use the phone.

I wonder if I should call Amy and make sure she's not mad. I feel a little guilty lying to her about having to baby-sit. I guess it's not too late to change my mind. I think about calling her up and saying that Debra came home early and gave me the rest of the night off, but don't consider this plan very seriously. I'm too comfortable where I am. I take my book from the end table and find the grocery receipt I'd tucked in to mark my place.

I read a page or two, before noticing that nothing has actually entered my brain and been registered there. My eyes were moving over the printed words, but my mind had been wandering. I get up and make a lap around the kitchen, thinking. I drink a glass of tap water and then sit down to try again. This time I succeed in immersing myself in *Sister Carrie*, and don't look up again until I hear Jeffrey's key in the door.

He comes into the playroom from the entryway, dropping his briefcase alongside the diaper bag I had deposited there earlier. He looks tired. He woke me up this morning at seven, on his way to work, and it is now past ten. This is why I can't very well complain about *my* long hours.

He manages a half-smile when he sees me. He takes off his suitcoat and drapes it over a chair. He has left his shoes in the hall. "Hey, Michelle," he says.

"Hi. You look tired."

"Oh, man, this perfume spot is kicking my ass. I could work these long days when I was just out of college, but I'm getting too old for this bullshit."

Jeffrey works in advertising, producing TV commercials. He is a vice-president of his ad agency -- something I found very impressive until I learned that almost everyone above mail clerks and receptionists are vice-presidents. Actually I guess he is pretty important. He has a couple of Clio awards up in the living room on the second floor.

Debra also works in advertising. She is an Art Director at a competing agency. They met at one of the editing facilities. They were both there working on different spots in neighboring editing rooms. Debra has a very loud, distinctive laugh. I won't say it's obnoxious, just that it gets your attention. Anyway, Jeffrey heard this laugh coming from the next room, and when he went to investigate, it was love at first sight.

Jeffrey, having shed himself of his jacket and shoes heads for the kitchen to look for something to eat. I follow him, bringing my book. He opens the refrigerator and peers in at the assortment.

"We don't have any food!" he says. He says this every day.

"Sure we do," I tell him. I push him out of the way and begin handing him jars and containers. "What do you call this?"

"Leftovers."

"How come you didn't eat with your clients tonight?" I ask.

"They were ordering up Chinese again. I've had Chinese every day for five days. I couldn't take it." He has discovered something to his liking and eats straight from the jar, with his fingers. I hand him a fork.

"Beer?" I offer.

He nods, his mouth full. I get a beer from the fridge and slide it to him across the counter. He mumbles his thanks. When he finishes chewing he drinks deeply from the beer bottle, draining half of it with his eyes closed. Revived, he stands at the counter and sorts through the mail while he eats.

"So, Michelle, how was your day?"

"It was pretty good. Amy's mad at me though."

"How come?"

"She wants me to go out with her all the time. I don't feel like it." I start to scrub out the sink, though I've already scrubbed it once tonight.

"Did Jake have fun at tumbling? That was today, right? Yeah, it's Tuesday."

"I guess he had fun. He was happy when he came out." I tell him about singing "Old Mac Donald" on the way home. He chuckles.

"God, I haven't seen the kids all week. Except when Jake got up last night for some water. He probably doesn't remember that."

"Yeah, he does. He told me about it this morning. He asked me when you're going to take him to the park."

"The park?"

"Remember? You told him that when you were done with your important work, you would take him to the park and watch him on the big slide."

"Right. The big slide." He takes another long drink of beer.

"And how's the baby?"

"Adorable."

"Well that goes without saying. Is her colic getting any better?"

"She only went for an hour and 45 minutes tonight. Besides, all the books say that it usually disappears by three months. We're almost there."

"Let's just hope Miranda's not the exception."

"Really."

Jeffrey drinks all but the last inch of beer in the bottle then hands it to me. "Want the rest?"

"Did you backwash?"

He smiles. "Nope."

I take the bottle and close one eye, looking inside. "Ugh, pretzel crumbs." But I drink it anyway.

We are startled by the sudden buzz of the intercom, and then Debra's voice: "Jeffrey?"

"Yes," he says.

"You're home."

"It appears that way." He winks at me. "I'll be up in a minute, Deb." There is a pause, and then the sound of the intercom clicking off.

"So, play group tomorrow?" Jeffrey asks, wiping his mouth of crumbs.

"You know it," I say, back at my sink scrubbing.

"Okay, well," he turns toward the stairs. "Guess I'll be moseying on upstairs now."

"Okay," I say, "'night."

He starts walking away and then stops and turns back to me. "Oh, Michelle," he says.

"Yeah?" Still scrubbing away, putting my back into it now.

"Try to leave some of the enamel on, will you?" He nods at the sink, then smiles.

I laugh. "*Good-night*, Jeffrey." I listen to him climb the stairs as I throw away the empty bottle and wipe the counters one more time. There is a rush of water through the upstairs pipes. Looking around me, listening to the house, I walk all around the bottom floor, turning off lights and checking locks. I make sure the burglar alarm is on, then brush my teeth and climb in bed. I turn out the light and hope that maybe tonight I can sleep.

*　　　*　　　*　　　*

I must have slept because I am awakened by a noise. A noise from the staircase, and then from the playroom just outside my door. I am still half asleep and a bit disoriented, having gone so abruptly from dreaming to waking. I roll over towards the clock next to my bed. The luminescent green numbers read 1:14 AM.

My doorknob turns slowly and then light appears in the widening space between door and jamb. A figure in the doorway blocks the light from behind. A voice whispers: "Asleep or awake?"

"Awake." I sit up. There is a crackling sound as one of my cassette cases is crushed underfoot.

"This *room*."

"Sorry." I giggle. "Is she asleep?"

"What do you think?" There is a groan of bedsprings, as they protest the added weight.

"I didn't think you were coming. I went to sleep."

"I should be asleep too. But I couldn't. I kept thinking about you."

"Maybe my insomnia is contagious."

"Must be. But I'll take *whatever* you've got."

TWO

Sometimes it's amazing to me that I am so far away from what I used to know, and live such a different life from Joanne, who I was nearly joined with at the hip this time last year.

I met her at freshman orientation. I didn't know anybody and was wondering if maybe college was a mistake after all when I saw this little girl reading a book in the middle of the dorm lounge. I say "little girl" because at first glance I thought she was twelve years old. I figured she had to be either a student's kid sister, or else a child prodigy. She turned out to be eighteen, and six months older than I was. Anyway, much to my surprise, we ended up being roommates, and eventually, best friends. At the end of freshman year, we picked out a room in our dorm for next year, and had it all decorated in our minds. Much harder than telling my parents I was moving to New York, was telling Joanne that I wasn't going back to school with her in the Fall.

I will never forget the look on her face when I told her. We were sitting in McDonald's across the street from my mom's office, where I worked that summer. The air-conditioning was on full blast, and we shivered over our milkshakes.

She was telling me about a party she had been to the night before. Who was there, who went home with whom, and who puked their guts out -- all the vital information. I wasn't really listening. I had heard this tale all summer long, only the details changed. It wasn't that I was disinterested, but I was waiting for an opening to introduce the subject of New York. I nodded my head and made all the proper responses: "You're kidding," "No way," and "Oh, my God," being the most frequently used phrases.

She began talking about next year and how fun it was going to be, and my stomach went all queasy. I'd blame it on the Big Mac, except that I hadn't touched my food. I started to think that maybe I should forget about New York and just go back to school instead of telling Joanne that all her plans were for naught and that she'd be flying solo come September.

"...right?" I heard her saying.

"Right, what?"

"You're bringing your microwave, right? I'll bring the mini fridge and the stereo, and you bring the microwave and blender." She looked exasperated with me.

"Well..." I really felt ill.

Joanne narrowed her eyes. "What is *wrong* with you Michelle? You haven't eaten anything, you haven't been to a party in three days, and you're zoning out on me. What is up?!"

I felt so guilty. Here she was all concerned for my welfare and I was about to ruin everything. "Nothing's wrong," I say. "It's just that, well, I have to tell you something and I don't want to do it."

"Oh, God. You're not pregnant are you?" Her hand came up to cover her mouth in the classic horror mode.

"Nooo!! Jeez, Joanne, give me some credit!"

"Well *what* then?!"

"Okay," I leaned back in my chair and ran both hands through my unruly hair. How can I ease into this gently? "Well, you know how my parents said they'd only pay for my first year of college?"

"Which is why you're working this summer instead of going to the beach."

"Right, but..."

"Which is why you're supposed to be saving every penny that you earn for tuition and housing and why I've been footing the beer and entertainment bills all summer long, *right*?" She was getting mad. There were two little points of color on her cheeks that were getting to be a deeper red every second.

"Well, yes, that *was* the plan..." She was not making it easy.

"What do you mean *was*? What's this past tense crap?" She grabbed my arm across the table, and looked me right in the eyes.

"Michelle, did you spend that money? Did you spend all your college money?"

"Well, not exactly."

"So what's the problem?"

I took a deep breath and looked out the window at the people passing on the street -- people leading carefree lives who didn't have to say to their best friends what I was about to say to mine. Without looking away from the window I said, "Joanne, I'm not going back to school." I waited for a shriek or a slap across the face -- anything -- but there was nothing. Still not looking at her, I said again, "I'm not going back to school in the Fall."

"You mean you're *dropping out?*" she asked quietly.

"No, not necessarily. I'm taking a year off. At least a year. I'll graduate a little later, is all." I wasn't even convincing myself. Just the night before I had written in my journal: *I'm never coming back.*

"What are you going to do, work in your mom's office? Live at home? Be a bum? What are you going to do when everyone else is in school?" At last I turned to face her. Her nose was wrinkled up as if she had smelled something foul. Sometimes she can be a snob. In her esteemed opinion, anyone without a college degree is worse than trash.

I was a little annoyed at her attitude. "Listen, you can fuck around in college all you want. You can believe whatever those professors tell you and waste away for all I care! No, Joanne, I'm not going to be a bum. In fact I'm getting the hell out of here. I'm moving..." And here I arranged my face in a smug little grin, "...to New York City." I shrugged, as if nothing could be more commonplace.

Her face was like a stone mask. I didn't know if she'd heard me. Surely the magic phrase 'moving to New York City' should elicit more of a response than that! I had nothing to add to my declaration, and she apparently had no intention of making a comment, so we both sat in silence. Joanne eventually picked up her cheeseburger and began to nibble around the perimeter, taking small, even, bites and chewing them mechanically, with an absolutely blank expression on her face.

When I could stand it no longer I started to explain myself, hoping to get her caught up in the excitement I felt so she would forget about being mad. But the moment I opened my mouth to speak:

"How could you?!" came flying from her lips with great violence and assorted sesame seeds. "How could you do this to me, for one thing, but more importantly how could you do this to *yourself*?! How can you just throw away your whole life like this. Thirteen years of school for nothing? So you can run away to New York? What are you going to do there, Michelle? Have you thought of that? Do you know how expensive it is to live there? You've never even been there!"

"Oh, like you have!?" I hated it when she treated me like I was so naive and in need of her guidance.

"Well, I'm not the one picking up and moving away on some whim. I swear, Michelle, sometimes you just don't think things through. Have you even given a *thought* to how you'll support yourself? Especially without a college degree!"

"Listen, Joanne, You're not my mother, okay? What I was about to tell you is that I have the whole thing figured out."

"I'll bet."

"Will you *shut up*?" I was starting to lose my temper. I couldn't understand why Joanne was giving me such a bad time. I'd told my parents the day before, and hadn't met with anything like this. They had expressed little interest beyond relief that they would no longer have to shelter, clothe and feed me.

Joanne said, "Okay, what's this big plan of yours?" She sat back, her arms folded across her chest, her cheeseburger abandoned to the flies.

I cleared my throat. "Well," I began, "I'm going to be an *au pair*." I said this last word timidly, unsure of the pronunciation. Joanne raised her eyebrows. "A nanny," I said.

Joanne sat up. "What the--? You don't even *like* kids!"

"Sure I do. Kids are okay. Besides, I get my own room and TV and phone and 150 to 200 bucks a week! Sweet, huh?"

Joanne stared at me in amazement, seemingly unsure what to ask me first. "Wait a minute. You get room and board *plus* 200 bones a *week*?"

"Yeah!" I nodded vigorously. "Well, I might only get 150, it depends on the family I work for."

"Well, who are you going to work for?"

"I don't know yet."

"You don't even have a job yet? You put me through all this and nothing is for sure?"

"Everything is for sure except the details. I am definitely doing this, Jo. I'm signed up with an au pair agency and everything." This time, I said the word with a bit more confidence, knowing that Joanne didn't know how to say it, or even what it meant.

Joanne shook her head slowly, looking at the table top. She picked at some dried catsup with her thumbnail. Then she said, very quietly. "All right. Tell me everything. Tell me from minute one."

Oh boy, where to begin? I shrugged and started, "I got to thinking that I really don't know what I want to major in, and as you know, my grades are terrible." She rolled her eyes. "I'm just not interested in school right now. I mean, it's a blast -- the lifestyle, the dorms, the parties, the guys -- but it doesn't feel like real life. It feels like *camp*. I'm learning what my professors think, but not what I think. I want to get away from college life and be a real person in the world. I feel like a white rat in a maze. It's like, 'Find the cheese, find the cheese. Don't look around, don't explore, don't stop and contemplate. Learn the maze and find the cheese.' It's stupid, and I don't want to do it anymore. I especially don't want to do it if *I* have to pay for it!"

Joanne looked unconvinced. She loves academia, and plans to become a professor so that she can live the college life forever.

"So, I started thinking about what else I could do. Working in my mom's office has been very illuminating on one point. I don't ever want to work in an office."

"I thought you like working there." She nods toward the glass tower across the street.

"I like it fine for three months. But I can't even think about being a full-timer. It makes me sick. The office politics, the secretaries that sneak out every half an hour to have a cigarette, the cheap polyester dresses they wear and the scuffed-up shoes. They make the shittiest money and they get no respect. Plus, the air up on the seventeenth floor is *vile*. It just circulates and recirculates all through the building. You can't open the windows or you'll get sucked out or something. That place hasn't seen fresh air in years. I get a headache just thinking about it."

"I get the picture. You don't want to work in an office. So where did this nanny thing come from anyway?"

"I was reading the Help Wanteds last Sunday and I saw this ad. Here, I have it with me. I showed it to my mom this morning. She wanted to call the agency to make sure it's not a white slavery ring." I handed her the smudged scrap of newsprint that I had been fondling for the past week and a half.

Suspiciously, she took the paper from my hand, watching me carefully. Then she read, "'Child care/Au Pairs. Busy New York City families need you for child care and light housekeeping. Own room and TV. 1 year commitment. Call collect.' I take it you called." She was beginning to look resigned.

"Not right away," I admitted. "It seemed like such a big step to even pick up the phone. I saw the ad on Sunday, and then on Monday proceeded to have the most hellacious day imaginable. The bus was crowded and I had to stand the whole way, I screwed up a phone call at work and got yelled at, I got in a fight with my brother... let's just say that all the signs pointed to New York. So Tuesday morning before work I dragged the phone into my closet and made the call."

"So, what was the place you called? This is an *agency*?"

"Yeah, they match up nannies with families that need them." My appetite was returning, and I munched on a cold french fry.

"Do you have to pay for this?" Joanne was always the skeptic.

"Nope. The families have to pay the fee. The nannies don't pay for anything. Not even the plane ticket."

Joanne raised her eyebrows yet again. "Really?"

"Well, the way it works is that the family pays for your ticket out there. Then they take the price out of your salary. When your year is up, they pay your way back home. Assuming you go home."

"So what makes you think they'll take you?"

"They already took me. I sent in my application and they said it looks great. It's not like it's brain surgery. You just have to be eighteen and have done some baby-sitting. I don't even think you have to be a high school graduate. In fact, they're impressed with me because I've had a year of college. I'm like the intellectual nanny."

We both laughed. I was relieved to see her smiling again. Still smiling slightly, she asked, "So what happens now? Do you fly out there for interviews? Can I go with you?"

"I wish. No, actually, they do the interviews over the phone. They know everything about me anyway. I had to give them all these baby-sitting and personal references, write a letter to my prospective employers saying why I wanted to be a nanny, send a recent picture; they even wanted to talk to my parents to make sure they know what I'm doing and I'm not running away or something."

"So now you wait for them to call?"

"Yeah, but it's not like I just get a call from a total stranger. Barb, the lady from the agency, tells me who she's sending my "packet" to, so if they call I'll know something about them."

"And has she told you about any families yet?"

I nod. "Two. One is a film producer whose wife died and he has a six year old son, and the other is this English lady. She's a stewardess and her husband is a lawyer. They have two little girls."

"That sounds cool. I don't know about the bachelor father business though. It sounds kinda sketchy to me."

"Well, I don't think he'll call anyway. Barb said he was almost decided on hiring this girl with more experience, but that she would send him my packet anyway. I was worried at first that no one would want to hire me, but Barb said there are so many more families that need nannies than there are decent nannies that anyone who wants to can get a job. I was worried that I don't have much experience, and she told me that I could get any job based on the fact that I'm white and American. I guess back there they think girls from the west are particularly wholesome."

"Wait'll they get a load of you." she said.

She was all right after that. She even started to get a little excited for me. Since I would be leaving soon, it made spending time together imperative. We went out almost every night, and I called in sick two or three times a week. What did I care? I was leaving anyway.

Joanne and I also raided my savings account. Since I wouldn't be using the money for college, my plane ticket would be taken care of, and I would soon be rolling in tax-free cash without constraints of rent, utilities or even grocery bills, we took it upon ourselves to spend everything but two hundred dollars.

Every evening she would come over after work, and we would wait for the phone to ring until nine o clock New York time. Then we figured it was safe to go out. We saw movies, ate every night, and haunted the mall, searching for the perfect New York Nanny wardrobe. My mother wondered if I would have to wear a uniform, but we set her straight on that matter.

I was a bit discouraged by the small amount of inquiries I got from the "busy New York City families." I got two or three calls, but they seemed only mildly interested. I started to get stressed out. It was only early August, but I wanted to be gone by the time school started.

Barb, from the agency, told me to hang in there, and that the right job would turn up. One day she called me at work and told me that she had just gotten a frantic call from a family with whom she had placed three previous nannies. They were a terrific family, she told me, but their most recent nanny had up and left without any warning. It seems she was a manic-depressive (a fact she had failed to mention on her application) and had taken off in the middle of the night, leaving the poor family in the lurch with no nanny for the three year old and a new baby due within the week. They needed someone immediately, and Barb thought I would be perfect for the job.

Barb had faxed my packet to the woman's office and they called me that night. Joanne listened on the extension. I talked to both the mother and father and the little boy. They asked all the same questions that the other families had, but something about their manner, their sense of humor, the way they didn't take themselves so seriously, I liked right away. I knew that I wanted to work for these people, and told them so.

I spent the next day agonizing over every word I'd said. Was I too flip, too familiar? Was it pushy to tell them I wanted the job? That night they called to tell me they had put my plane ticket in the mail, and they would see me on Friday. "Does this mean I'm hired?" I asked. They laughed and said yes. When I hung up the phone I let out a giant whoop and picked up the phone again to call everyone I knew. Joanne rushed in from the other room and we jumped around like a pair of fools before we started crying.

Immediately, I began making lists of what to take and things to do before leaving. I had three days. I packed up a bunch of winter clothes and books and things and sent them ahead of me, had my hair trimmed, and sent in change of address forms to my magazine subscriptions.

Joanne threw a huge going-away party for me the night before I left. Everyone I knew was there. My parents, brother, aunt and uncle, all our friends from the University, some of my old friends from high school and even one of my old teachers. There was a cake with a big apple and the words Good Luck Michelle, We Love You! written in icing. Everyone gave me presents and we promised to write and cried in our beer. It seemed my head had just hit the pillow that night when Joanne was outside my window honking her horn to take me to the airport.

It was still dark out when we loaded my two big suitcases and bulging carry-on bag into the trunk of her car. We were silly from lack of sleep and I was shaking from cold and nervousness. We sang along to the radio. At the airport we parked her car and had a hell of a time getting my bags to the terminal. Neither of us are very big, and the bags must have weighed at least fifty pounds each. We dragged the two big ones along, even though they were the kind without wheels, and kicked the carry-on ahead of us. We got the bags checked and went to find a snack bar. My stomach was in knots and I could only look on in disgust as Joanne devoured a four-dollar hot-dog.

My flight was announced and we hurried to the gate. There were only a few people boarding, and I let them go ahead of me. I turned to Joanne. "Well..." I said.

"Well," she said back.

"I guess... this is it, then."

"Guess so."

"I'll call you as soon as I get in." I offered.

"Okay."

They were about to close the door. I turned and jogged down the ramp toward the stewardess motioning me towards her, waving her stack of boarding passes. As she tore off my seat assignment I looked back at Joanne and called, "See you in a year!"

By the time we took off, the sun had come up. It was a beautiful clear day, and I spent the first half of the flight with my face pressed to the window. We had a stopover in Dallas/Ft. Worth, and the pilot had a southern accent. I have a weakness for that sort of thing, not to mention the uniform, and fought with the urge to visit the cockpit.

Captain Dallas, as I thought of him, loved the sound of his own voice and was on the intercom continually, telling us what we were flying over and what could be seen. I drank a Coke and ate some peanuts, enjoying the view. I had the whole row to myself. I had brought three different books to read, but I was perfectly content to sit back and feel the sunlight through the window.

As we got closer to Dallas, wispy clouds appeared, and the sunlight no longer streamed onto my seat. When the plane landed, reality hit me like a freight train. I realized that I was on my way to

New York, where I didn't know anyone and no one knew me. What was I thinking?! How could I have let things go this far? My first thought was catching the next flight back to Seattle. I wondered if my remaining two hundred dollars was enough.

Captain Dallas, as he pulled the airplane into its parking spot, informed us of the weather and advised us all to have a wonderful time in the Dallas/Ft. Worth area. He went on to say that those of us continuing on to New York/La Guardia should just sit tight, and we'd be taking off within 45 minutes. Of course we were free to venture into the terminal, but we should leave one of the little signs on the seat, for when we re-boarded the aircraft.

Passengers getting off in Dallas gathered up their belongings, and pushed through the aisle, bent on making the terminal and baggage claim ahead of everyone else. The other people, who would be traveling with me to New York, were much more relaxed, waiting until the others were gone before standing up, stretching, and leisurely making their way out to the airport bar or gift shop -- wherever they were heading.

I myself was paralyzed. Some odd physiological phenomenon had taken place and I was effectively welded to my seat. My butt had chemically bonded to the polyester of the seat cushion, and escape was impossible. Who would help me now? Captain Dallas was gone, probably tossing back martinis in preparation for his next flight.

Then I thought of the only person I knew in Dallas. A guy from school who was at home working for his father during the summer. I had dated him briefly at the beginning of freshman year. The only thing I had liked about him was that Texas drawl. Beyond that he was a waste of time. What would he do if I showed up on his doorstep? I had his address somewhere. I rummaged around in my bag for a moment or two before realizing how ridiculous I was being. Of course the only real solution was to go home and admit that I, Michelle, had once again made a grievous error in judgment.

I could imagine vividly my parents' reaction to finding their first-born back in the nest. Two nests, I should say. They've been divorced since I was ten and my brother Brian was six. Mom had always wanted to have a sailboat, so she bought one and lived aboard. Although it's big for a boat, it's not quite big enough for two kids. So, contrary to the popular divorce custom of the time, my dad got the house and custody of my brother and I. He is a musician, and works nights playing saxophone in small jazz clubs, so Brian and I didn't see much of him.

I'd have to say that Brian and I raised ourselves, or maybe we raised each other. Dad didn't get home from work until two or three in the morning and slept until noon. Brian and I got ourselves up, made breakfast, packed lunches and went out to the bus stop. I didn't play with the other kids after school because I had to be home to watch Brian. We made dinner for ourselves if Dad didn't take us to the drive-through. We never had a bedtime. We just had to be in our beds and at least feigning sleep by the time Dad got home.

Despite all this, I think we grew up relatively normal. At least no major psychological disorders had yet reared their ugly heads. I was a bit more serious than most of the other kids my age, and even in high school found it difficult to cut as loose as my friends did. I did go out and have fun, but it was a restrained sort of fun, my mind being on other, more domestic matters.

It wasn't until I got to college that I really learned how to have a good time, to live in the moment. Joanne had played a big role in that. She encouraged me to worry about things later, and enjoy the present. This philosophy would probably account for my dismal grade point average, but at last, at nineteen, I was acting my age.

My parents had made a deal with me that they would pay for my first year of college. After that, it was up to me. Most of the time I was happy just to have the chance to go at all. I had an awful lot of high school friends that were still living at home, working crappy jobs and going to community college at night. But on the other hand I knew even more kids at the University whose parents were giving them a free ride. They paid for tuition, housing, books, car, even gave them an allowance. That seemed too easy, and I was unspeakably jealous.

Mom and Dad took the news of my moving to New York rather well. So well, in fact, that I felt a little insulted. Aside from my mother's white slavery fears, they hadn't voiced any concern for my safety or questioned the wisdom of dropping out of college. They didn't seem all that heartbroken about losing the pleasure of my company either. But this wasn't surprising. My family, rather than a close-knit unit with clearly defined roles of mother, father, sister, brother, was more like a collection of individuals who sometimes shared living space. We were like distantly related roommates.

Even so, I didn't relish the idea of returning home with my tail between my legs and having to say that I hadn't gone because I was too scared. Oh, God, and all the people at my going-away party. What would I tell them? No way. I couldn't do it. I would rather face a firing squad, and a hundred New York muggers than go home a failure.

It's just that I hadn't really thought this far ahead. I'd thought about moving away, and I'd thought about being gone. About what people would say about me when I was gone. How, when school started again everyone would ask where I was and be told, oh, Michelle moved to New York. What a response that would get. That cool, sophisticated Michelle! If she can make it *there*....

But instead of observing my *in absentia* success, I was here. I had to live it. That never entered my mind before. Oh, I'd toyed with the idea. I had a little nanny fantasy of escorting the adorable children to the museums and libraries, the kids looking up at me adoringly, myself cool, efficient, and vaguely glamorous. But I hadn't thought of the day-to-day stuff, the getting there and meeting them and figuring out what to do. And I didn't like the idea at all. A fine mess.

It was a bit late to think of all that. Passengers had begun filing back onto the plane. Some finding the seats they had left behind, and wiping their mouths of airport cuisine, the new people consulting their tickets, looking for their seats, and stowing their luggage overhead. A middle-aged man and his young son sat next to me. The wife and daughter were across the aisle. I thought that the boy must be about the same age as the little boy I was going to take care of, but then overheard him tell the stewardess that he was six. I guessed I still had a thing or two to learn about kids.

The plane took off, this time with a new pilot, whose voice wasn't nearly as nice, and seemed in a bad mood. He didn't tell us what we were flying over, but it was just as well because we couldn't see a thing. The clouds had settled in thick and gray. We could have been on the ground for all I could see. It was like that all the way to New York, adding to my apprehensive mood. I was more anxious because I couldn't see where I was going. It was like having a blind date with destiny.

When the morose captain announced that we would soon be starting our descent into New York/La Guardia and called our attention to the fasten seatbelt sign, I had a fleeting, but intense wish for the plane to crash and burn before I had to step off it, and into my new life. I leaned my cheek on the chill glass of the window and cursed my fate. Me and my stupid ideas. How could I get myself out of this? Suddenly, I saw something in my peripheral vision -- something out the window.

The plane dropped down below the cloud cover and I got my first glimpse of the Manhattan skyline. It was raining, and the city looked like a huge granite monolith. It literally took my breath away. It was Atlantis, El Dorado, Oz. Whatever else you can say about it, New York doesn't disappoint.

Then the man in the seat beside me started whistling. He leaned over to his son and whistled a tune in his ear. When I realized that it was "New York, New York" I almost cried. Instead, without thinking, I reached over and squeezed the little boy's hand. I laughed. I wasn't afraid anymore.

I was out of my seat before the plane had even stopped taxiing, and had to be restrained by a flight attendant. Even so, I shoved past everyone, and was first out of the chute. Inside the building I was a bit taken aback by the pushing and pulsing crowd of unknown faces. I felt a flutter of the old fear. I looked around for something familiar, trying not to crane my neck in an obvious fashion. *Please let them be here*, I thought. Then I saw what I came for. A small boy sitting on his father's shoulders holding a hand-lettered sign that read: Michelle West. I smiled and walked towards them.

I was a bit surprised at what Jeffrey looked like, the way you often are when you see a favorite disc jockey after years of listening to them on the radio. Jeffrey's low, even voice had led me to imagine a tall and slightly serious man, despite his sense of humor.

What I saw in La Guardia airport was very different from the image I had conjured up in my head. Though he had looked rather tall from across the room with Jake perched on his shoulders, when I approached him I saw that he stood only two or three inches taller than myself. But what he lacked in altitude, Jeffrey Goldman made up in attitude. He was deeply tanned, it being the end of summer, and his teeth, when he smiled at me in greeting were straight and very white. His hair was light brown and receding slightly from his forehead. It was cut so that it stood up in a youthful, jaunty way at the top of his head.

Holding Jake in place by one ankle he shook my hand vigorously. His hand was warm and dry to the touch. "You must be

Michelle," he said. He smiled like this was a great joke in which I was included, which saved me from an idiotic response.

I let my gaze wander upward to the small boy. Jacob Elijah Goldman looked down at me suspiciously with giant blue-green eyes framed by black, curling lashes that contrasted with his dark blonde hair. His face was thin and heart-shaped, his chin coming to an elfin point. His little mouth was set in a stubborn scowl as his father urged him to say hello to me. Jake shook his head and refused.

Feeling I'd already failed with Jake, I smiled weakly and said, "That's okay, Jake. You can say hi to me later." I hoped that Jeffrey wouldn't sense my ineptitude and put me back on the plane before I'd had a chance to meet Mrs. Goldman.

Jeffrey lifted Jake down from his shoulders and spun him around once before setting him on the floor. He held Jake's hand firmly and we three walked to the baggage claim. As we waited for the bags to appear on the conveyor belt I hoped that Jeffrey wouldn't be angry when he saw my two huge suitcases. I asked him if my boxes had arrived in the mail. He said they hadn't come yet.

I tried to think of something to say, but Jake would have nothing to do with me, and Jeffrey seemed perfectly content to stand and rock back and forth on his heels. He had a slight grin on his face, and I thought his mind must be on something more amusing than the baggage claim. Finally I spotted my suitcases, and rushed forward to grab them before any of the criminal element beat me to it. From Jeffrey's disparaging glance at my shabby luggage, I gathered that I had nothing to fear.

"Looks like these have been around a while," he said.

"Around the world is more like it," I said in defense of my bags. "My father used these when he was touring."

Jeffrey looked at me strangely, and said, "Oh, right, your dad's a... a..." He snapped his fingers, trying to summon the word.

"Musician. Tenor sax."

We made our way out of the terminal to the parking garage. Jeffrey easily lifted my monstrous bags, that I had so recently learned to be ashamed of. Since both his father's hands were full, Jake was forced to hold onto my hand when crossing the street, and was very distraught.

In the car I got a slight smile from Jake when I suggested that he ride in the front seat while I took the back, but Jeffrey quickly vetoed that idea. Jake burst into tears and fought and kicked when

Jeffrey buckled his seat belt. Jake cried angrily until we got onto the expressway. I looked back cautiously, not wanting to set off another tantrum by showing my face. He was sound asleep, his face streaked with tears.

"He's not usually like this," Jeffrey said, glancing at his son in the rear-view mirror. Debra went into the hospital this morning, and he's worried about that."

"She did?!" I was surprised. I knew the baby was due any day, but I didn't expect it to be the day I arrived. "Well, did she have the baby yet? Why aren't you there? I could have taken a cab!" I felt awful. Here I was making them shuttle me around while Debra was in the hospital all alone having that baby. I sank down in my seat. This was all wrong. Jake already hated me, Jeffrey hated my luggage, and Debra was probably cursing me from her delivery room. I wondered if I faked a psychotic episode, Jeffrey would turn the car around and take me back to the airport.

"Relax," Jeffrey said. "Debra was in labor sixteen hours with Jake. She's only been in the hospital since eleven. She likes to take her time. I'll drop you and Jake at the house and then head for the hospital."

He was completely calm and in control of the situation. I found myself relaxing a bit, and looking at the scenery. I soon wished I had kept my eyes off the road, as Jeffrey was serenely weaving in and out of traffic like the dangerous erratic driver in the Driver's Ed movies in high school. No one honked their horn at him, or even noticed because all the other drivers were engrossed in their own giant slalom race. Every hundred yards or so the car shuddered as it hit a pothole at sixty miles an hour. Abandoned cars lined the shoulder of the road. Most had been stripped, burned out, or both. This, I was to learn, was the infamous Brooklyn-Queens Expressway. We passed or were overtaken by every imaginable vehicle. The number of stretch limousines nearly equaled the beat up junkers with thudding bass and fuzzy dice.

I gripped the door handle and tried not to grit my teeth for fear they would shatter in the impact of the collision that was surely imminent.

It had been getting darker as we drove along, and by the time we got onto what Jeffrey told me was the Manhattan bridge, all the lights of the city were glowing and beckoning. My first thought was that it looked like Pleasure Island from Pinocchio. It was like a post card, and I closed my eyes briefly and willed myself to never forget what I had just seen. I wanted to remember exactly what it was like.

Jeffrey turned on the radio and I smiled at the novelty of the station call letters beginning with a 'W' instead of a 'K'. The announcer said, "It's six-fifty-five in the Big Apple," and I felt the same giddiness as when the man on the plane had whistled "New York, New York."

I swore to always remember it, and I do. The first song I heard in New York City was "The Girl From Ipanema."

The sun's last rays streamed through the windshield into our faces. Strange to think that it was the same sun that had warmed my face in Seattle only a few hours earlier. I blinked against the sun and when I looked over at Jeffrey I noticed that his eyes were so dark as to be nearly black. They were so darkly black that they seemed not to reflect the light, but instead swallow it into their depths. I wondered why I hadn't noticed before.

I was pondering how a person's eyes could be that color (or non-color, as the case may be) when Jeffrey pulled the car up to the curb on Bank Street and announced that we were home. Getting out of the car I stared up at the house in amazement at its size and antiquity while Jeffrey removed my bags from the trunk. Looking at the house, with its elaborate facade and pinkish brick, it dawned on me how old New York is.

Climbing the stone steps up to the leaded glass double doors that led to my new home, I imagined myself as an Edith Wharton character, and felt out of place and oddly unfeminine in my jeans and T-shirt.

Inside the house I walked slowly and gingerly through the dim rooms, fearing I'd disturb some ancient spirit there. The ceilings were twelve feet high, and the woodwork was elaborately carved. Though the walls had been painted recently, they were done in muted, old-fashioned colors. I couldn't believe that I lived there. The furniture was sparse but comfortable. Though modern in style it didn't seem out of place.

Jeffrey gave me a hurried tour, depositing the still sleeping Jake in his bed on the top floor. He then took me down to the kitchen, gave me the phone number at St. Vincent's Hospital, and left me to my own devices.

I unpacked my bags and arranged my new room the way I liked it. Around ten o'clock, I could stand it no longer and went into the kitchen and made some toast. I hoped no one would be mad that I'd helped myself. The phone rang and it was Jeffrey announcing that Debra had just had a baby girl, seven pounds, five ounces. Both mother and baby were doing well, and Jeffrey would be home shortly.

After debating with myself for a few minutes on whether or not to do it, I went upstairs and woke Jake. I figured that he should know. I went into his room and whispered his name from the doorway. I didn't want to frighten him. He didn't respond, and I felt a sudden panic and rushed forward to lay a hand on his back. He was breathing. He chose that moment to roll over in his sleep, and I shook his shoulder gently.

His eyelashes fluttered and then opened.

"Jake," I said, just above a whisper, "Jake, your mommy had a baby. You have a new sister."

He sat up slightly, his eyes still unseeing.

"Her name is Miranda. Isn't that great?"

His eyes focused on me at last, and as he recognized who I was, he began to cry piteously. I instinctively reached out to hug him, but he pushed me away and cried harder.

"Jake, I know you don't know me yet, but we're going to be friends. It's hard to have a new babysitter isn't it?" More crying. "It's hard for me, too. But we'll get used to each other. Tell you what. Your daddy is going to be home in a little while. Would you like to come downstairs and wait for him?" Still crying, he nodded and lifted his arms to be carried.

When Jeffrey came home he found us asleep in the playroom armchair, Jake in my lap. I was so exhausted from the excitement of the week, my farewell party, my early flight, and the stress of all the newness, that I didn't say a word as Jeffrey lifted Jake from my lap and carried him upstairs. Shuffling into my brand new room, I fell on top of the covers, and slept for twelve hours straight.

In the two days before Debra and the baby came home Jake learned to accept me as his only link to food and other necessities, but was still very distant. Kids had always taken to me quickly -- probably sensing that basically I was one of them -- but Jake took a long time to warm up to me.

The house was thrown into chaos when the baby came home. I'd heard stories about children having a terrible time adjusting to the birth of a sibling, and probably behaved that way myself when Brian was born, but I was not at all prepared for the hell that broke loose on Bank Street. Jake, when he was not trying to hit the baby while she nursed, was systematically forgetting all his toilet training. I have never seen a sadder kid than when Debra and I were giving the baby her bath and Jake stood silently in the corner and pooped his pants.

Debra was just as I had pictured her. She was thin with a sort of boyish body, and she had dark, shoulder length hair with a slight wave to it. Her eyes were gray and quick, darting here and there, and her mouth was set in an efficient, but not grim expression. For having just given birth she had a lot of energy. I later discovered that this was due to the fact that she could fall asleep anytime, anywhere as soon as she lay her head down, and could rack up twelve or fourteen hours a day that way. She was extremely lucky that both of her children were great sleepers from the beginning -- something they obviously inherited from their mother.

She was friendly enough -- went out of her way to tell me the best places in the neighborhood to shop and to meet people -- but she was very business-like in her manner. I got the feeling that this was not aimed at me personally, but rather the way that she had always conducted her life. She was not fond of small talk or joking around, but neither did she join in the debates over politics or literature that Jeffrey and I would wage each night at dinner.

Debra did not ruminate over the past or contemplate the future. She was purely a creature of the moment. Abstract ideas had no place in her world, which is not to say that she was unintelligent, but that she gave her attention only to things that required it. Art and music could survive with out her she would say.

Jeffrey was just the opposite. He loved to talk. It wasn't so much that he liked the sound of his voice, but that he was curious to hear what he would say next. He could talk for hours on any subject, which is not to say that he was overly intelligent, but that he had a passing familiarity with any subject you could name, and had a gift for bullshitting. He was also easily the funniest person I had ever met. He had the quickest, sharpest wit, and could imitate voices, too. I laughed so hard my eyes would tear up and Jake would say "Why you cwying, 'shell?" Debra would give me a look like: *don't encourage him*, and Jeffrey would just beam.

Debra had a one month maternity leave, which she claimed was insufficient, but as the weeks went by, she began to seem anxious to get back to work. She spent a lot of time on the phone with her office, and occasionally had lunch with clients or co-workers.

Debra thought it would be best to keep the two kids apart until Jake's violent streak passed. I didn't see how it was going to pass if he never had the chance to get used to the baby, but it wasn't my job to tell her this.

It was still very much summer in New York, and Jake and I spent most afternoons in the park. There were kids he knew from playdates, and through them I met a few nannies. Fiona was one of them. I don't think I would have become friends with her on my own because she seemed so standoffish. It was easy to assume that she was a snob because she worked for the Bouchets. But Jake and Katy loved playing together, and by spending many afternoons in Fiona's company, I discovered that she was shy and reserved, but very nice. I loved the way she talked, and would come away from the park with a slight brogue in my own voice for an hour or two. It's funny the way accents are contagious.

While I kept Jake occupied, Debra spent her time napping with Miranda. When I came back to the house, she would take Jake out to a museum or on a playdate while I stayed with the baby. I rarely saw Debra for more than a few minutes. Jeffrey would come home in the early evening (I guess it was a slow time at work) and we'd have dinner. When it was nice out, we'd take a walk, Jeffrey carrying Miranda, and Jake between Debra and I holding both our hands. We would count to three and then swing him up in the air between us, and he would laugh and laugh and want to do it again.

Jeffrey would point out things he thought I would be interested in: old buildings, funny shops, locations of famous crimes. Interspersed were bits of his personal history. He'd point out the barber shop where he'd gotten a really bad haircut when he was ten, or the building where he had his first apartment after college. Debra was originally from New Jersey, and said that when we went to visit her parents in Paramus, she would show me all *her* old haunts.

We walked along smiling and joking and swinging Jake in the air. It was warm, and the sharp edges of the city seemed softened as the sun dipped lower.

I remember one evening the air was hot and still under a thick cloud cover, but we were reluctant to give up our walk. Outside, noises were muffled as if it had snowed. There was a nervous tension in the air, as people hurried their steps toward home with frequent glances at the sky. I wondered what the big deal was. After all, I was from Seattle: I knew rain.

I didn't see the first flash of lightning, but there was a sudden rumbling from all sides. At first I thought the buildings were falling down. Then it rained. In Seattle, the rain is a slow, steady drizzle, with bursts here and there of harder rain, which quickly lose momentum and return to dripping. I was therefore surprised to find myself soaked through within seconds of the first raindrop. The Goldmans ran for cover, and after a few stunned seconds, I followed them under a store awning. Jake took my hand and told me that there was nothing to be afraid of, that he would protect me. I fought back the urge to scoop him into my arms and cover his little face with kisses. But I didn't want to push my luck.

Jeffrey, after surveying the storm, and the distance between where we stood and home, announced that we would wait it out in a diner around the corner. We walked under awnings, avoiding the down spouts, laughing at ourselves. When we were seated at a table, Debra discreetly nursing Miranda under the tablecloth, Jeffrey insisted that I have an egg cream. I was worried that it was the sort of concoction that Rocky drank while in training. I remember that as we all simultaneously slurped at the bottom of our glasses, I thought that I had found the family I had missed out on, and even though I knew I couldn't be a daughter to them, maybe I could be like a niece or long-lost cousin

THREE

It's officially winter now, just a week before Christmas. It just doesn't get cold like this in Seattle. There it gets below freezing just two or three times a year, and they cancel school for a half-inch of snow on the ground. New York is a different story, as it is in most respects. Here they have a thing called a *wind chill*. This has some complicated meteorological equation to it, but what I understand is that it takes however cold it is, (which believe me was already cold enough for my taste) and makes it twice as cold as that. In fact, that may be the equation right there: Twice as cold as too cold. Too damn cold squared.

Before I left Seattle, Joanne and I had bought a coat that we thought was suitable for a New York winter. It's impossible to buy a coat in August. No matter what you try on, it's unbearably hot and bulky. Yes, yes, my mother warned me that I wouldn't be warm enough -- I just had no idea that such extreme cold was possible. When the first true winter wind came barreling through the valley of skyscrapers and into my face I was so surprised I said, "Hey!" This wind had the nerve to blast right through my jeans and sting my shins!

The kids and I are on the way to play group, it being a Wednesday afternoon. Miranda, in her enormous down snowsuit is too bulky for the Snugli and so is riding in the back of the recently-acquired double stroller. Jake, equally bundled in the front seat, hangs over the side looking for dog crap. Every time he spots a pile -

- sometimes so fresh it's steaming -- he points and yells: "Watch out, 'shell! Poop! I see dog poop! Gross!"

When we reach the building, the doorman calls up to the apartment to announce our arrival. He even pushes the elevator button for us, which I'm sure he sees as a courtesy, although Jake is very insulted. Button-pushing is very high on his list.

Upstairs, Summer is waiting for us at the door. "It's about time," she says.

"Hi, Summer," I say. "Sorry we're late. This stroller takes some getting used to. It's so heavy with both kids in it, that I have to jump on the handle to get it up the curb!"

Summer is not amused by my anecdote. She stands aside to let me wheel past her into the apartment. Carmen, Camille, and Katy all cluster around Jake squealing. Benjamin, the boy Summer looks after, throws a truck.

I work quickly to release Jake from his bonds while he wiggles and whines. Finally, he is free and all four kids go running off to Benjamin's room where they slam the door behind them. I reach down to lift Miranda out, but she's fallen asleep. Perfect. Just the way I like her. Not wanting to wake her, I carefully unzip her snowsuit so that she won't get overheated, then wheel her over next to the couch and sit down.

Fiona and Amy are also in attendance this afternoon. They both say hi and then go back to what they were doing. Amy sits in one corner of the large sectional couch reading a magazine, and Fiona is in the kitchen fixing a snack. Summer is folding laundry, angrily snapping out the wrinkles. Something is wrong. Usually, I walk into a riot every Wednesday afternoon. Since we take turns hosting, sometimes the riot is at my house. This time it's too quiet. Everyone is keeping to themselves, their mouths grimly set. The prime indicator that all is not well is Amy's near-catatonic state. Although she flips the magazine pages as if she were Evelyn Wood, and swings one leg over the sofa arm, for Amy this is practically motionless. I wonder if they've been fighting.

"Someone want to tell me what's going on here?" Shrugs and blank looks all around. "Why is everyone acting so weird?"

Fiona puts down her spoon and comes into the living room, wiping her hands on her jeans. "It's Molly."

"Yeah, I was just going to ask where she is. Isn't she coming?" Molly is another Irish girl. She's only been here a couple of years, but she's worked for the same family the whole time. Taken care of their little boy since he was a week old.

Fiona quiets me with a stern look. "Molly's been let go."

"What?"

Summer looks up impatiently, flailing a freshly laundered pair of boxers. "She got fired, Michelle! You want it in semaphore?" She goes through the motions with the boxer shorts, most likely Mr. Leibowitz's.

Fiona ignores her and continues. "The Robinsons are moving to a smaller apartment and don't have room for her. They're going to hire a live-out. Probably someone from the Islands."

"Jeez. What's Molly going to do?"

"Well, she's got to find a job fast, before immigration catches up with her. The Robinsons didn't give her any warning. She came home one night and they'd tacked a note to her door telling her to be out by the weekend. She came right to my house. She hasn't gone back to work. She figures it serves them right to have to scurry around for a last-minute baby-sitter." Fiona twists her mouth in an attempt at a smirk, but fails miserably and retreats back into the kitchen.

"After all that time, this is how they treat her? That sucks."

Amy stands up, the magazine falling from her lap. "I'd say that's an understatement, Michelle."

"I can't believe that! They seemed so nice."

Fiona says from the kitchen, "They're all nice as long as it's convenient to be."

"Poor Mol," I say. "How's she holding up?"

"Not well," Fiona says sadly. "She sits around the house and watches TV. The Bouchets don't know she's staying with me -- they wouldn't approve -- so she hides out in my room. She hasn't told her parents yet, but they'll know soon enough, now that she's not sending any money home." Fiona is silent for a moment, carefully spreading jelly onto the peanut butter sandwiches. "Plus, she's been drinking." She doesn't look up.

"Oh." Everyone agrees this is not the best course of action. We decide to keep our ears open and try to find a position for Molly before she's too far gone. Beyond that there isn't much we can do for her. Amy and I would sign her up at our agency, except that Molly isn't legal. Our agency only deals in American nannies.

To break the spell on our depressed group there is a sudden thud and then a piercing scream from Benjamin's room. Summer and Amy hurry in to see whose head has split open. I gently rock the carriage, trying to keep Miranda sleeping.

Summer comes back in the room carrying Camille, who is still screaming. The kids had been playing Peter Pan, and against her wishes, Camille was elected Captain Hook and therefore pushed off the bed and into the waiting jaws of the crocodile. Camille's face is bright red and she's crying so hard she can't catch her breath. Amy takes her from Summer and holds her in her lap until she calms down. The first intelligible word out of her mouth is "ice", which Fiona brings in a zip-lock bag. For reasons unknown to me, ice is the magic cure-all of the preschool set. Band-Aids of course are extremely desirable, but you have to bleed to get one, and picking a scab doesn't count. Ice, however, can be acquired with any old bump on the noggin and a few tears. Camille happily runs back to Neverland with her bag of precious ice.

The first crisis of the afternoon taken care of, we settle in around the dining room table to eat junk food and bitch about our jobs. Since it is nearly Christmas we compare bonuses and vacation time. Fiona is the grand champion of bonuses. She got two weeks' pay and a couple hundred dollars' worth of department store gift certificates. She also gets to accompany the family on their three week trip to the South of France, where her boss, the magazine editor, has a chateau inherited from her uncle.

The rest of us are incredibly envious, but Fiona insists that this "vacation" will be much more like a punishment. She will have to take care of Katy 24 hours a day while the Bouchets go to Monaco on a friend's yacht. She says that the house is an awful old dusty run-down cavernous thing and besides, she can't stand the French. I think I speak for all of us when I say that we would trade places with her in an instant.

Amy got gypped in the bonus department, getting only a week's salary and a card. But she requested and was granted a full two-week vacation. She is going home to San Francisco for her cousin's wedding, and then skiing in Tahoe with some friends.

Summer and I came out about even. She got cash and a portable CD player. I got a round trip plane ticket to Seattle, but I can only stay three days. Neither Jeffrey nor Debra can take much time off of work.

Summer is also from Seattle, though I didn't meet her until I moved to New York. In fact, she was one of the first people I met. She used to work for a family that lives down the street from the Goldmans, the Eagans. She also had dropped out of college, although she was in her Junior year when she left. She had seen the same newspaper ad, and arrived three weeks or so after I did.

I ran into her in a deli on West Fourth Street. She was there with three kids, one twelve, one six and one nearly two. She got my attention because she looked way too young to have three kids, and she had that harassed, confused, brand-new nanny look that I'm sure I recognized from my own mirror. Another thing I noticed was that she was wearing a T-shirt with the name of an obscure Seattle band. After three weeks of New York accents and attitudes, she was like an oasis in the desert. I asked her if she was from Seattle, and we struck up a conversation.

She had only been there for a few days and hated her job. On the phone she had been told that she would be working for a psychiatrist and his wife who was a psychotherapist. They described to her a lovely bedroom on the top floor which was to be hers, and gave glowing reports of their wonderful children. They described her daily activities as dropping off and picking up the two boys from their schools, and playing with the toddler. What they left out was that the whole family was absolutely insane, and her bedroom consisted of an empty room with a futon on the floor. She was expected to stow all of her belongings in the closet during the day so that the room could be used as the psychotherapist's meditation chamber. The kids were dreadful, the six year old given to asking "Want to smell my gas?"

Summer was miserable and looked half dead. She was working twelve to fourteen hours a day, and had never had the chance to adjust to the time difference. When she told me about her job she started to cry. I invited her and the kids over to my house.

I sent the kids into the living room and put on a Disney video for them to watch. Back in the kitchen I handed Summer tissue upon tissue until she'd cried herself out.

"The only thing I can think to do is run away from the Eagans and go find a nice park bench." She said, miserably.

"Summer, is it really that awful, or is it just different than you expected?"

"It's that awful. I'm not the Eagans' only slave. There is this Czech guy who's remodeling the kitchen. He barely speaks English. He's saving all his money so that he can bring his family over here. Then there's this little ghost of a girl. She's Japanese, but she's from Brazil so she speaks Portuguese. I used to wonder if she was real, because I'd only seen her from the corner of my eye. The Eagans never mentioned her. Then last night, she came and knocked on my door. She sat on the end of my futon and told me that I should leave. That I am too young to be in a place like this. It was like The Amityville Horror or something! So this 'girl' turns out to be thirty years old. Her parents made her come here. When she wasn't married by the time she was thirty they kicked her out.

"It's so weird, you learn about immigration in elementary school, and there are pictures of Ellis Island and then of course Vito Corleone in Godfather Two. But I never thought about it still going on. The same old thing. It's really sad." Summer looked out the window for a minute or two. "It just makes me mad the way they treat these people. They speak to them like they're very slow children. Even though Dr. Eagan is the same age as the Czech guy, he orders him around like he's an animal. And the ghost girl sleeps on a cot next to the washer and dryer! It makes me ashamed to be an American. I felt like apologizing on behalf of the whole country! New York is supposed to be so sophisticated and liberal. I never expected to find this kind of stuff going on." She looked ready to cry again.

"Why don't you just go home?" I said, hoping she wasn't as offended as I would be if someone suggested the same to me.

"I wish I could. But I could never face my parents. I only had a year left of college, and they still can't believe I quit. I wouldn't listen to anyone, I had to go to New York. Now I'm stuck here."

"Have you told them how awful your job is?"

"No way! I feel like such an idiot for not asking better questions on the phone or holding out for a better job. I was so anxious to get out of there that I took the first job I was offered. You know something? This sounds like 20/20 hindsight, but when I first talked to Mrs. Eagan I got a weird feeling, and then again after I accepted the job. But I ignored it. Some part of me knew that it wasn't right."

"That's happened to me before. Now I have a rule that I always go with my first instinct. I liked the Goldmans right away, and it's worked out great. I love this job."

"I can tell. I mean, I just met you, but I can see that you're really good with the kids. I was looking forward to being a nanny so much. I'm going to be a kindergarten teacher when I get my degree. I thought this would be a great chance to learn about kids."

"I just had a thought."

"What?"

"On my first day here -- or the morning after I arrived -- the agency called me to see if I got here and if everything was okay. Did Barb call you, too?"

"Yeah."

"Did you tell her how awful it is?"

"No, I didn't have the chance. Mrs. Eagan was in the room staring at me when she called. Someone is always listening when I get a phone call. And, of course, there's no phone in my cell."

"You know what, Summer? I think that Barb is not the kind of woman who would knowingly let this happen. I'll bet she has no idea what the Eagans are really like. I'm going to tell her." Summer started to look nervous. "Look, you can't stay there, and you say you can't go home. Barb told me that there are ten families for every nanny, so there's got to be something better than the Eagans."

I picked up the phone and dialed the agency. Barb was extremely apologetic and understanding. She told Summer (while I listened on the extension) that she was to go right back to the house and tell the Eagans she wasn't going to stand for this kind of thing and that she would be leaving immediately. Barb then called the Eagans herself and told them the same thing, adding that her agency would not be providing them with another au pair because they had misrepresented the job on their application.

Summer went to talk to the Eagans, but was told that in all their years of hiring nannies, no one had seen fit to complain and that she must have a very active imagination. They even suggested that she seek professional help for her delusions. Summer grabbed her suitcases, which she'd never unpacked, and walked out. Barb let Summer stay with her until she found her a job with the Leibowitzes two   weeks   later.

Although I felt I had effectively maneuvered Summer through a crisis situation and deserved a debt of gratitude, she apparently disagreed. Since moving uptown she has been rather cold. We get together for play group and once in a while see a movie together, but it is all very polite. I've given up trying to be her confidant. She has a smart-ass mouth and can be very sarcastic and abrasive, but I like her anyway. We have a lot in common besides the Seattle connection. We also have similar tastes in music and she is one of the few people I know who actually reads books. Jeffrey is another.

Besides bashing Jenny Hunter and her small circle of hangers-on we mostly enjoy gossiping about our employers. Although their kids play together once a week, none of the parents have ever met. Despite this, they like to keep track of what the others are doing: where they're going on vacation, what big-ticket items they've recently purchased, who their friends are and where they shop. Debra is always interested in the latest report from play group. It never has dawned on her that I tell stories about her and Jeffrey that get tossed around to the Maxwells, the Leibowitzes, the Bouchets and the Robinsons (although it looks as if the Robinsons, having shafted Molly, will now be out of the loop.)

The exciting news this week is that Mrs. Maxwell, Carmen and Camille's mother, went in for an ultra sound and it was determined that the new baby is a boy. She is due in April. Amy is so excited she can hardly stand it. She loves babies. She can barely keep her paws off Miranda most of the time, and is beside herself at the prospect of her own little one at home. Carmen and Camille can't imagine that there is only one baby in there. They think everyone is a twin.

After we've plowed our way through a bag of chips and a whole jar of salsa, the kids come tearing through the room, insisting that they are dying of starvation. Fiona distributes the peanut butter sandwiches, thoughtfully cut to each child's specifications. Jake demands triangles, while Benjamin likes his sandwich intact but crustless. Carmen and Camille prefer theirs cut into sixteenths.

As the kids feast on sandwiches and apple juice, I hear a faint cry from the stroller. Miranda stirs, and looking at the time I decide to cut short her nap so that she will sleep tonight. I want her in bed early because I really am baby-sitting this time. Debra and Jeffrey are having dinner with some friends in Brooklyn, and although they claim that this is a boring social obligation and they will be home early, I've heard that line before and know that it will be long after midnight before they get back.

I change Miranda's diaper while I'm waiting for her bottle to warm. Debra says not to bother warming it up anymore, but I can't stand to give her that disgusting soy formula cold. Amy begs for the honor of feeding the baby, and I hand her over.

The kids have finished eating and are trying to cajole some kind of desert from Fiona. They first ask for ice cream, but she talks them down to goldfish crackers. I make the rounds of the table wiping peanut butter off hands and faces with a warm washcloth. When each child has received exactly ten fish in their cupped hands, they start back to Benjamin's room, walking carefully, so as not to upset their treasure.

Amy clears her throat and announces: "By the way, I met Montana Sue last night."

"Who?" asks Summer.

"The girl from Montana. Susan. She's from the agency."

"So," I say, helping Fiona clear the table. "What did you think of her? Is she cool?"

Amy casts up her eyes, deep in thought. "Well, I wouldn't say 'cool' exactly. She's very quiet. It was like pulling teeth to have a conversation with her. The thing is, she's beautiful. I mean, this girl is absolutely, stunningly beautiful. I've heard that about those mid-west types, but I never believed it."

"What's so beautiful about her?" Summer asks, with a hint of hostility. She is very good-looking herself, tall and wide-eyed.

"She has perfectly blue, enormous eyes, long, thick naturally blonde hair, and a little turned-up Barbie nose. And she has *no idea*. She thinks she's a normal-looking human being. I would have gotten a total complex sitting there with her, except that she's so shy and nice. I could tell she was disgusted by the Rail, but she smiled and ordered a wine cooler. You should have seen Bud's face when she did, too!" Amy bursts out laughing at the thought of the hugely fat, bearded bartender.

It is pretty funny, but I have to ask: "You took her to the Rail? When was this?"

"Last night, like I said before." She burps the baby. "Oh, come on, Michelle. You expect me to go into hibernation because you have to work constantly? You know, you're only obligated to baby-sit two nights a week. It says so in the contract. If you really wanted to go out, you could. I just got sick of waiting for you."

"Nobody said you had to wait for me. You can do whatever you want. I hope you and your Barbie doll will be very happy together." I say this sarcastically, and they all laugh, but I can't help feeling a little hurt.

Since it is so close to the holidays, and we will be scattered all over the globe, we say our good-byes as we leave play group. We will reconvene when Fiona gets back from France. I will be seeing Amy up until she leaves on Friday, and Summer and I have made arrangements to do lunch back in Seattle.

Although it is, as the weatherman puts it, 'bitter cold', I walk the whole way home. It is dark already, and the lights on Fifth Avenue are beautiful, seeming to sparkle even brighter in the cold, clear air. I tell Jake that the little white lights are fairies, cousins to Tinkerbell. He looks at me skeptically, but waves and calls out "Hi, Tinkerbells!"

I love Christmas. I am not religious, in fact have only seen the inside of a church at weddings. But the season has always had this invigorating effect on me. Even as I get older, the Christmas spirit hasn't yet started to wane. As we walk down the Avenue, I feel happy and alive and am actually looking forward to seeing my family. I know I will be disappointed by their lack of enthusiasm -- in fact, my Dad's outright hatred of the season -- but I am anticipating the large, traditional dinner at my aunt and uncle's, where I envision myself as the conquering hero, the girl from New York City.

Back at the house, I am surprised to find Debra already home. I tell her about our day, omitting the part about walking seventy blocks home in the cold. Debra seems agitated. She sits at the kitchen table picking the polish off her nails.

She cuts me off in the middle of a sentence saying, "Michelle, I have to talk to you. Come sit down."

"Okay," I squeak, in an attempt at nonchalance. I wrack my brain, trying to come up with what I may have done, what offense I must have committed. In the seconds it takes me to deposit myself in the chair opposite, I run through the entire catalogue of what I was supposed to do today and can't come up with any missed items.

She doesn't look at me, but continues to pick at the pale pink polish. "Michelle, I have to tell you something I don't think you're going to like hearing."

Oh God, I think. *Why didn't I think of it before? She must* know. I draw my lower lip between my teeth and hold it there firmly, arranging my face into what I hope passes for a look of innocent curiosity.

"You know I've been working on the fried chicken account for months." I didn't know, but am so relieved I smile and nod my head. "Some problems have developed, and it turns out that I'm going to have to work over Christmas. In fact I'm going to have to go to LA."

At first I wonder why she is suddenly sharing this information, until I realize what it has to do with me.

"So, you're saying I can't go home."

"'Fraid so."

"I can't go home for *Christmas*?" I can't believe what she's telling me.

"I thought you said you weren't particularly religious."

"Well, I'm *not*, but..."

Debra pushes back from the table and stands up. She smoothes her skirt as she says, "Look, I'm sorry this had to happen, Michelle, but there really is no way around it. I'd reimburse you for the ticket, but since we paid for it..." She smiles tightly.

"Great," I say, standing up. "Merry Christmas." I walk to my room and slam the door, not quite making it before the tears.

I stay in my room until Jeffrey gets home at six. Debra doesn't dare ask me to help with dinner, although I spend some time thinking of all the choice words I'd have to say if she did. I listen to her struggling with both kids in the kitchen. Jake is whining, and the baby is getting an early start on this evening's fit. The colic did not disappear with her three month birthday. I'm beginning to think she just has a bratty streak to work through, and chooses to exercise it when she has the biggest audience.

I hear something like a pot lid clatter to the floor and then a "God*damn* it!" I laugh to myself. I hear Jeffrey come in, drop his things in the entryway and walk into the kitchen. Jake squeals when he sees his dad, and a slight grunt escapes Jeffrey when a three-year-old projectile makes contact with his stomach. I hear him say hello to Debra and then the infuriating pause for a kiss. I decide now would be a good time to put in an appearance.

I trudge slowly through the playroom, sniffing loud enough for them to hear. I've already checked the mirror to make sure it's apparent I've been crying, but that I don't look too bad.

"What happened to you?!" Jeffrey asks when he sees me.

51

"She's upset because she can't go home for Christmas," Debra says.

"Why not?"

"I have to *work*," I say.

Debra tells him about the chicken fiasco. She's defensive and upset and starts to cry. Jeffrey puts his arms around her and makes soothing noises.

I send one extremely evil look to the back of Debra's head, and go back to my room. Jeffrey taps on the door a few minutes later. I'm about to tell him to go away, when he opens the door.

"So, it's just you and me this Christmas?" he says, grinning.

"Oh, sure, you *would* be happy about it. This stinks! I can't believe you guys are doing this to me. Why can't *you* take care of the kids? It's only for three days."

Jeffrey lowers his voice and says, "You take care of the kids and I'll take care of you."

"Shut up," I say without much enthusiasm. "It's not even going to feel like Christmas at all."

With a quick glance toward the door, Jeffrey comes over to where I sit on the carpet. He puts his hands -- still icy from outside -- on either side of my face. He gets this look on his face, and I glance toward the door myself, feeling a momentary panic. He leans down and kisses me long and deep. I lose myself in it, and then when he pulls away at last, and before he opens his eyes, I smack him in the shoulder, and say, "Stupid! She's *right there*!" I point in the kitchen's general direction. I'm a bit annoyed that he would come in here thinking that all he has to do is kiss me and it will make everything okay, but I have to admit that I am slightly thrilled by his boldness. Up to now, nothing has gone on between us unless Debra has been either out of town or safely asleep.

Jeffrey stands up and ruffles my hair. "Well, I have to go get dressed." He heads for the door.

"For what?"

"Dinner. We're going to the Kaufman's tonight." And I am mad all over again.

When they leave I stomp around the house, and find myself speaking sharply to Jake. Then, feeling guilty, I decide to let him stay up and watch a movie. When Miranda is upstairs in her crib, Jake and I pile pillows and blankets on the living room floor, making ourselves a 'nest'. We make a bowl of popcorn and settle in to watch

'The Little Mermaid' for the second time this week. I always get choked up during the song "Kiss the Girl."

When Jake is in bed I call home and give everyone the bad news about Christmas. It's nice that they're disappointed, but no one offers to 'fix it.' I know I'm silly for being so upset about this. It's not like Christmas is all that great anymore. Every year I have an expectation that it will be like the old days -- before the divorce.

I remember sitting in the living room on Christmas Eve with only the light from the fire and the tree. We'd hang up our stockings and sing carols. Brian and I would sit in Mom's lap and Dad would play his saxophone so softly it was almost a whisper. Then Brian and I would go off down the hall in our feet pajamas, our faces still warm from the fire. Those nights my house seemed like the warmest, safest place in the world.

Christmas morning we'd come into the living room shielding our eyes from Dad's movie camera with the giant light bulb mounted on top. There were so many presents. All the brightly wrapped boxes from out of town relatives that we'd been shaking and prodding for days, were drug out from under the tree and torn open. The hearth was piled with toys from Santa, Brian's loot on one side and mine on the other. Opening presents seemed to take hours, and when we were done the floor was covered in wadded wrapping paper and bits of ribbon.

Since Mom and Dad split up, no one seems to take much of an interest in Christmas. Our new ritual is to spend Christmas Eve on the boat with Mom and her new boyfriend, then go back to Dad's Christmas morning. We would always be in a hurry to get home and see Dad and have our second Christmas. Always we were disappointed. Dad's misery was contagious. The living room would be filled with harsh, winter light from an overcast sky. Dad didn't bother with Santa Claus except for a bag of M&Ms or a couple of batteries in the stockings we'd hung the day before.

The only good part of Christmas anymore is going to my aunt and uncle's for dinner. My dad's brother is an engineer at Boeing, and though he can be morose in his own way, he loves a party and is always happy to have lots of people over for the holidays. My aunt is a domestic goddess -- a latter-day Hestia. Although it's not currently in fashion to excel at such things, I can't help but be in awe of the woman. She cooks, sews, quilts, paints -- anything creative to do with her hands.

Dinner at their house is always the same. That's what I love about it. My aunt brings dish after dish to the table, one of the few times a year I get to eat 'real' food. Dad and my uncle trade corny jokes and stupid puns. My cousins and I compete for the center of attention and kick each other under the table.

One year, Dad decided he wanted us to have our own Christmas dinner. We sat around the house watching "Blue Hawaii" while Dad slept in the recliner. We finally woke him up around eight to ask what we were going to do about dinner. He took us to Denny's, where we were served rubbery spaghetti and meatballs by an understandably ornery waitress.

That was the worst Christmas in recent memory, but this one is shaping up to be the all time champion. It's not even going to seem like Christmas. The Goldman's just don't know how it's done. I'm going to have to insist on getting a Christmas tree.

After I clean up the kitchen and disassemble mine and Jake's nest, I sit down with a Diet Coke at the kitchen table and write out my Christmas cards. I start by enclosing nice little personal notes, but half-way through the list I'm just scrawling my name and stuffing them into the envelope.

Debra and Jeffrey come in as I'm licking stamps. They're home early, it's only eleven. I can hear Debra laughing from the entryway. They come into the kitchen, Debra tottering on his arm. They're drunk, and when she goes to toss her handbag onto the countertop, she misses, and the contents of her bag go flying everywhere. She finds this hysterical and drops to her knees to clean it up.

"How were the kids tonight?" Jeffrey asks me. I notice that he is watching me with the stamps. Every time I lick one he winces as if in pain. I decide to torture him and let the stamp linger on the tip of my tongue a fraction longer than necessary.

"They were fine," I say.

"Still mad at us?"

"Yes." I put a stamp in the corner of the last envelope and pound it down with my fist.

"Well, we feel really bad. We want to do something nice to make it up to you."

Debra stands up and brushes off her knees. She turns to me and gushes, "We really do, Michelle. We think you're great. We don't want to lose you." She must have had quite a few tonight.

"You don't have to do anything. I'm not going to leave."

"You're not? Oh... we just love you! We want you to stay forever!" She comes towards me and throws open her arms, engulfing me in a hug. She smells like perfume and vodka. Jeffrey comes over and hugs me from the other side, seizing the opportunity to seize my butt.

Debra leans on me heavily, and stumbles a bit. She doesn't drink very often. Extracting herself from the hug, she holds her head on with both hands. "Woah, maybe I'd better lie down."

"Good idea. I've got some things to do down here, and then I'll be right up." Jeffrey walks her toward the staircase.

"But I want you to come to bed with me," Debra says, looking at him from beneath her lashes and affecting a slight pout. I try to keep my disgust to myself. I'm wondering just how Jeffrey is going to put her off, when he follows her dutifully upstairs without even looking back.

I'm surprised but not discouraged. I go through my nightly routine, and settle down in the playroom armchair to read. Every time I turn a page I check my watch. After an hour and a half it finally becomes apparent to me that he's not coming back down.

I pick up the phone and call Amy. If it rings more than once this time of night it means that by some miracle she has gotten to sleep, and I will hang up. She picks up halfway through the first ring.

"I have got to get out of this house," I tell her.

"What's wrong?" She sounds alarmed. I tell her about Christmas.

"Want to meet me at the Rail?" I say, putting on my shoes.

"Oh... sorry, Michelle. I knew you were baby-sitting tonight, so I told the Maxwells I'd sit too. They're staying at the country house overnight. Do you want to come over here? Me and Susan are just talking and stuffing our faces."

"*Susan's* there?"

Amy lowers her voice, "Mick, don't be like that. Just come over, okay?" She waits for my reply. "*Okay?*"

"I'll be there in ten."

"Good." She hangs up.

I put on my coat, disarm the burglar alarm, and quietly slip out the door. Once outside I walk quickly, trying to keep warm. The Maxwells have an apartment on Perry Street, a few blocks away. When I get to the building, I see Amy standing in the doorway. She opens the door and motions me inside. I wonder why she didn't just buzz me in from upstairs.

"Why did you come all the way down?" I ask, following her up the stairs.

"I wanted to talk to you alone for a minute."

"About Susan?"

"I just want you to be nice. She's really upset. She called me about nine 'o clock and asked if she could talk to me. So I told her to come over. She lives in Gramercy Park."

"Well what's wrong with her?"

"She had her purse stolen."

"Oh no. Where?"

"Penn Station."

"That figures."

Amy lets us into the apartment. It's quiet and dark. I follow her into the living room, where I can just make out a human form by the light of the television.

"Susan," Amy says "this is my friend Michelle West."

"Oh, hi." The shape stands up from the couch and comes toward me, wiping her eyes.

"I heard you had a little trouble today," I say, trying to appear casual while I stare. If this is what Montana Sue looks like when she's upset and has been crying all night, I don't think I want to see her on a good day. Except that she not wearing any makeup and her hair is without benefit of a wind machine, she looks like she could have stepped off a magazine cover. I have never seen anyone this beautiful in my life. Not in the movies, not on TV. I am surprised out of my trance when she speaks.

"Yeah, some guy took my purse. He bumped into me, and like a fool I said 'excuse me.' Then I realized that my purse was gone. I feel like such a dummy."

"Did you tell a cop? Oh, forget it, there probably weren't any around for miles. I think even *they* are afraid of Penn Station."

"Well, no, actually there were quite a few. Three or four of them took down my statement. Then one of them walked all over the station with me to see if I recognized the guy who did it. But he was gone."

Amy and I smile. I can imagine the reaction of New York's Finest to finding Montana Sue in distress. I'm surprised they didn't give her a police escort to the mayor's office.

"But you're okay, right?" I say.

"Yeah. When I got home I told the Connollys about what happened and they told me it was my fault!"

"Let me guess," I say, "you were carrying your bag wrong and you weren't walking the right way."

She opens her mouth, her eyes wide. "Exactly! They told me that I was asking for it, and that criminals can spot a victim right away. They weren't sorry at all, they just thought I was stupid."

I take her arm and head for the kitchen. "Susan, the same thing happened to me when I'd been here two days. The Goldmans had no sympathy for me either. I think it's just something that you have to go through -- a rite of passage. Now you can say you're a New Yorker." We sit at the table and Amy gets some ice-cream from the freezer.

"I don't feel like a New Yorker. I don't think I want to be one. Why are they so mean?" Susan says, her eyes filling again.

"I don't know. Maybe they have to believe that there's a certain walk and attitude and way to carry your stuff that keeps you immune. Otherwise they'd all be too scared to leave the house."

Amy sets two heaping bowls of ice-cream on the table. She hoists herself and a third bowl up on to the kitchen counter, her favorite perch. Susan takes a bite of ice-cream and swirls it around her mouth experimentally.

"Hmm," she says, "This needs something. Do you have any chocolate syrup?"

"I like this girl," I say. Amy reaches behind her for the syrup and hands it around.

Susan swirls the syrup over her ice-cream. Do you guys like being nannies?" she asks.

"Yeah," I say.

Amy shrugs. "It's okay."

"I guess I like it," Susan says. "But it's really hard to know where I fit in sometimes."

Amy and I nod knowingly. "It's tough at first," Amy tells her. "How long have you been here?"

"About six weeks. I just thought I'd be more into the routine of things by now. I mean, the baby is great. I didn't really know what I was doing at first, but Mrs. Connolly didn't either, so it wasn't that bad. The problem is Mr. and Mrs. Connolly. They want me to call them Ed and Jane, but I just can't do it. I wasn't raised that way."

"Force yourself," I advise. "If you can't call them by their first names don't call them anything at all. It's a yuppie thing. You make them feel old."

Susan nods. "I guess I could try. The hardest thing, though is that I feel so awkward around them. After they come home from work I feel like I should leave and let them have their life to themselves. Plus, every night they invite me to eat dinner with them. I know my food is included in the contract, but I never know what to do. I don't know if they really want me to eat with them or if they're hoping I'll say no."

Amy slides off the countertop landing with a thud on her bare feet. "I was the same way. I didn't know if they wanted me out of their face or if they would think I was antisocial if I didn't eat with them. Here's what you do: make a schedule for yourself. You eat with them every other night. Of course if they go out and you're home with the kid, you don't worry about it. And weekends don't count."

"Yeah, what about weekends?" Susan asks. "I know it's my time off, and I should leave them in peace. But I'm usually so tired that I just want to watch TV in my room or talk on the phone."

"That's something you really have to be careful about," I tell her, enjoying being the voice of experience. "You should go out no matter how tired you are. If you're around they'll be tempted to ask you to baby-sit 'just for a minute' while they run to the store or go work out or read the paper. Then you never have any real time off, and you'll resent them and you'll be cranky with the kids and the whole thing gets ugly."

"Yeah," Amy adds, "You have to understand something, Susan. No matter how much they like you, they will take advantage of you every chance they get. See, to them you're just a hick girl from Montana."

Susan looks down at her bowl of melted ice-cream. "I can't believe them sometimes. They think Montana is the wild west or something. They think we get around in covered wagons and use outhouses."

We laugh. Amy says, "My first morning here, we were having breakfast and Dr. Maxwell asked me if I knew what a bagel was!"

"They're ridiculous," I say. "They think New York is the only *real* place, and the rest of the world is just background." Everyone agrees with this theory.

Susan steers the conversation back on track. "I do need to get out of the house when I'm not working," she says, then sort of shame-facedly admits, "But I don't have any place to go. I can only go to so many movies. I met a couple of nannies when I first got here, but..."

"Jenny Hunter?" I ask. "Amy told me how she wanted to audition you."

"Yeah, and I was so desperate to meet people that I went along with it. I don't want to sound mean, but she's a little bit strange."

Amy and I burst out laughing at this understatement.

"I met her for coffee one evening after work, and I could have sworn she had a British accent. But then we went out that weekend and it was a Southern accent. Where is she from?" Susan looks genuinely perplexed.

"She's from Cleveland," I tell her. "If you hang around her long enough you'll also be privy to her Long Island accent, her Boston accent and her Valley Girl accent, which I'd say is her best work."

"You don't like her?" Susan guesses.

"Let's just say this, " Amy says "In our agency there are two distinct nanny factions. There are Jenny Hunter and her toads, and there are the cool people."

"Another thing," Susan says, "The Connollys pay me in cash every week. I don't know if they take taxes out or what."

Amy and I look at each other.

"They don't take taxes out," I tell her.

"So I'm going to have to save up, and pay in one big chunk?" she asks.

Amy shakes her head. "No. See if you declare that income, then they're supposed to pay Social Security and all this other stuff. It's a lot simpler to keep everything under the table."

"Won't we get in trouble?"

"I guess not," I say. "That's just the way it's done."

"I don't feel right about that. I should be paying my fair share of taxes like everyone else." Susan draws herself up self-righteously.

Amy laughs. "Look, it's tax-free income. Enjoy it while you can."

"I don't enjoy breaking the law."

"Well if you file a return," I say, "Then they're going to want to know why the Connollys aren't declaring it on theirs. If you make that kind of trouble for them, they're likely to send you home, and find someone who plays by the rules -- *their* rules, I mean."

Susan looks miserable, but resigned to being what she considers a criminal.

"You know, Susan," I say, cautiously, glancing at Amy. "A few of us get together on Wednesday afternoons. It's sort of a playgroup thing. I know Riley is only 18 months, so he'd be a little younger than the other kids, but you should think about coming. The other girls are pretty nice."

"That would be great. Thanks so much. I didn't think I could stand hanging out with Jenny one more time." She looks so grateful, like she'd been rescued from disaster in the nick of time. I feel guilty that I didn't want to meet her before.

We adjourn to the living room to watch a video. Amy pulls me aside and thanks me for inviting Susan to join playgroup.

"No problem," I say. "She's nice. No one should be subjected to Jenny Hunter. Besides, I feel sorry for her. I remember feeling weird and confused and alone when I first got here, too."

We arrange ourselves on the living room sofa to watch the movie. Amy rented "...and God Created Woman" which is my favorite movie, but when I see that she's gotten the remake, I'm very disappointed. I think about going home, but know I won't be able to sleep, and I don't feel like going out in the cold. Amy and Susan settle in to watch the movie, and I flip through a magazine. It's Mrs. Bouchet's latest issue. How many articles can you have in one magazine about how to please your man, or how to trick a man? Interestingly, there is an article on The New Nanny - Destroying the Mary Poppins Myth. It discusses the pros and cons of live-in nannies versus live-out, and what to watch out for so that you don't inadvertently hire an evil nanny who's purpose in life is to molest your children and seduce your husband.

Why aren't there any articles for nannies on how to screen prospective employers? How to get through a phone interview and tell if they're lying. How to ask the right questions so that you don't move three thousand miles away from everything you know and end up with a family like the Eagans. I could just as easily have gotten that job. I was really lucky to get the Goldmans on the first try.

The movie's credits are rolling, and Susan is wiping her eyes. Amy is asleep at the far end of the couch.

"Don't look at me," Susan says. She blows her nose on a paper towel. "I always cry at the end of a movie -- no matter how stupid it is."

"Don't worry about it," I tell her. "I won't tell anyone." Hoping to preserve the confidential atmosphere, I check to see that Amy is sleeping soundly before I ask her:

"Susan, has Mr. Connolly -- what's his name? Ed?"

"Yes."

"Does Ed ever... act like maybe he... What I'm trying to say is does he ever, y'know, *hit on you*?" I immediately wish I could take the words back.

Susan's eyes are wide and she looks a little angry -- offended or something. "No!" she says, "Of course not! What a thing to ask!"

"I'm sorry, I'm sorry. That was a really stupid thing to say. Forget I said anything, okay? Please? Pretend I never opened my stupid mouth." I'm desperate now, wanting to defuse this situation before we wake up Amy.

"Well, okay. I guess I overreacted or something, but it just seemed so weird that you would say that." She looks perplexed and still a bit upset. We sit there in the dark while the television screen turns to static. I get up to turn off the set. From the darkness I hear Susan say, as if it has just occurred to her: "Michelle, has Mr. Goldman ever done it to you?"

"Jeffrey? No way."

Christa Charter

FOUR

It is Saturday afternoon, and Jake's birthday party is in full swing. He turns three today. Both the playroom and the living room upstairs are teeming with kids. Their parents line the walls and staircase, drinks in hand. They talk animatedly, having to supplement their speech with gestures and facial expressions to be understood over the roar of the children. The living room is draped in crepe paper and balloons. Jake wanted a Ninja Turtle motif, but Jeffrey refused to give in to commercialism, and went with plain old blue and white.

I stand mutely in the center of the room, searching for something to do with my hands. None of my friends are here, nor are they expected. Birthday parties are a parent event. This will be the first time that many of the parents will meet, and it is a big deal to them. Susan and Amy wanted me to go shopping, but I couldn't do that to Jake. He would be so hurt if I missed his birthday. Summer and Fiona are conspicuously absent also. Katy and the Bouchets are not coming because they had three other birthday parties this weekend -- children whose parents are big in the publishing business. Summer was going to come, but Benjamin was running a fever last night, so she called this morning and canceled. So I am abandoned by my friends, alone in a sea of parents and toddlers.

I am utterly useless. I can't even pretend to busy myself with Miranda. Debra has installed herself and the baby at the far end of the couch, and is holding court there. The mothers are all fawning over Miranda, as if she has just sprung from Debra's forehead, fully formed, dressed in pink ruffles, with a ribbon in her sparse blonde hair. Never mind that I am the one who got up with Miranda this morning, fed her breakfast, and then bathed and dressed her while Debra sat in the kitchen with her coffee having a nervous breakdown.

Jeffrey is making the rounds, glad-handing the men, and bestowing kisses on the women -- the consummate advertising man. I follow him with my eyes. Surprisingly, I'm not jealous at the way women react to him. Rather, I feel proud and superior in a way. I know something they don't know. At least I hope they don't.

The doorbell rings, and I trot for the door, glad for anything to do. The Maxwells are on the stoop, present in hand. Carmen and Camille's party dresses are identical except that Carmen's is pale yellow, while Camille's is seafoam green with matching satin ribbons tying back their hair. They are each holding one of their father's hands. I have only seen Doctor Maxwell once before. He is one of the only practicing obstetricians remaining in the city, and it seems he has to deliver every baby born in the Metropolitan area. Chris Maxwell is resplendent in a floral garment the size of a tent. Her face is pale and she shifts her bulk uncomfortably from one foot to the other. Her baby is due in three weeks. Although she looks ungainly and a bit humorous, there is something about her belly, swelling with vitality, that makes me happy and envious at the same time.

I usher the Maxwells inside, and unburden them of their coats and gift. Since they have never met the Goldmans, I am important for a moment, as their liaison to the party inside. The twins run screeching for Jake and the rest of the kids. Doctor Maxwell sheepishly heads for the bar, and strikes up a somber conversation with an accountant friend of Debra's. When Chris Maxwell enters the room, revealing all her pregnant glory, the women gravitate towards her, and she is soon happily inundated with questions and patting hands. I myself feel an almost primal urge to lay hands on that rising loaf of baby. But I have more pressing matters to attend to. I have corners to lurk in, hallways and stairways to slink through, hoping to remain unnoticed.

I wander over to where the children are gathered around a pile of brightly painted wooden blocks. Each child is busy with his or her own construction while they debate who is scarier: The Wicked Witch of the West or Ursula the Sea Witch.

"The Wicked Witch," says one of the neighborhood kids.

"No," puts in another, "Ursula. She's an *octopus.*"

Jake, who is carefully balancing a triangular block at the apex of his creation says in an offhand manner: "Yeah, but the Wicked Witch is scarier. She's *green.*"

I smile and turn away, thinking of all the times Jake has commanded me to fast forward the "green witch" so that he will be spared the scariest parts. As I walk away I hear Jake informing the gathered masses that the Tinman has no tongue. Camille counters with the information that Batman has black pee.

The Connollys have arrived, and enter the room apprehensively. Jane carries Riley in her arms, and Ed Connolly carries a beribboned package with his fingertips, as if his masculinity might be in jeopardy at the very touch of the bunny rabbit wrapping paper. He is a professor at Columbia, and has dressed the part. The graying beard, the pipe, even elbow patches. Jane, a former student of his, is dolled up in a party dress and tights. She even has an Alice in Wonderland band in her straight, blonde hair. Poor Riley, I am dismayed to see, is nauseatingly attired in short pants with suspenders and a bow tie.

Jane's face brightens at my approach until she remembers that I am only the nanny. "Hello, Michelle," she squeaks. She always squeaks. "I'm surprised you didn't go shopping with the other girls." She refers to us as 'the girls' although she is Fiona's age.

"Well, I couldn't miss Jake's party!" I say, taking the present from a very grateful Mr. Connolly.

"Oh, you had to work, huh?" She looks at me in mock sympathy. Why is it so difficult to understand that I *want* to be here? I don't even attempt to explain. I lead Jane over to Debra, and introduce her as Riley's Mom. They do their smiling, nodding thing. Since Debra has lost her audience, she lets me take Miranda off her hands. Overwhelmingly grateful for something to do, I take the baby down to the kitchen to mix up some formula.

I don't recognize them until it is too late. Quickly, I avert my eyes, and walk faster, hoping they won't say anything. But it's no use.

"Why it's the lovely young Michelle!"

"Hi," I say weakly, my smile so phony the corners of my mouth twitch.

James and Rachel Zhering, the hip couple of the decade. They look almost incestuous together they are so alike. They are both tall, with darkly tanned skin and thick black hair expensively coifed. Rachel's is short and chic, displaying her tastefully sized diamond earrings to full advantage. James has his hair slicked back in a GQ style with some substance that is probably fifty bucks a tube. Both wear dark suits, as they have only 'popped in' on their way to the office. Their wide white smiles are so similar that you'd think whoever capped their teeth used the same mold on both of them.

Whenever I see them, or even hear Jeffrey or Debra mention their names I feel an inward cringe like remembering the time in the second grade I couldn't get my overalls undone in time and wet my pants. Seeing them is like experiencing the shame and humiliation all over again. I imagine I can almost smell the stale urine from all those years ago. I always associate the two -- humiliation and the ancient smell of pee drying slowly on denim.

The first time I met the Zherings, I had been working for the Goldmans for only a few weeks. It was after Summer quit her job with the Eagans and moved uptown, but before I had met any of the other girls. I had seen Fiona in the park, but we hadn't really connected yet. That time was what I like to think of as the blissfully ignorant stage of my nanny adventures. I was still enchanted by the Goldmans, and was fancying myself a Goldman-elect, a distant, but well-loved family member.

Debra had been back at work for a week. She had been very concerned that I wouldn't be able to handle both kids at the same time -- probably because she found it overwhelming -- but I was having fun. Jake went to preschool in the mornings, and I would put Miranda in the Snugli and run errands, or else get some things done around the house. Later, I would nap when Miranda did, but in those days I was still sleeping at night.

In the beginning I never felt like I was intruding on their lives, or that I should make myself scarce and let them enjoy their family in privacy. It never occurred to me that they wouldn't want my company, or that what I had done that day wouldn't be of paramount interest to them -- especially since it involved their children. I just chatted away like I had known them all my life, which is what it felt like.

After dinner, if the weather wasn't nice enough to go for a walk, we would rent a movie. We'd put the kids in bed, open some beers, and sit around the TV in the living room. They seemed to enjoy my company: they asked my opinions on what was going on in the world, and they told me about all the places they'd traveled together before Jake was born. They even laughed at my wisecracks. I enjoyed all this so much, that when Barbara called from the nanny agency to invite me to a party planned for the next weekend, I told her that I had other plans, and made it pretty clear that I wasn't interested in socializing with the other nannies. I didn't really have any plans, I just couldn't bear to give up an evening with the Goldmans.

Every once in a while Debra would suggest that I go to a museum to see a certain exhibit, or ask me if I'd met any friends. I took this to mean that she was concerned for my well-being and that maybe I would be bored hanging out with people so much older. She often joked about me being half their age, and I would joke back that I didn't think they were *quite* ready for the nursing home.

Anyway, Debra decided to have a dinner party to celebrate her first week back to the old grind. She invited the Zherings, another married couple, and a girlfriend of hers from college who she was trying to set up with a single white male from her office. The girlfriend, Trisha, had reached the advanced age of thirty-five without having experienced wedded bliss. She was almost a lost cause, but Debra, in her compassion, decided to give it one last shot. Never mind that the intended man was grievously unattractive, and had the annoying problem of spit collecting in the corners of his mouth when he talked -- a bachelor was a bachelor.

Debra got up early Saturday morning, and spent the day cooking. Oddly enough, this also meant that I spent my day off with the kids, "keeping them out of her hair." At the time I didn't think twice about this arrangement. After all, what older sister would refuse to look after the younger kids while "Mom" prepared the feast? I was just being a dutiful daughter. I continued to keep the kids occupied while Debra showered and changed and got ready for the party.

Debra was walking through the house smoothing things -- her dress, the tablecloth, Jake's hair -- when the guests arrived. Jeffrey had spent all day in the office, and breezed in with the rest of them. Everyone sat around in the living room and Jeffrey played bartender. The kids were in their pajamas when the party began. They were trotted in to be admired, and with that finished, were trotted out again, and upstairs to bed. Debra orchestrated this maneuver, the proud and doting mother. When she came back down to announce that both kids were sleeping like little angels, I snuck upstairs to read Jake his story. "Don't ever go away," he warned.

"I'm not going anywhere tonight," I said.

Downstairs in the dining room Debra was serving dinner. Jeffrey was in the kitchen below loading the dumbwaiter, which he sent up to Debra, who put the dishes on the long dining room table. When everything was in place Jeffrey came upstairs. We all sat down, Jeffrey and Debra at opposite ends, and myself seated between James Zhering and the ugly guy from Debra's office. Jeffrey raised a toast to Debra and her career, and we all drank.

Dinner seemed to go well. All of the guests asked me what Seattle is like, and what I thought of New York so far. I told them that I loved the city, and rhapsodized about how big and exciting it is. They then began drilling me on what I'd done and seen since moving here.

"Been to the Met?"

"No."

"The Whitney? The Guggenheim?"

"Unh-uh."

"Lincoln Center? The Empire State Building?"

"Well, not yet." I started to feel like a criminal being cross-examined.

Trisha, directly across the table, leaned forward on her elbows, directed her hatchet-face in my direction and asked: "What *have* you done, Michelle?" She said my name like it was a dirty word.

"Well, I guess I ... just...I take care of the kids..."

James Zhering put his arm around me and said, "Jeffrey, you're working this poor girl to the bone!" He gave my shoulders a condescending little squeeze and everyone laughed. Then they moved onto the topic of some new movie that was so scandalous they had to invent a new rating for it. I took the opportunity to volunteer to fetch the coffee and dessert.

"Well *thank you*, Michelle," Debra beamed at me.

Downstairs in the empty kitchen I brewed the coffee and made a note to go and visit some of the places that had been mentioned. I was in New York, after all. I really should see something of it. Maybe I would take the kids to the Museum of Modern Art.

I began to load the fragile wedding-present dessert set onto the dumbwaiter. I hummed a little to myself, and as I turned to get the coffee I heard voices floating down through the dumbwaiter shaft.

"...she hasn't seen anything of the city," a male voice said. Sounded like James. "You ought to let her out more often."

"*Let* her out?!" Debra laughed. "I can't *get* her out!"

Everyone chuckled at this.

"Well what's the matter with her?" Trisha.

Debra sighed. "I don't know. I've tried everything I can think of. I've made all sorts of suggestions, I've left brochures for night school in her room, I'm at my wits end. She just won't leave. She's always here, hanging around. I don't know what to do with her. She's wonderful with the kids, but I'm thinking I may have to send her back. I'm too young to have a teenage daughter."

"Michelle's a home-body," Jeffrey said in my defense. "She's a nice, sweet girl from Seattle. I'd like to keep her that way. Much better to have a nice little babysitter than a wild one that runs around at night and gets herself knocked up."

"Well, I guess you're right," someone agreed.

"Well..." Jeffrey said, ready to change the subject. But Debra couldn't let it drop.

"You won't believe what she said the other day," she continued. "She actually said that she wished her parents were more like Jeffrey and I! Can you imagine?! God forbid that Miranda would grow up to be a *nanny*." She laughed bitterly at the thought.

Someone said, "Hmm..." and there were a few moments of complete silence. I realized that I had stopped breathing and my jaw was clenched so tight the muscles in my neck were beginning to ache. I was in such a complete state of shock that I wasn't sure my body would respond to the commands of my brain, but I began to pull on the rope that sent the dumbwaiter up into the dining room. It squeaks very slightly -- it seems everything in this house does -- and at the sound, Jeffrey exclaimed, "Well, there's the dessert!"

I considered running outside and catching a cab to the airport, but only for the briefest of seconds. I walked up the stairs like a convict to the gallows. When I came into the dining room, Jeffrey was dishing up the cake, and I slipped back into my seat. More than anything, I didn't want them to know that I'd overheard them. Then I would *have* to leave.

I drew patterns in the cake with the tines of my fork. I kept a half-smile upon my face, and looked around the table, not really seeing anyone. Rachel Zhering began telling about how she had to fire three maids in a row because their English was so poor they couldn't understand her instructions. Besides, she had reason to believe that one or all of them were pilfering her good silverware.

I smiled like I thought it was funny. I smiled like my guts weren't laying on a chafing dish in the center of the table. I looked toward Jeffrey's end of the table, not quite able to meet his eyes.

It suddenly struck me that I was not a creature on par with the Goldmans, the Zherings and the rest. To them, I was one of many nannies, maids, handymen, and other various slaves. I was a walk-on bit-part in the drama of their lives. And in that instant I also realized that in their eyes I no more belonged at the dinner table eating with them than would be the man who runs the newsstand on the corner, or the old woman who goes through the trash looking for cans and bottles to turn in for small change.

In my bed that night I lay awake. I tried to understand how anyone could think of me the way they obviously did. I gave that up and spent the rest of the long night trying to think of a plan. Some way that I could prove myself to the Goldmans -- and to their asshole friends. I would become so unbearably hip and cool and sophisticated that they would never want me to leave. And they would realize that I really was one of them.

The next morning, after the first of many sleepless nights in New York, I called Barbara at the agency and told her I had changed my mind about the party and I wanted to go. As soon as I hung up the phone I left the house and didn't return until after dinner. I walked all the way to Central Park, and then went to a movie by myself. I stopped in at the Metropolitan Museum of Art, but it was Sunday, and the lines were too long. So I stood outside on the wide, white steps eating a hot-dog from a street vendor's cart and feeling like a tourism ad. See the Big Apple! Glamour! Excitement! A caste system!

Back at the house that evening, I came in to find Debra and Jeffrey absolutely frantic. They didn't know where I'd gone, and thought I'd been murdered somewhere, because, let's face it, I didn't know the correct way to walk, and I carried my bag all wrong. I was very evasive about where I'd spent the day, and told them not to worry about me because I was nineteen years old, and could take care of myself. Jeffrey and Debra exchanged a bewildered glance. I kissed the kids, yawned dramatically, and went into my room. Jeffrey knocked on my bedroom door a little while later to see if I wanted to come upstairs and watch a movie with them. "No thanks, " I said lightly, without opening the door.

All that next week I made sure that if I wasn't baby-sitting, I was out of the house the minute they got home from work. I saw every movie showing below 23rd Street, investigated stores and tried out the local diners and delis. I was running out of things to do when I went to Jenny Hunter's nanny party and met Amy. From then on, my social life was pretty well taken care of. I got to know enough girls so that if I was free some evening there was always someone to go out with.

I think that the Goldmans must have had an idea that I'd discovered what they really thought of me. What else could they make of my dramatic personality change? But they never said anything about it, and I eventually got over feeling betrayed by them, and learned to relate to them not as surrogate parents, but employers and house-mates. The only thing that brought it up again was the mere mention, sight, or sound of the Zherings.

The Zherings, through their smiling teeth, tell me how good it is to see me again and ask if I've done anything *fun* lately. A horrible taste rises up in my throat and I tell them that I've done plenty of fun things, but nothing I could relate in mixed company. They laugh it up for a minute, then make their way upstairs to the party.

As soon as they go I lay my head against the cool refrigerator door and take some long, slow breaths. I have my eyes so tightly shut that I see patterns on my eyelids. They move and seem to dance as I shift my eyeballs from side to side. They feel smooth against the moist inside of my eyelid.

Miranda suddenly shifts in my arms, and nearly dropping her, I realize that I'd been asleep. I have been so tired for so long now that I have reached a new level of tiredness. I wonder if this is the way to nirvana or the loony bin? It's funny, but not very, that for the life of me I can't get to sleep at night in my bed, but I can drift off perfectly nicely standing up with a baby in my arms and the appliance logo pressed into my brow.

On automatic pilot I mix the baby's bottle, and grab myself a Diet Coke. I roll the ice-cold can across my forehead before popping the tab and drinking most of it in one pull. I almost laugh at what James and Rachel Zhering would do if I let loose the enormous belch I have on deck in my throat. But I suppress it. Someone might hear it through the dumbwaiter and figure it was just typical of a white-trash nanny girl.

Upstairs again at the party, Debra is trying to corral all the kids into the dining room to cut the cake. The kids turn it into a chase game and go fleeing across the room in mock-horror, giggling and tripping over toys and each other. Debra wipes her hair out of her eyes and looks exasperated. I could tell her that if she would just strike a single match to light the birthday candles every child in the room would be at her side instantaneously, but I don't think she wants my advice.

Jake runs past me, and I put out a hand to catch him, but he shrugs me off. He is too busy with his friends. Miranda squirms to be put down. I find a relatively safe corner for her and she lays on the floor and wriggles on her belly -- 'creeping' they call it. The stage before 'true crawling'. Her pink dress gets caught up underneath her, and she screams in frustration. I try to untangle her, but she wants to do it herself and swats me away.

Being rejected by both kids, I go sit on the sofa next to Ed Connolly. He is making small talk with one of Jeffrey's clients. I open my mouth to add something to the conversation, but close it right up again. Who needs that kind of aggravation? So I sit there with my Diet Coke trying not to look like I have no one to talk to, and no role to play. Out the window I see our friendly neighborhood bag lady going through the trash. I want to knock on the glass and tell her to come back after the party when there will be lots more to choose from. For a minute, I almost wish I was out there with her. At least she knows where she fits into the scheme of things. Either that or she's so delusional she doesn't care.

Inevitably, my eyes stray to where Jeffrey stands at the stereo, changing the CD from Beethoven to the Rolling Stones. At the first strains of "Honky Tonk Woman" he moves slightly to the music, and his hand pats out the bass line on his thigh. He looks up, and we make eye contact. I try to hold his eyes with my own, to tell him to come talk to me, to rescue me from anonymity, to show everyone at this party that I matter, at least to him. But his black gaze has moved on to something more interesting.

I begin to wonder if I exist at all. Do I just think I'm here? Am I invisible? Am I dead and don't realize it? I sometimes think this way. Amy and I went to a late, late showing of an old French movie called "Les Jeux Sont Fait." In it, when people die, they hang around, walking among the living, but they are invisible and intangible except to other dead people. They also, like vampires, cast no reflection in a mirror.

I'm about to go consult the nearest mirror for proof that I'm alive when Debra calls out that it is time for cake. The parents, sluggish after a few drinks, hoist themselves out of chairs and sofas with various grunts and moans. Everyone shuffles into the dining room where Jake sits at the head of the table, the bottom half of his face hidden by the enormous cake with a candle shaped like the number three. I can see by the look on his face that he wants desperately to reach out and touch the dancing yellow flame, but doesn't dare. Debra and Jeffrey stand on either side of him like a damned Norman Rockwell portrait, and Jeffrey leads us in singing Happy Birthday. The four and five year olds in the group add the extra verse at the end that goes "...you look like a monkey, and you smell like one too." All the parents get a big rise out the cleverness of their offspring.

I am thinking that I could easily disappear into my room, and no one would be the wiser, when Debra tells Jake to blow out his candle before it gets wax on the frosting. Jake looks frantically around him. "Where's 'shell?" he says. "She has to help me blow."

Scooping up Miranda, I step out from behind the crowd, and present myself in front of Jake. He grins, says, "Now we have the whole family!" and blows out the candle. For this moment I belong. I belong more than the Zherings or the Connollys or the neighbors and business associates. I belong because this is Jake's party. And I'm the one who makes him breakfast and packs his lunch box. I'm the one who grills his cheese sandwich to a perfect shade of light brown, the one who reads him to sleep and who he never wants to leave. I'm the one he loves, and everybody knows it.

If only I could say the same for his father. I also belong here because of Jeffrey, but no one here would guess that except in their wildest imaginings. I almost want them to guess. I want them to know that whatever they may think of me, I am more than that to Jeffrey. I find myself wishing that he would do something -- a word, or a gesture that would acknowledge me as someone who matters to him. I know I do, but somehow it isn't enough. This has been going on for months now, and I'm getting a little tired of being such a well-kept secret. It makes me feel like I'm something to be ashamed about, or embarrassed by.

If these people here could have seen us last night... They would certainly look at me in a new way. Instead of the quiet little nanny from Hicksville, USA, who has to be pried out of the house with a crowbar, they would get an eyeful of the real Michelle West.

I look across the room, always keeping tabs on Jeffrey, gauging his distance from me, and monitoring his mood. Our eyes meet once again, and I search his eyes for something of what I saw there last night, but there is nothing. I wonder again if I am here at all.

Last night Jeffrey got home early and brought in two big bags full of crepe paper decorations and balloons. Debra took one look at them and groaned. "I thought we weren't going to do decorations this year."

"Well, I couldn't help myself. I found a place that was going out of business. I got all this for thirty bucks!" He spread his arms to indicate his bounty.

"Jeffrey, I still have to pick up the cake and meet with the caterers. I don't have time for this!" She started to whine.

"You don't have to lift a finger, Deb. I'll do it. Michelle will give me a hand, right, Michelle?" Jeffrey and I were on the other side of the counter, and he moved his left leg against my right, where Debra couldn't see.

"I guess so," I said, and swallowed hard, a spear of lust shooting through my belly. Even after all this time, he still had that effect on me. I felt physically weakened around him. Sometimes, I'd be standing there talking with him, and I'd suddenly feel that I could fall over from loving him so much.

After dinner, we all went up to the living room. Debra sat on the sofa watching a movie. Jeffrey and I watched from across the room where we sat Indian-style on the floor blowing up balloons. The baby had gone to bed early, and Jake was nearly asleep with his head in his mother's lap. Jeffrey and I took our time on the balloons. There was only so much decorating to be done, and we needed to make it last. Once, we each blew up a balloon half-full, then traded, and blew up each other's, like a couple of Junior High kids. We laughed, and blushed at our own sappiness. Debra turned at the sound, and we pretended that we were laughing at the movie.

The room had grown dark, and there was only the light from the television and the streetlights through the unshuttered windows. Making sure that Debra was engrossed in the movie, Jeffrey reached over and slowly ran his hand up my leg, his wedding ring catching the light. I couldn't tear my eyes away from it.

Finally, the movie ended and Debra asked Jeffrey to come take Jake off her lap and carry him up to bed. When he came back she said, "Well, it looks like there's still a lot of decorating to be done. I'd help you, but since you two volunteered..." She waved at us, thinking she was cute, and went upstairs. I had to laugh. She had played right into our hands. She thought she was so smart, and we had gotten exactly what we wanted.

We did end up decorating for the party. We kept the stereo very low and listened to some old Marvin Gaye songs. We stood on stepladders and furniture, stringing crepe paper streamers across the room like waves. I can't remember what we talked about, only that it seemed important at the time. Most likely we argued. That's one of my favorite things about Jeffrey: he realizes how much I love a good debate, and tries to accomodate me at every available opportunity. Although we are pretty like-minded politically, if we get on to philosophy and the question of whether man is basically good or evil, we can get some pretty good arguments going. We don't argue because we're angry with each other, only that it's fun. It's a flirtation for us -- almost foreplay. He usually ends up by shaking his head and telling me that I'm much too smart to be a nanny and that I should go back to college. Which he always qualifies by saying: "But not too soon."

The one subject I know we didn't discuss was "us." That was something we didn't even dare to get close to. Even though at times I wanted him to shout out to the world that I meant something to him, we both knew that the minute either one of us broached the dread subject of "us" -- which could only lead to worse subjects like what are we doing and where is it going -- then everything would be different. Once the words were spoken they could never be taken back, and everything would change.

When the balloons were put up and the fate of the world had been debated, Jeffrey fell quiet. He turned off the stereo, and the house was silent and dark. We both stood there, listening. Jeffrey held up one finger in a gesture for me to wait. He went upstairs and stood outside their bedroom, listening for any noise within. He came back downstairs and flashed me the "okay" sign. The coast was clear. My adrenaline started pumping as he walked closer with that knowing, anticipatory look on his face. I started to head for the stairs, assuming that we'd go down to my room, but Jeffrey had other plans. He caught me by the arm and smiled. He pointed down at the oriental rug.

My eyes widened. "You can't be serious?!" I whispered, although I knew he was. He pulled me into his arms and kissed the side of my neck. "You're insane," I said, closing my eyes.

"I am insane, " he agreed, his voice a low, growling whisper. "This is what you do to me -- make me crazy. You're like some kind of poison. I know it's dangerous, and may even kill me, but I keep coming back for more."

I wanted him to keep talking. I wanted to hear it all. But I covered his mouth with mine, and he didn't say any more.

We lay down on the rug in the center of the living room, with the ceiling twelve feet above. If anyone had come in, there would have been nowhere to hide, nothing to scramble behind and fumble to put our clothing back in order. It was so open and exposed, we may as well have been center court at Madison Square Garden. It felt like an arena of some kind, and that we were players in some ancient Roman ritual.

At one point a drop of perspiration rolled slowly down his forehead and fell, with a perfect little 'plop' into my left eye. I looked up at the ceiling, and for a moment, my vision was miraculously clear -- all the edges sharply defined, the colors seeming to glow. The only sound was our rapid breathing, and as it quickened, I shouted at him in my mind to tell me something. I couldn't even *think* what I really wanted him to say. Even in my thoughts I used the euphemism 'the L-word'. And, as if he had received my telepathic message, he did say the l-word. Unfortunately, it was used in conjunction with the F-word. But, I thought to myself, at least it's something.

Jeffrey is at the door, saying good-bye to the Maxwells. He tousles the twins' hair, and gives Chris Maxwell's belly a pat. People are beginning to collect their coats and their children, ambling out into the early evening to get on with their Saturday nights. The kids whine and fuss -- they need their dinner. Jake cries because one of the little boys insists on taking home the present that he came with. I grab the toy away, and take Jake into my lap, showing him that the toy is safe and sound. The other kid starts screaming. I am in no mood to try to massage his ego, and when his mother comes to collect him, she gives me a dirty look. I see her talking to Debra and looking towards me on her way out. Now I'll probably get in trouble.

The place is almost empty now. I roam around gathering beer bottles and paper plates. I drag the big waste paper basket into the center of the room and start shoveling in wrapping paper, empty boxes, plastic forks, and streamers that have come down during the festivities. In one corner, I find a dirty diaper that someone has left. They very thoughtfully balled it up and secured it with the tapes, but you'd think they could find a garbage can! This reminds me that Miranda hasn't been changed in a while. I find her picking cake crumbs off the carpet. I take them out of her hand before she can pop them in her mouth. She shouldn't be eating off this floor, especially after last night.

Jeffrey and Debra stand at the door, their arms around each other's waists, waving at the departing guests. Sickened, I take Miranda upstairs. As I'm changing her diaper I think about how Jeffrey's paid barely any attention to me all day. He left to play tennis before I woke up, and then spent the rest of the morning in the office. Come to think of it, he hasn't spoken to me since last night.

Sometimes he does that, though. After a particularly intense evening in my company, he often is distant for a day or so. Early on, I thought maybe he was feeling guilty, but I don't think that's the case. It seems the more he likes me the more it pisses him off -- like I'm doing something purposely malicious to him. Ridiculous! He's the one who started it!

Maybe this time he's finally through with me. Maybe last night was too much for him. Oh well, I guess I knew this would happen some day. I hope I can handle it. I hope that it doesn't kill me to sit across the table from him and remember what it used to be like. Maybe I should leave. Maybe that would be the best thing for everyone.

I hear the toilet flush in the master bath. I finish Miranda's diaper, and get her clothes back in order quickly, in the hope that whoever is coming out of the bathroom doesn't see me. I don't feel like having any sappy, condescending chats with any of the parents. I pick up Miranda and cross the nursery with my head down. The bathroom door hasn't opened yet, and if I can just make it to the stairs...

"Hey," a voice says softly. Jeffrey catches me by the arm.

"Oh, hi," I say. "You scared me." I should be relieved, but the way my thoughts have been going the last few minutes, Jeffrey is the last person I want to see.

Jeffrey looks toward the stairs, and seeing no one, takes my elbow and steers me back into the nursery. "I know I haven't been paying much attention to you today," he says. He's moving me back, back into the corner of the room.

"Well, you were busy," I say.

"That's no excuse. I know you need your fair share of attention."

"I know it's stupid..." I look down, ashamed at my pettiness. "It's just that sometimes I think you don't like me anymore." I am well aware how pathetic and pleading I sound, but the words come out before I can stop them. I blink hard, trying not to cry. How dumb, I think, hating myself. How utterly dumb to let anyone make me feel like this! I lay my cheek on Miranda's head, breathing in the smell of baby powder and strained peas.

Jeffrey gently takes Miranda from me. I still won't look at him. "Listen," he says, "how could you think I don't like you? Come on, I'm crazy about you! Can't you see that? Would a sane man behave the way I do?"

I have to laugh. I shake my head. "I guess not."

He leans in closer, close enough so that I can feel his body heat and smell the sweet rum on his breath. "Michelle," his voice is low. "I want you all the time," he whispers, "even in my sleep." He sways in to kiss me, but changes his mind and drops the kiss on Miranda's plump cheek. "Lucky you can't talk yet," he tells her.

FIVE

From the window of the Connolly's apartment I can see the last of the blossoms drifting down from the trees in Gramercy Park below. The winding paths and benches are empty except for one woman walking slowly through the trees with her eyes on the ground, as if looking for something she's lost. In the room behind me are gathered what remains of our playgroup. Molly, not being able to find another job, returned to Ireland to marry a distant cousin. We haven't heard from her in months, and don't even know her husband's name to get in touch with her. Summer and Benjamin sit on the floor looking through a stack of video taped cartoons. Susan carries Riley back and forth across the floor. Miranda has just learned to pull herself up on the furniture, and is making good use of an end table.

Jake stands near the door. He has recently had his hair cut in a big-boy way, and it amazes me how his face has thinned out and matured over the past several months. He's really growing up. I notice that he is fidgeting around quite a bit.

"Do you need to go pee?" I ask him.

"No." He shakes his head.

"Then why are you such a wiggle worm?"

Jake laughs and begins exaggerating his motions, sticking his butt out and swaying it back and forth. He waves his arms around and sticks out his tongue. "I'm a wiggle worm!" he declares. "I'm a wiggle squirm, a squirmy worm!" He collapses to the floor in a fit of giggles. Benjamin, not to be outdone, announces that he is a snake, and starts squirming on his belly and sssssssss-ing.

"You guys are silly," Susan says affectionately. The kids are all wound up this afternoon because we are expecting Amy at any minute. She hasn't been to playgroup the last two weeks, so this will be our first sighting of the new baby, Cameron Maxwell.

"I think I hear the elevator!" Benjamin says. But it's a false alarm. I look out at the park again, and wonder why no one thought to make a playground. It's a perfectly beautiful spring day, and here we are cooped up in the apartment. Maybe some fresh air would wake me up.

There is a light tapping on the door, and the kids start screaming and jumping around. Susan pushes them gently aside to let Amy in. "Hi!" we all say at once. It feels like we haven't seen each other forever. Amy pushes the carriage into the apartment. The twins are walking beside the carriage, secured with stretchy plastic cords running from the handle to bands around their wrists. There is probably some trendy yuppie term for this device; I prefer to think of it as a leash. Amy insists that they would go off in all directions if allowed to run loose.

Susan and I have discussed this beforehand, and we make a big deal over the twins before we even look at the baby. We are dying to peek in at the sleeping bundle, but give the girls hugs and attention and tell them how big they are getting. They smile and show us their new shoes. Then Carmen says, "Want to see our new baby?"

Susan and I look at each other. "Well... okay," she says.

"You hafta be very gentle," Camille warns us. "He's little."

Jake and Benjamin push up to the carriage, and the girls push them back. "I wanna *see*!" Benjamin whines.

"Ben!" Summer says sharply. "Come over here and wait your turn." He does as he's told.

When she's sure she has everyone's undivided attention, Carmen slowly pulls the baby's blanket down and whispers, "Hi, Camera, wanna meet my friends?"

"*Camera?*" I ask Amy.

"That's what they think his name is. I've tried to tell them it's Cameron, but they insist." She shrugs. She looks tired. My guess is that it's been a hectic couple of weeks.

Cameron opens his red, toothless mouth and squeaks. His tiny fists wave in the air, trembly in that newborn way. The kids all take a step back and then say quietly, "Hi, Camera." It's pretty funny, but they're being so serious and sweet that we manage not to laugh. Jake puts out a finger tentatively, and looks up at me to see if it's okay. I look at Amy.

"Tell you what," she says, leaning down to the kids, "Let's wash our hands to get the germs off, and then you can all have a turn holding *Cameron*." The kids run for the bathroom, and Summer takes on the task of lifting them up to the sink one by one and helping them wash. I guess they get a bit carried away squirting the liquid soap judging from the shouts and laughter, and Summer's insistent: "Stop that *now*!"

I take the opportunity to get the first shot at holding the baby. As I reach into the carriage, I spot Amy's anxious expression. "Relax," I tell her. "Remember, I've done this before." I nod toward Miranda, who has pulled off one of her socks and stuffed it into her mouth. She grins at me around a mouthful of white lace trimming. It's hard to believe that this big, active girl was once a little lump like Cameron. Holding Cameron, I look back and forth, comparing the two. Cameron has a thick, dark thatch of hair that will probably fall out in the next few months and be replaced by his true hair. When Miranda was born she was absolutely bald, tiny and red. Cameron looks like he is already two or three months old. Besides the full head of hair, he weighs almost ten pounds, and is healthy and vigorous. He fills up those vigorous little lungs and lets loose a cry that brings the kids running in.

We sit them down in a row on the couch: Jake, Carmen, Benjamin, and Camille. Amy puts the baby on each of their laps in succession. Riley is too little to hold him, but stands over whoever's got the baby at the moment, and peers down into his face intently. He suddenly laughs and says "Bay-bee!" It is his first word. Susan jumps up and twirls him around the room. We all get up and join in the jumping saying "Yay, Riley! Good boy!" Riley smile widens and he says: "Bay-bee, bay-bee, bay-bee!"

When everyone calms down again and Amy has Cameron safely restored to his carriage, Summer asks Susan when the Connollys are going to give Riley a little brother or sister. Susan gets quiet, and licks her lips nervously. She nods towards the kids and shakes her head.

"Hey, guys!" I say, "Why don't we go in Riley's room and watch a movie?!" They jump and clap their hands. When they are settled in watching a video and eating microwave popcorn, Summer, Amy, Susan and I pour a round of Diet Cokes and gather in the living room. Miranda sits on my lap with her bottle of apple juice.

"So what's up?" Summer asks.

"You guys won't even believe this," Susan says. "The Connollys are breaking up."

"What!?"

She nods, and tucks a few stray strands of blonde hair up into her baseball cap. "It's been going on for a week or two. They yell all the time, slam doors, throw things -- it's like living on the set of a soap opera."

"Well, what happened?" Amy asks.

"I guess -- and this is just what I've put together from bits and pieces that I've overheard -- Ed has been having an affair with one of the students in his ethics class."

"No way!" Amy says, her eyes wide.

"Well, isn't that how he and Jane got together in the first place?" I say. Susan nods. "She shouldn't be too surprised then."

"Yeah, but...." Susan looks towards the kids' room and makes sure the door is still shut. She lowers her voice. "This is a *male* student."

We are all too stunned to speak. It occurs to me that if Susan hadn't been the one telling us, she would have responded: "Eww, gross!" But nobody says anything.

Finally, Summer says: "Well, what's going to happen? Are you going to have to leave?"

"I don't know. In a way I want to. All the things that keep happening to me..."

"Oh no. Did you get mugged again?" I ask.

Susan laughs. "Twice more. It's getting so that I don't want to leave the house. I'm afraid someone will abduct Riley. We were on the subway the other day and this guy came around shaking a paper cup full of change. He was a veteran or something. He kept saying 'Spare some change? Spare some change for a Vietnam veteran?' and jingling the cup in everyone's face. His breath reeked like booze, and he smelled like he'd peed in his pants."

"He probably had," Amy observed, adjusting Cameron's diaper.

Susan wrinkled her nose at the thought and continued: "Anyway, I thought about giving him a quarter -- I mean, my *uncle* was in Vietnam -- but no one else was giving anything, so I pretended not to see him. Then he stopped right in front of me and goes: 'How 'bout you, blondie? Spare some change?' I just froze and stared straight ahead. I was saying over and over in my head, please God, don't let him touch Riley. I even squeezed my eyes shut for a second, and when I opened them he was shuffling toward the door to the next car. Just as he was about to leave, he turned around and started *screaming*! I can't remember exactly what he said, he was really drunk and hard to understand, but it was something about how he fought for his country and saw his buddies get killed. Then he said something about Agent Orange. He took off his shirt to show everyone how the Agent Orange had burnt him. He had all this gross, rashy stuff all over his chest and arms. I covered Riley's eyes. The guy sort of slid down into the corner and sat there with his head on his knees, mumbling. It sounded like he was crying. It was *awful*. We were still three stops from home, but we got off the train at Bleeker, and walked the rest of the way."

"I think I've seen that guy," Summer says. "It's not that big a deal, Sue. Why does that make you want to leave?"

"It's not just that. It's all the things piled up on top of each other. As my granddad would say: It's just one goddamn thing after another." She smiles slightly, thinking of home. Then she shakes her head. "But I'm not going to quit. I can't leave Riley in the middle of this mess. He gets so scared when his mom and dad fight. He picks up on the tension and gets cranky and starts whining. Then they yell at him for interrupting their fighting."

"So who's going to take him if they get a divorce?" I have to ask.

"You know, the sick thing is that neither of them seem to want him. Jane wants revenge, and Ed just wants to get away from Jane so he can be with his... his... y'know..."

"Lover," Summer finishes.

Susan cringes. "Yeah, that. Anyway, I think if I left now they'd forget poor Riley even exists." There is a sound from the hallway, and we look up to see Riley standing there with his thumb in his mouth. I just want to die from the look in his big, innocent eyes. He has no idea that his whole world is about to end. The poor kid probably just came in to get more juice. Susan opens her arms and Riley smiles and rushes into them, burying his head in her shoulder. She holds him tightly and sways back and forth for a long, long time. When she finally lets him go, she turns away to wipe her eyes.

I can't stand to watch this, so I go to collect the kids from the other room. They are sitting cross-legged in a semi-circle around the television set, entranced by the cartoon. I come up behind Jake and kiss the top of his head. For once he doesn't whine and push me away. He's too busy watching to notice me.

"Hey!" Amy calls from the living room, "Guess who's here? Katy and Fiona!" They kids run out to see their friend, and I follow at almost the same speed. I haven't seen Fiona in weeks. Oh, we've said hello as we pass in the hall at preschool, but they've always got somewhere to go, so I haven't spent any real time with her.

Fiona is glad to see us, and awkwardly accepts our embraces. We all begin talking at once, everyone along the lines of where have you been, we never see you anymore. Fiona nods guiltily. "I know. It's dreadful of me. I should have called or something, but I didn't quite know how to explain."

"Explain what?" Summer asks, her hands on her hips.

Fiona looks at the floor. "The new playgroup," she admits. "You see, Mrs. Bouchet wants Katy to play with these other children..."

"What other children?" Amy demands.

"The parents are all business contacts for the magazine -- big advertisers, publishers, distributors. The kids are all different ages, and don't really like each other, but it's a big deal for the parents. Katy hates it. She cries and says she wants to play with Jake and Benjamin.....and the twins, of course," she smiles at the girls playing princess under the dining room table with Katy. The boys are trying to cross the moat. Jake calls out: "'Punzle, 'Punzle! Give us your hair!"

"So," I ask, "do youmean you're not coming to this play group anymore?" I'm afraid I already know the answer.

"I'll come whenever I can, but I don't think it will be very often. The new playgroup meets twice a week, plus they've signed her up for music and French." She shakes her head. "It's too much for a little girl. She needs to have time to look at books and play on her own once in a while. They have her so busy, I'm afraid she's not getting enough rest at night."

"She's still going to be at tumbling, right?" I ask. At least I'll see her on Tuesdays.

"Only until June. Then she starts tennis lessons."

"Tennis?!" Summer yells. "That's ridiculous, the racket will be bigger than she is!"

"I agree, the whole thing is silly. I tried talking to Mrs. Bouchet about it, and I even left an article on overextending your children on her dressing table where she would be sure to see it. I couldn't get her to listen. Mr. Bouchet is rather reasonable, but he's never around."

Fiona looks toward Katy, who is still under the table, brushing Camille's hair. "It breaks my heart to see this happen. I'm really fond of Katy." Susan and I look at each other. Fiona is much more than 'fond' of Katy.

"So why don't you quit?" Summer asks.

"I tried to," Fiona says softly. "But they gave me a raise -- a very large raise. One of my sisters is coming over in August, and I want to be able to help her out with money."

"Which sister?" I ask. I feel like I know them all, I've heard so many stories.

"Dorothy," she says, and smiles.

"Is she going to be a nanny?"

"What else? I couldn't talk her out of it. I'm going to save every penny of my raise, and maybe in a couple years we'll be able to get an apartment and go to secretarial school."

Fiona is a smart, responsible girl, and I care about her a lot. Hearing that her biggest goal is to be a secretary, makes my stomach turn. I guess I'm a bit of a snob, but Fiona deserves a better life than that.

Fiona looks at her watch. She immediately starts gathering up the toys that Katy has scattered on the floor. "We must be going," she says. "We have to be at the children's museum by three-thirty. It was grand seeing you all again."

"Well, wait!" Amy calls, in a panic. "We'll see you again, right? You still have Thursday nights off?"

Fiona shakes her head. "No, they changed me to Monday. We'll be going to the Hamptons every weekend starting next week. But call me. I'm home in the evenings. Call me after Katy's in bed." She walks into the dining room table and leans down. "Katy, it's time to go." Katy pretends she can't hear. "Katherine, I'm going to count to three."

Katy shakes her head violently. Ben starts yelling: "One more minute, just one more!"

"One..."

Katy rolls herself into a ball and refuses to move. The other kids cluster around, protecting her.

"Two....Katherine Bouchet you'd better start moving..." Fiona looks to us for a moment and then says: "Okay...Three! Come out of there this instant!" She reaches under the table and starts dragging Katy out. Katy screams at the top of her lungs, and all the other kids join in. They hold her legs while Fiona pulls her arms. The rest of us rush forward to disengage our particular kid from the struggle, and they all begin crying. Finally, Fiona gets Katy out of the apartment and the door slams behind her. The remaining members of play group are sprawled on the floor. We nannies are sweaty and out of breath from the struggle, and the kids are sulking, wiping their eyes with fisted hands. I'm thinking that we're probably going to have to have a Big Talk about what happened, but Amy starts giggling and then gets the hiccups. Everyone is laughing soon after and everything is okay until Cameron wakes up and howls for his bottle.

In a few minutes we have everyone settled at the table for a snack. Riley decides he wants a big-boy seat, so I put Miranda in the highchair and sprinkle some Cheerios on the tray. Susan adjusts a telephone book under Riley's bottom, and we retire into the living room, leaving the kids to their juice and crackers.

Summer tells us that the Leibowitzes have just leased a house on Fire Island from June until September.

"Hey!" I say. "We're going to Fire Island too. Is it their house or a share?"

"Share. We'll be out every other weekend."

"We'll see you there then. We can hang out."

"I don't know if I'm going to last 'till then," Summer says.

"What do you mean?" Susan asks, picking toys off the floor.

Summer looks at her impatiently. "You really *are* a blonde, aren't you? What I mean is that this job is getting on my nerves and I'm going back to the University in the Fall. My contract isn't up until September, but I need to get home before that to get all my shit together for school."

"Oh, no!" Susan says.

"Hey, it's no tragedy. I'm so sick of the whining and potty training... I don't think I'm cut out to work with kids. I'm considering changing my major."

"Yeah, it is hard sometimes," I try to sympathize. "I wish you were staying though." My friends are dropping like flies.

Amy laughs and shakes her head. "It's weird that you would want to cut your contract short. Mine's up next month, but I can't leave when Cameron's so little. In fact, I might sign up for another year."

"Are you crazy?!" Summer yells.

"It sounds funny, I know. But I can't imagine leaving them. Cameron's so helpless and brand new. He really needs me. And I don't know what the girls would do without me. Who would love them as much as I do?"

"Amy," I say gently. You should give this some thought. In another year you'll be even more attached to the kids, and it will be harder to leave. It's not like you're going to be promoted to mommy someday. You'll always be the nanny."

"Oh, you should talk!" Summer says sarcastically. "You are the worst offender, Michelle. You tell Amy not to get attached, but look at yourself. You act like these kids are *yours*!"

"They feel like mine," I say under my breath.

"Leave Michelle alone," Amy says, narrowing her eyes at Summer. She can look quite scary when she wants to. "You have to get somewhat attached to be able to stand this kind of work. Besides, maybe Michelle has other reasons for wanting to stay in New York. I know I do." She raises her eyebrows.

"What?" Summer asks.

"She has a new boyfriend," I explain.

"Well this is interesting. Do tell." Summer takes a seat and folds her arms across her chest.

Amy stands up and paces the floor as she talks, every once in a while giving a little skipping hop or a twirl to accentuate her point. "His name is Gunter." Summer starts to laugh, but Amy flips her off and continues. "He's from Germany, and he's been in New York for four years. He's 24, and has long blonde hair and a mustache."

"Gross," says Susan. "I hate facial hair."

"Me too," I agree.

"Shut up you guys," Summer says lightly. " I want to hear this. Where'd you meet him, Ame?"

"In a club. I went to see a band I like, and the opening act was a band called The Intensers. Gunter's the lead singer." She shrugs and smiles, as if to say 'and the rest is history.'

"Well how long have you been seeing him? How serious is it?"

"I'd say pretty serious," Amy says. "I've only known him a month, but I think this may be it."

Summer turns to me, "Have you met him, Michelle?"

"Only for a minute. He seems cool." I shrug. In truth I'm not crazy about him, but that may be partly due to the fact that he has snatched my friend away from me. I feel sort of betrayed. I mean, I know I'd probably do the same thing in her place -- how many nights have I stood her up to stay home with Jeffrey? -- but I'm still not happy about it.

Summer leans back in her chair and puts her hands behind her head. "So," she says to Amy, "are you getting any?"

Amy twirls and drops a curtsey. "Constantly," she says. We give her a round of applause. Susan blushes slightly. I have strong suspicions that she's a virgin.

Summer turns to me, her eyes wide in mock innocence. "Hey, Michelle, maybe that's your problem. You can't sleep because you're sexually frustrated. What you need is to get laid." Everyone cracks up at this, and Susan hides her face in her hands. I smile and nod, thinking of this morning -- Jeffrey and I standing up in the bathroom, the door banging in its frame. Sometimes it's hard to keep my mouth shut when I just want to tell it all.

Summer is asking Amy if Gunter has a friend for me. I start shaking my head before she can open her mouth.

"Yeah! He has this friend who's dying to meet her, but she won't have anything to do with him."

"Michelle West! What is your problem?" Summer scolds.

Even Susan looks annoyed with me. "Why won't you go out with him?"

"I just don't feel like it, okay? Will you all please leave me alone?"

"Ohhhh...." Summer says. "I think I know what this is all about. Michelle has a big fat crush on her boss."

"I do not!"

"Oh come on! You talk about him all the time, you never want to come out. You say you're attached to the kids, but I bet who you're really attached to is Mr. Goldman."

Amy comes to my defense. "Summer, shut up. That's stupid. Anyone can see she loves those kids."

"Yeah, then why won't she go out with Gunter's friend?"

"How should I know? Maybe she likes girls." Amy laughs.

This elicits an "Eww gross!" from Susan.

"Oh very funny," I say. "I do not like girls, *or* Jeffrey."

"You know you do, so you might as well admit it," Summer says.

"I'm not admitting anything! This is stupid! I'm not listening to this." I start over to the table to refill the kids' juice cups.

"Okay. We believe you." Summer winks at Amy, then adds, "You'd better give up, Michelle. He's married. He's twice your age. It's never going to happen."

I have never been so close to telling them. But I go into the bathroom and sit on the edge of the tub until I calm down. I can't let them know how insulted and angry I am. That would be a dead give-away. I go back into the living room and drop to the floor on my knees. I throw my arm back over my forehead and pretend to swoon.

"At last," I cry dramatically, "The truth is out. I have a terrible, desperate case of unrequited love for Jeffrey Goldman! I can't hide it anymore!" I pretend to sob, and mop my face with an imaginary handkerchief. They all laugh, but the kids are a bit concerned, turned around in their chairs looking at me. "You're right, Miss Summer, I must give him up. Never again shall I pine away the evening thinking of him." I collapse to the floor in my rendition of 'the dying swan.' There is a patter of applause for the second time this afternoon.

I get to my feet, laughing.

"So does this mean you'll go out with Nicky?" Amy asks, only half-seriously.

I groan, "It's too soon after my heartbreak."

"No, really," Summer says. "You should go."

"Yeah, go Michelle, you might have fun." Susan puts in.

"Come on, Mick, whaddya say? You, me, Gunter and Nicky. Tonight. Eight o' clock. CBGB's."

"Well..." I say.

"Yes! I knew we'd wear you down eventually," Amy says triumphantly. She gives Summer a high-five.

"Oh, God," I groan. "What have I gotten myself into? Amy, listen, I have to make sure Debra doesn't need me tonight. I'll call you when I get home."

Amy looks at me suspiciously. "Okay, but if you bail out on me, I'm going to call the house to make sure you're really baby-sitting."

Everybody laughs, but she has just taken away my plan for getting out of this. I'll have to think of something else. Maybe I can convince Debra to lie for me.

    *   *   *   *

Debra has served up some mysterious slop for dinner that has suspicious-looking blobs that may or may not be tofu. I don't know what they might be if they're *not* tofu, and I'm not about to venture a guess. I'm certainly not going to ask. Debra is very sensitive about her "cooking." I smoosh the stuff from one side of my plate to the other, and wish the Goldmans had a dog that I could sneak it to under the table.

There is wine with dinner, as always, and Jeffrey is on his third glass. He tosses it back like it's water, maybe trying to kill the taste of the meal. He spoons up the glop and shovels it into his mouth while humming along with the radio. He is staring into space, oblivious to Miranda, who is painting his jacket with applesauce from her place in the high chair. I don't call his attention to it. It would be like waking a sleepwalker.

Meanwhile, Debra and I take turns coaxing Jake into eating his dinner. I don't tell Debra that he's eaten the equivalent of a whole box of crackers with his friends this afternoon. She'd just start on some tirade about proper nutrition, blah, blah, blah. I'm losing my patience with her. I tell Jake that the peas on his plate are sad because they want to be with their friends that have already gone into his tummy. I tell him there is a big pea party happening down there, and everybody wants to go. Every time he picks up a pea in his spoon, I say in a high-pitched pea-voice: "Thank-you for putting me in your tummy, Jake! Now I can go to the party with my friends!" And as he pops them in his mouth the peas say: "Wheeee!" as they slide down his throat.

Things are unusually quiet until Debra asks if I have any plans for the evening.

"Why, do you need me to baby-sit?" I perk up at the thought.

"No, no, you've had the kids every night this week. You need some time off."

"Well, that's really nice of you, but could you possibly tell Amy that I *am* baby-sitting?"

"Why would you want me to do that?" She rises from her chair and starts clearing the table. I follow her lead, and go to the sink to rinse them and load the dishwasher.

"It's really stupid..." I start, and laugh uncomfortably. "See, Amy has this new boyfriend, and she wants to set me up with one of his friends." I grimace, to let her know exactly what I think of the idea. I notice that Jeffrey has discovered Miranda's art work, and is wiping at the applesauce with his napkin. I'm pretty sure he's listening now, because otherwise he'd be swearing up a storm about his jacket.

"You want me to lie for you so that you don't have to meet this guy, is that it?" Debra says, sort of amused.

"Something like that," I say, and laugh. I've got her now. She'll do it. We girls stick together.

Debra puts her hands on her hips and shakes a scolding finger in my face. "Now, Michelle, why wouldn't you want to meet a nice boy? I think it's high time you got yourself a little boyfriend! What's his name?"

I shrug. This is not going as I'd hoped. "Nicky or something..." I say flatly.

"*Nicky*?" Jeffrey rolls his eyes. "What kind of name is that? What is he, some Mafia hood?"

"How should I know? I've never met the creep! He saw a picture of me at Amy's and for some reason wants to meet me. Amy's been hounding me for weeks to do this, and I've run out of excuses, unless..." I turn toward Debra.

"No way." she says, enjoying this. "This is great. It's about time that a boy noticed you, honey. Of course we think you're wonderful, but you should have a special friend who appreciates you. Don't you think so Jeffrey? Jeffrey?"

"Huh? What?"

Debra sighs, and gives me a look like: *men*. "Don't you think it would be nice if Michelle had a boyfriend?"

Jeffrey looks at me and twists his mouth in an ironic sort of smirk. "Yeah!" he says with enthusiasm. "That would be great! Go for it, Michelle." He turns back to reading the paper.

Now I'm really pissed. Not only did my so-called friends gang up on me, accuse me of lesbianism, and imply that Jeffrey is way too good for me, but now Debra says that *no* males of the species would be interested in the likes of me, and that I'd better jump at the chance while I can. And as if that weren't enough, Jeffrey goes along with it all. I know he's got to keep up appearances, but I'm still unhappy.

"Well, you know," I say, my tone changing to flip and casual, "Maybe you're right Debra. I think I *will* meet this guy. I'll call Amy right now." I start toward the playroom to use the phone in private, but changing my mind, pivot on my heel and pick up the kitchen extension. I talk loudly and giggle quite a bit, throwing in plenty of innuendoes as to how much fun we're going to have, how drunk we're going to get, and where the evening might lead. I'm sure Amy must be wondering what in the hell is wrong with me, but it's not for her benefit that I'm having this conversation.

When I hang up the phone Jeffrey rustles his paper, calling my attention. I look at him, annoyed. "What?" I say sharply. "I have to get ready to go."

"I was just going to suggest that you wear that new red sundress of yours."

"It's not red, it's *raspberry*." I say. It is his favorite. He bought it for me a couple weeks ago for our six month 'anniversary.'

"What sundress?" Debra pipes up.

"Oh, haven't you seen it?" Jeffrey says, playing with both of us. "It's quite....fetching."

"Sounds like a dog," I mumble.

"I still don't know what you're talking about, Jeffrey."

"Sure you do. It's that short little sundress that shows off Michelle's tan."

I could strangle him. Debra is casting up her eyes, thinking. Slowly she nods. "Oh, yes. I think I know the one you mean. It's *fuschia*." She turns and leaves the kitchen, taking Miranda with her.

Jeffrey is such an idiot. I'm too mad to bawl him out for taunting Debra like that. I can't believe that he's encouraging me to go out with someone else. Not only that, but to wear the dress *he* gave me! If that's the way he wants to play, then so be it.

"I think you're right," I say. "I will wear my new dress."

He looks a bit surprised, but quickly recovers and says, "Go ahead." He turns back to his paper, and doesn't look at me.

"Okay, I will." I say.

"Fine."

"Fine." I turn and head for my bedroom. He makes a big deal about rattling the newspaper around so I will know how engrossed he is in his reading. Boys never change. They act the same stupid way at forty as they did at fifteen.

On the other hand, I am incredibly mature. I slam my bedroom door, and crank up the stereo, tuning to a pop station that plays the latest dance music. I normally can't stand the stuff, but my point is that I'm young and free while Jeffrey is old and has got to stay home with the ball and chain. Laughing to myself, I dance around the room in my bare feet. I'm going to make him suffer.

Half an hour later I emerge from my room in a cloud of perfume -- this, also courtesy of Jeffrey and his Platinum Card. I flounce through the playroom and into the kitchen, the full skirt of my dress swirling around my bare legs. I make a lap of the kitchen, modeling my outfit for Jeffrey and Jake, who are at the table working on a coloring book. Jake looks up and his jaw drops. For a second he seems unsure as to who I am. I have really pulled out the heavy artillery.

"Hey!" Jake says, recognizing me at last, "That's 'shell in there!"

"Sure is," Jeffrey agrees.

"She looks like a *princess*!"

"Yes, she does. And you know what she's going to do tonight?" Jake shakes his head. "She's going out to kiss a frog."

"If the frog is lucky," I say.

Debra comes back in with the baby, who is freshly bathed and in her jammies. "Mmmm.... What's that I smell?" Debra asks.

"That would be me," I say, twirling around for her approval.

"Well, don't you look nice? So that's the famous sundress I've heard so much about. Very nice." She looks me up and down and makes me turn a few more times. "I've never seen you like this, Michelle. You're going to knock that boy's eyes out."

"Thanks," I say, blushing. I do love a compliment.

"What kind of perfume is that?" she asks. I tell her the name, sort of sheepishly. "Wow!" She looks astounded. "That's pricey stuff. Where'd you get that?"

"Christmas present." I tell her.

"From whom?" She doesn't look so happy anymore.

"Oh, just someone back home."

"An old boyfriend?"

"Something like that." I'd really like to get off this topic.

"Well, he must still like you an awful lot, to give you something like that for Christmas. Even *I* don't have that perfume! Jeffrey, when are you going to buy me some expensive perfume?" she asks, sort of teasing, and sort of pissed off at the injustice of her hired help having nicer things than she does.

"When I get a raise," Jeffrey jokes.

"Oh!" I say, looking at the kitchen clock. "I've got to go! Thanks so much for talking me into this, Debra." I look her full in the face so she can see that nothing is wrong here.

"Sure, honey," she says, smiling, relaxed now. "Have a good time."

"Thanks!" I say, heading for the door. I fairly skip out of the kitchen and through the entryway. Once out on the sidewalk, my pace changes, and I trudge to Amy's place on Perry Street, dragging my feet all the way.

*   *   *   *

It's fairly early, and CBGB's is almost empty. Not many people come to see the opening bands, since there may be four or five before the main attraction. CBGB's, is a long, shoe box-shaped establishment that glories in its filth. The walls are covered in decades worth of graffiti, and neon beer advertisements.

Amy and I are sitting in a booth across from the long bar. It is towards the front, away from the stage, where there are already gathered a small crowd of die-hard music fans. No one has yet taken the stage, but these people are staking out their territory early, in preparation for the crowd that will be filtering in as the night goes on. I sip at my beer, thinking that I should probably get really drunk before this Nicky idiot shows up, but not having the stomach for it. I had been so busy cajoling Jake to eat his peas, that I sort of forgot to eat my own dinner.

Amy sits quietly, almost still except for the tell-tale tapping of her shoe against the table leg, and the constant movement of her cigarette to her mouth, to the ashtray, and back. I watch the orange glow of the lit end for a while. She spends so much time flicking her ashes off, and then rolling the burning end into a perfect point, that I don't believe she ever smokes more than a fraction of each cigarette. Even so, there is something graceful and fascinating about the ritual. It almost makes me want to take up smoking. Hell, maybe just for tonight -- it might scare off Nicky.

I'm reaching for Amy's lighter when a band comes out on stage and Amy bolts up in her seat in anticipation before realizing it isn't what she was waiting for, and blowing out a lungful of smoke in disgust. I'm feeling bored already. If I weren't so annoyed with Jeffrey, I'd fake some illness and go home. Unfortunately, I've got to stay out late tonight -- at least until after I'm sure he's gone to sleep. Jeffrey's got to think I had a great time, no matter how miserable I really am. This band is quite possibly the worst I have ever heard in my life, and that includes the pot and pan jam sessions Brian and I used to have back home. Their set is twenty minutes long, and they play approximately forty songs. They are all thirty seconds in length, and indistinguishable from one another. There are three guys and a girl with black-rimmed eyes, who screeches some sort of lyrics into a megaphone. Just when I think I may catch a word here and there, the song is over, and the guitar player leaps into the air and comes down as the drummer crashes the final beat. It's the only way of determining the end of one tune and the beginning of another. Amy and I look at each other in astonishment. It's too bad to be funny. By asking around, we discover that the Intensers are not up for another hour, so we go next door for a slice of pizza.

When we come back, the place has filled up a bit more, and someone has taken over our booth. But apparently, the band on stage is the Intensers, since Amy grabs my hand and pulls me up front. When we get closer, I recognize Gunter, who is busy adjusting amps and wires and stuff. Amy blows him a kiss, and he comes over and says, "Hey babe." Amy grabs him by the ends of his foot-long curls and pulls his face down to hers. I look away before I have to see any tongue. Some weirdo with a pock-marked face and black leather pants tries to make eye contact with me, so I just stare straight ahead at the curtain behind the band, silently cursing Amy for bringing me here.

To my surprise, Amy pulls me back toward the booths and we sit with a couple of bike messengers from Queens. I ask Amy why she doesn't want to be up front and she explains that Gunter finds her distracting, and that it's bad PR for the fans to know the lead singer has a squeeze. So Amy sits back regally with her gin and tonic, smiling serenely at the young girls clamoring to the front of the stage. If they end up getting married I wonder if she'll become domesticated, or if she'll insist on an engagement diamond for her nose?

The drummer counts off, Amy grips my hand, and the Intensers launch into their first song. It's nothing amazing, it's sort of plodding and predictable, but they aren't bad. The lyrics are incredibly silly, but sound more interesting in Gunter's German accent. He struts around the stage and swings his hair around like every other lead singer since the dawn of man. Amy is entranced, and I have to give her a sharp kick in the ankle to get her to let go of my hand. "Look at him," she murmurs, almost to herself. "Will you just look at him?" I shake my head, dismayed. She's got it bad.

I start to move a little with the music. I don't want to enjoy this, but there's something about the bass line. It doesn't quite fit with the rest of the amateurish band, it's a mix between funk and jazz, and I find myself thinking that Jeffrey would have some knowledgeable comment to make about it if he were here. When I find myself wishing that I was here with him instead of Amy, I remember I'm supposed to be mad at him, and banish him from my mind for the remainder of the evening.

Trying to avoid looking at Gunter because he makes me want to laugh, I check out the other members of the band. The drummer is hidden behind his equipment, and the guitarist is sporting a goatee and a pained expression. So I focus in on the bass player. He's obviously a more accomplished musician than the rest of these goons. He strikes me as a white-bread type with fine blonde hair that just barely brushes his collar, wire-rimmed glasses, and dressed in a simple button-down shirt and jeans. He looks like an algebra class geek, and I look instinctively for a pocket protector. Not finding one, I do happen to notice that the geek has these incredible forearms. I'm not much into muscles, but it kills me how his shirt is rolled up just below the elbow, and the way the tendons in his arms move as he plays his bass. He keeps his eyes closed as he plays, but somehow it doesn't seem phony. Every so often he leans forward to his microphone and adds some backup vocals to the mix.

One of the sorry excuses for a waitress comes up, but I wave her away. She's blocking my view. They go into a cover of an old Motown hit, and I tune out Gunter's mangling of the words and just listen to the bass. I don't know what it is about this guy, but he makes the song sound like the Detroit version of Bolero. It's pure sex, and I look around to see if anyone else is blushing. What is wrong with me tonight, I wonder? Without taking my eyes off of him I get Amy's attention and tell her that the bass player is sexy in a nerdly kind of way. She starts laughing and when I ask what's so funny she just shakes her head and turns back to the music.

When the song ends, Gunter tells the crowd that this will be their last song. The groupies up front moan their disappointment. Gunter motions to the drummer who taps gently on the rim of his drum, then the goatee guy comes in playing softly. There's something familiar about it, and from the bewildered looks all around, everyone else is trying to figure out where they've heard this before. Amy obviously knows what it is -- she's smiling smugly over the rim of her glass. Gunter steps back a few paces, over next to the drums, and the bass player steps forward. He scans the crowd nervously before taking a deep breath, closing his eyes, and starting to sing in a clear, tenor voice: "Michelle, my belle. These are words that go together well, my Michelle..." All around me people sort of chuckle, not knowing if it's a joke or not, but by the time he breaks into French, everyone is singing along. I move my mouth a little, but I am too blown away for anything more than a squeak to come out. I don't even look at Amy. No one has to tell me that the bass player with the great forearms, sweet voice and perfect French is Nicky.

*   *   *   *

Bud kicks us out of the Rail at five in the morning. He'd let us stay half an hour past closing, but seeing that we were having such a good time, and didn't seem inclined to leave, he finally told us to go home. We've had quite a bit to drink, and amazingly, no one gets sick or mean or belligerent. By some happy accident, all four of us are flushed and silly and affectionate. Everyone is beautiful and best friends. Even Gunter can't get on my nerves tonight.

I can't account for it, but Nicky and I have really connected. We've been having a non-stop conversation for hours, never running out of things to say. We like the same things, and I don't even miss arguing. He's so open-minded and enthusiastic about life. It's quite different from Jeffrey's studied indifference.

After we leave the Rail, we walk slowly west, enjoying the freshness of the sunrise after the stale beer and cigarette smell of the bars. Even the panhandlers are in congenial spirits. They don't ask for donations, but call out "God bless!" as we pass. Amy and Gunter walk ahead of us, their arms wrapped around each other, her head leaning on his shoulder. I barely notice when Nicky takes my hand, it seems so natural and friendly. We swing our arms back and forth, exaggerating the fact that we're holding hands, so it will seem like less of a big deal.

Amy and Gunter leave us at Hudson Street. They are on their way to Gunter's apartment. I can't imagine how she's going to drag herself out of his bed and back to work in only two hours, but she must be getting used to it by now. Nicky walks me to the house on Bank Street. The brick looks very pink in the early light. Nicky laughs when I cover my mouth and yawn. I think if it was still dark I'd want him to kiss me, but it doesn't seem right now. I have the feeling I'll be seeing him again. I tell him that he can call me later in the day, and stand on tip-toe to plant a kiss on his cheek before going into the house.

I take off my shoes in the entryway, and head for the window to watch him walk away. Before I reach my room, I hear a noise and turn to see Jeffrey sitting in the playroom armchair. He's so still that for a second I think he's asleep, but then I see the glint of his black eyes, and he says: "Home so soon?"

His voice is raspy, as if he hasn't spoken in hours. "Hi," I whisper. "What are you doing up so early?" I ask this although I suspect that he hasn't been to bed at all.

"So how's old Nicky?" he says, ignoring my question.

"He's okay. Sort of a geek, but I could stomach him for one night." I feel guilty saying it, but I don't feel I have a choice. "Why," I add. "Jealous?"

"A little." He opens his arms and I crawl into his lap, curling up the way Miranda does. I'm so sleepy and he's so nice and warm, I could fall asleep right here. I close my eyes and listen to him breathe, feeling the rise and fall of his chest under my head.

"Michelle..." he says.

"Shhh," I say without opening my eyes. "Let's stay like this forever." I feel like going to sleep, but somehow my thoughts stray to Nicky, standing at the microphone strumming his bass and singing that old Beatles song. He's the last thing I should be thinking about, and I feel a momentary panic rise up in me. I sit up straight and look straight at Jeffrey. "Do you want me to go out with other guys?" I demand.

He looks a bit surprised. "No, I don't *want* you to, but I can't stop you either."

"Yes you can." I mumble.

"I don't have the right to do that," he explains, "I mean... I've got Debra..." he spreads his hands and trails off.

I stare at him, squinting, trying to see through those black eyes back into his brain. I try to make him understand that he has every right to ask anything of me, all he has to do is claim it. All he has to do is make me his. I find myself looking at him as if for the first time. Not like when I saw him in the airport with Jake, but as if I'm truly seeing him at last. There are lines around his eyes that I've never noticed, and furrows in his forehead that appear deeper in the shadowy room. It finally sinks in how much older he is. When I was born he was already a senior in high school. I probably wouldn't have been his first choice for a prom date.

I lean forward and kiss him, trying to impress upon him all that I think he ought to know. It doesn't seem to be getting through to him, and I'm too tired to keep trying. I tell him that I'm exhausted, and I'm going to try to get a couple hours of sleep before the kids wake up. He goes up the stairs and I go into my room. As I undress I listen to him squeak his way back to his and Debra's bed.

Although I feel about ready to drop, once in my bed and under the covers, I can't switch off my mind, and I run through the events of the evening over and over. As the luminescent green numbers on the clock steadily go through their paces, clicking the early morning away, I lie there and think about Jeffrey. I think about how it all began.

*   *   *   *

After my unpleasant brush with reality via the Zherings I spent most nights out of the house seeing movies, shopping and talking with Amy. On the occasions that I was in the mood to party, Molly was the one I turned to. Molly O'Doyle was a large-framed, slightly chubby blonde girl that could pack away hard alcohol like no fraternity boy I've ever seen. She was loud and vivacious, and alcohol merely amplified her personality until she was screaming over the jukebox, dancing on tables or doing shots with the bouncers.

The nights I spent with Molly usually ended with me puking in the bar bathroom and Molly putting me in a cab heading downtown. She never seemed the worse for wear, and I would frequently call her the next day, hungover and cringing at every diaper I had to change. "I hate you," I would tell her, groaning. She'd laugh so loudly it made my head ache, and say things to try to make me puke.

"Michelley," she called me, "What color was it?"

"Was what?"

"Your upchuck, missy! Was it brown and chunky, or sort of yellow from the tequila?"

"Oh, God, shut up, Mol. I swear I'm going to barf again...."

"Oh, I'm sorry," she said, not sorry at all. Then, pretending concern: "Have you eaten anything today?"

"God, no. I don't even want to think about it."

"Well, maybe if you put just a wee bit of something on your stomach you'd feel better."

"I doubt it. I don't think I can ever look at food again."

"Oh but something real tasty like... oh, say.... a hot-dog milkshake?"

"Ohhh, stop it!"

"Or maybe a nice boloney and babyshit sandwich?"

At that point I'd drop the phone and run for the bathroom, her raucous laughter following me down the hall.

Despite her slightly sadistic tendencies, she was a lot of fun. She had a mass of blonde curls that shook and bobbed around her face when she laughed. Her cheeks were permanently flushed, and I don't think I ever saw her with her mouth shut. She would strike up a conversation with anyone: bums on the street, cops on the beat, bartenders, bikers -- anyone at all. She wasn't afraid of anything, and no one could intimidate her. I once made the mistake of pointing out a guy that I thought was cute, and within three minutes she had gone over to him, established enough of a rapport with him to introduce him to me as her 'new friend John' and had paired us off. She even supplied him with my phone number.

Molly had staked out a string of Irish bars on the Upper East Side that she liked to frequent. She knew everyone there by name, the employees and regulars alike. One night we'd been to Flemings, our favorite haunt, where we drank ourselves silly until we got kicked out at last call. I had been so determined to keep up with Molly that even after puking, I continued to match her drink for drink. We sat out on the curb for a while, Molly calmly smoking a cigarette while I sat with my head hanging between my knees swearing to myself that I would never again touch a drop of alcohol.

Molly stubbed out her cigarette, and stood up to hail a passing taxi. She gave the driver my address on Bank Street, and put me into the back seat. "I'd take it easy on the corners," she advised the driver, "Unless you want to be mopping up her sick." She slammed the door and waved as the cab lurched forward.

I don't remember the ride at all, but I think the cab driver must have removed me from his vehicle and set me down outside the house. I found myself leaning against the front of the building, trying to get my key in the door. Once inside, I stumbled through the entryway, careening off walls and furniture before collapsing in a heap at the foot of the stairs. I thought I'd just close my eyes for a minute. Rest.

The next thing I knew, I was being dragged to my feet for the third or fourth time that evening. I opened my eyes to find Jeffrey holding me up by my shoulders.

"Oh, fuck," I said.

"You're a mess," he said, conversationally.

"I am." I agreed, nodding my head slowly, and with a great deal of effort. "I am what I am. I yam what I yam...." I laughed and started to sing the Popeye theme.

"Let's get you to bed," he said. He didn't seem mad, just kind of amused. Or maybe I was the only one amused. He led me into my room, and without turning on the light, deposited me on my bed. He started to take off my shoes, and I sat up in a panic. I couldn't have him looking at my feet.

"What's the matter?" he said, looking worried. "Are you going to get sick?" He stepped back, as if expecting a burst of projectile vomit.

I laughed a little. "You mean puke? Already did, Jeff. It's a done deal."

He left the room, chuckling a little. I closed my eyes and the bed spun. I opened them and Jeffrey was placing a large plastic bucket next to my bed.

"Jeffrey...." I groaned.

"Hmm?"

"I'm sorry about this. I feel like a shithead. A *shitfaced* shithead." I giggled hysterically at my own wit.

"I'm not going to tattle on you, Michelle. Nobody has to know this ever happened."

"Thanks," I whispered. I whispered because suddenly he was so close to me. He sat on the edge of my bed with his arms on either side of me. His face was so close to mine that I could feel his breath on my face. My mouth went dry and I swallowed hard.

"Sleep tight," he said, and suddenly he was gone, closing the door with a click that echoed through the sleeping house.

Strangely, I didn't think much of that incident. I chalked it up to a drunken imagination. But in retrospect, I can see that it was the beginning. After that Jeffrey was a lot more attentive. He'd always debated with me, and joked around, but he began to sit closer than he had before, to brush past me just a little more often. He'd comment on what I wore, and notice when I changed the color of polish on my nails. One day he brought me a book that he claimed had jumped out at him from a store window. It was a mystery set in Seattle, and he tossed it casually in my lap, as if it were nothing.

It was maybe two weeks later that Debra had a big awards banquet to go to. She fussed over her outfit, and agonized over a speech she had to make. Jeffrey had his own client function to attend, and neither planned to be home until late. I was looking forward to it. I thought Jake and I could build a fort. Maybe we'd even camp out on the living room floor.

After a dinner of grilled cheese and chocolate milk, the kids and I went upstairs to play. We turned on the stereo and started dancing around the room. Jake gyrated in his awkward, toddler way, while I swung Miranda around in my arms. This went on for half an hour or so, until we tired and fell laughing onto the floor. The CD ended, and that's when I heard a noise from the hall. I looked up and Jeffrey was standing there, watching us. His expression was so strange, and far-away looking that it scared me for a minute. Then he smiled and came over to pick up Jake.

"Having a party, huh guys?"

"You're not supposed to be home," I said. "I thought you had that thing tonight?"

"I did have that thing, but I decided not to go. I wanted to come home and see these guys before they went to bed." He didn't look at me as he said it.

I was a bit disappointed, but what could I do? It was his house and his kids. He could do what he wanted. He wrestled with Jake on the floor and tossed the baby into the air. Miranda loved it. She shrieked with laughter, and Jeffrey tossed her again and again until, as I'd warned him, she'd spit up on his suit. While he was changing, I put Miranda to bed, and then we both read Jake his story and tucked him in.

Downstairs again, I headed towards my room, wondering if I could get hold of Molly, or she'd already gone out for the night. Jeffrey had followed me downstairs, and stopped me in the playroom. He asked if I'd had dinner yet, and offered to cook something. I was suspicious, but too curious to pass it up. I said I was starving, and didn't mention the cheese sandwich.

In the kitchen he tuned the radio onto a jazz station, and started to look through the fridge. I sat at the table watching him. He decided that eggs would be the safest bet, and proceeded to make two enormous omelets. We drank red wine while he cooked, and more while we ate. He opened a second bottle after we'd cleared the table, and we sat in the dim kitchen drinking and talking for hours. He told me about when he was a kid, and the trouble he used to get into in high school. He confessed that in college he'd edited the campus newspaper, and had aspirations about being a great journalist. But then he'd gotten a job at a small ad agency, and had never gone back to writing.

After awhile we fell into a comfortable silence. There was only the low whisper of the disk jockey and the sound of Miranda's steady breathing over the baby monitor. The phone jolted us both out of our individual thoughts, and for a second we looked at each other, uncomprehending, not knowing what the ringing meant. Then Jeffrey leapt up and grabbed it, before it woke the kids.

I could hear Debra's voice from across the room. I couldn't make out what she was saying, but I had a feeling. Jeffrey said things like "Yes, yes. Okay Deb. Have fun then. Fine. 'Bye." He hung up the phone. "Well, that was Debra. She said she's going out with some people from work. She probably won't be home for a couple hours."

I searched for something to say. "How did her speech go?"

"Oh. I don't know. She didn't say."

The silence was no longer comfortable. I loaded the dishwasher and started my sink-scrubbing routine. Jeffrey busied himself sweeping the floor, pretty pointless, since I'd done it that afternoon. Although there was nothing left to do, for some reason I kept standing at the sink. Soon he put the broom away and I could feel him standing behind me.

"I guess I should go to bed." I said, not turning around.

"Guess so," he answered.

I turned around to leave and he caught me by the waist.

"Don't go." he said hoarsely.

I've never believed in astral projection or any of that new age out-of-body crap, but at that moment I felt like I had no control over myself. It was like watching someone else lean back and let Jeffrey kiss her. It must have been some other girl putting her arms around his neck and kissing him back. It couldn't have been me.

We came up for air, and I broke away from him, saying: "Oh, Jeez."

I ran into my bedroom and shut the door, leaning against it as if pursued. I could hear Jeffrey laughing softly as he climbed the stairs. I sat there on the floor until I heard Debra come home. I waited another hour after that before grabbing my jacket and leaving the house. I wandered up and down Bank Street until stopping at a phone booth on the corner and calling Joanne. She answered in a sleepy voice.

"Hi it's me," I said, glancing around to make sure no one had followed me from the house.

"What time is it?"

"I don't know. Listen Jo, something has happened."

"What? Are you okay? Wait, let me turn on the light."

"Okay," I told her. "Are you sitting down?"

"I'm *lying* down, Michelle. Will you cut the dramatics and tell me what's wrong?"

"It's Jeffrey. He... well, he kissed me."

"Peck on the cheek?"

"No."

"On the mouth?"

"Um, yes..."

"Tongue?"

"*Joanne!*"

"Well?"

"Yes."

"Oh boy." She let out a slow breath. "How did this happen?"

"I'm not really sure. We were drunk." It sounded like a valid excuse, but even as I said it I knew it would have happened eventually with or without the wine.

"Well, I can't say I'm all that surprised, Michelle."

"Why not?! *I* was!"

"Come on. Were you *really* surprised?"

"Yes, of course!"

"You had *no idea* this might happen?"

"What are you trying to say?"

"All I'm saying is that ever since you got there you've been saying Jeffrey's so smart and Jeffrey's so funny and Jeffrey did this and said that..."

"So you're telling me this is *my* fault? You think I *wanted* this?"

"Well didn't you?"

For a moment I couldn't speak or even form a complete thought. I toyed with the idea of shouting 'fuck you' into the mouthpiece and slamming down the receiver. But instead, I said: "Look, I was there and you weren't. I don't need you to psychoanalyze me. I just felt like I had to tell someone."

"All right, calm down. Never mind what brought it on, what are you going to do about it?"

"I don't know! That's why I called you!"

Joanne was silent for a while, presumably turning my dilemma over in her mind. I thought she'd gone back to sleep when she announced: "You should come home. The sooner the better. Give them two weeks to replace you, and then you're out of there. If you start the paperwork right away, you can get re-admitted for Winter Quarter."

"You think I should *leave*?"

"Michelle! You *can't* stay. Even if it never happened again you wouldn't be able to stay."

"Why not?"

"Look, I think you're in shock or something. You're not thinking straight. You'll feel better when you get here."

"I'm not leaving, Joanne, so just forget about that. I need another option. Help me think." I appealed to her logical, problem-solving side.

She sighed. "I guess you'll have to say something to him, then."

"No way. I couldn't." The thought of Discussing the Incident made my stomach feel like it was falling.

"No, it'll be fine. You just say 'Jeffrey, I was drunk, you were drunk, let's just forget it ever happened.'"

"Oh, man, I hate this."

"Well you can always come home."

"Hmmm... well, I'll just have to think about it." She started laughing. "What's so funny?" I demanded.

"You. You're not going to do a damn thing, Michelle. I know you. You'll just keep your mouth shut and hope it goes away."

"Yeah, I probably will," I admitted.

We hung up soon afterward and I walked home. I sat on the front steps for a while, thinking. Finally I went inside to wait for the rest of the house to wake up.

I couldn't look at Jeffrey during breakfast, but I could feel his eyes on me. It wasn't much fun looking at Debra, either. Later that day Jeffrey called from his office and told me that he was a bit embarrassed "about what happened last night" and that he was sorry and didn't want me to feel weird or embarrassed. My end of the conversation was a succession of monosyllabic squeaks, and when he hung up I thought about leaving. Then Jake tripped over a toy and I had to run to the rescue and put ice on his head. All thoughts of leaving were gone.

It was weird for about a week. I avoided Jeffrey and even tried not to laugh at his jokes. But time went by and we fell into our former routine. Everything seemed normal again.

A couple of weeks passed without incident. Then one night I went out drinking with Molly and Amy. We met a bunch of Irish boys who were over here for a hurling match. We hung out with them all night, drinking, dancing, and finally pairing off for a bit of kissing and groping. When I got home that night I was drunk and fired up. I was looking for Jeffrey.

I found him in the living room, sitting in the dark, listening to music. I took the opportunity to sit down right next to him and start up a drunken conversation. I can't remember what it was about, but at some point I felt compelled to do something, anything, and so I grabbed his hand, and interlaced my fingers with his. Apparently it was the sign he was waiting for.

The next night at dinner, Debra announced that she was going to L.A. for a few days. We were eating Chinese take-out, and I was so surprised that my chopsticks clattered to the floor. Jeffrey laughed at me, and squeezed my leg under the table.

On the night she left, I had figured that Jeffrey would come home early from work. I was disappointed. He came in, looking cranky and exhausted just as I was getting Jake and Miranda tucked in. He read Jake a story, and held Miranda on his shoulder until her eyes were droopy, then put her down in the crib.

Jeffrey and I sat in the living room in silence. The TV was on -- some old James Bond movie -- and though my eyes were glued to the screen, I wasn't seeing any of it. I doubt he was watching, either. After the eleven o'clock news he stretched, yawned, and went upstairs to bed. I stood in the empty room for a minute or two, then went to bed without going through my sink-scrubbing, door-locking ritual.

I lay awake in my bed, and he lay awake in his. Sometime during the night, one of us got up and went to the other, who was waiting. It doesn't matter who went to whom, who visited the bed of the other. What matters is that we came together like a head-on collision, and didn't disentangle ourselves until morning.

Christa Charter

SIX

It is after three in the morning, and I can barely make out Amy's face through the stale, smoky air. On the table between us are a myriad of shot glasses, ashtrays, and empty matchbooks. Amy and I haven't been to the Rail together in a long time -- ever since she met Gunter, in fact. The only reason we're here now is because 'the boys' -- Gunter, Nicky and the band -- have a one week gig in Jersey. They'll be back tomorrow night, so I figure I'd better enjoy Amy's company before Gunter comes back to monopolize it.

Amy is behaving like an idiot. Although Gunter has only been gone a week, and she's talked to him every day on the phone, she acts like he's dead or something. A certain song comes on the juke box. Amy sighs dramatically and says: "This is *his* favorite song." She sighs once more and takes a long, meaningful drag on her cigarette.

"Come on, Amy. Snap out of it. Tell me a joke or something."

"What do you mean 'snap out of it'? I don't see how you can stand it. Don't you just *die* when Nicky's gone?" There is a pleading, pathetic look on her face that I'd want to smack off if it wasn't so melodramatic and ridiculous.

"Why would I die when Nicky's gone? I barely know the guy." I lean back in my chair, going for the casual look.

"You what?!" She comes out of her trance at this blasphemous statement of mine. "Barely know him?! Michelle, you've seen him almost every night for the past three weeks!"

I sit up in my chair. "What do you know?"

"Nicky told Gunter and Gunter told me." She shrugs at the simplicity of it. "I know everything, Mick, don't even try denying it."

"Denying what?"

"You like him."

"He's all right. He's a perfectly nice human being."

"You like him and you know it."

"I just *said* I did."

"I mean you *like* like him." She grins mischievously.

"You're full of shit," I inform her. "You don't know anything about it."

"Ha! That's a laugh! I know *everything*." She raises her eyebrows, challenging me. I don't respond. She begins ticking items off on her fingers: "I know about the phone calls, the letters, the flowers, the *song*..."

"He told you about *that*?" I say, mildly horrified.

"I dragged it out of Gunter. I have ways to make him talk." She lowers her eyes demurely.

"Oh, please," I mutter to myself. "Amy, I admit that I've talked to him quite a bit. I can't help it if he writes me letters and...stuff. Freedom of speech or whatever." I'm not very convincing, but maybe she's drunk enough to buy it.

Bud, the bartender who looks like a cross between Papa Smurf and Jabba the Hutt, waddles over to our table and begins collecting the empty glasses. "So, ladies, what's doin' over here?"

"Michelle here is telling me that she doesn't like Nicky." Amy rolls her eyes to let him in on the absurdity of it all.

"Nicky who?" Bud asks, narrowing his eyes. Although he encourages the consumption of vast amounts of alcohol, he can be very protective about his female clientele. On the rare occasions that creeps haven't gotten the message to leave us alone, Bud has been known to lift the offender up by his belt loops and shot-put him out the door.

"You *know*, Bud," I remind him. "The blonde guy with glasses. He's been in here with me a couple times."

"*That* guy?!" Bud yelps. He turns to Amy. " A *couple* times, she says. More like every night for the last month!" Amy grins triumphantly and Bud lowers his voice to ask her: "What's Michelle's problem? This guy married or somethin'?"

"No! He's not *married*!" I burst out with more violence than necessary.

"So what's the problem? You can tell ol' Bud,"

"Well for one thing, he's blonde." I say.

"No! *Anything* but that!" Bud cries.

"I *hate* blondes," I whine. "Besides, he's just not my type." I feel guilty saying it, it's so far from the truth.

"Bullshit." Amy pronounces, banging her fist on the table top like a judge's gavel. "You and Nicky are perfect for each other. You're soul mates. I have never seen anything like the two of you together."

My face feels hot. Against my will, I'm pleased by her confirmation of what I've suspected all along.

Amy continues, "You've seen them, Bud. You must have noticed the way they are together; their conversation goes a hundred miles an hour. They have so much in common that every three seconds or so one of them will say 'No way! Me too!'"

"Maybe that's the problem," I offer weakly. "We're too much alike."

"Honey, that's the biggest load of crap I've ever heard," Bud tells us, pulling up a chair and laying down as much of his voluminous backside that one seat can contain. "At one time in my life I had to choose between two women."

Amy looks at me, biting her lip in an attempt to stifle a guffaw.

"Yep," he continues, "One of 'em was my ex-wife, and the other was a girl named Candy. Now *there* was a *woman*. She was no brain surgeon or movie star, but I tell you the time I spent with Candy was the best damn time I ever had." Bud's eyes are closed and he nods his head slowly as if remembering.

"So why didn't you marry Candy?" Amy asks.

"Same stupid shit Michelle's trying to pull," he answers. "I thought that we had too much in common. I figured we'd get sick of each other."

"See," I say to Amy, "There you have it. Being alike doesn't work. Straight from the mouth of.... Bud."

Bud shakes his head rapidly, his jowls flapping. "No ma'am. That is not what I meant at all. Turning Candy loose was the biggest mistake I ever made. Marrying Delores was the second biggest." Bud cracks himself up.

"See," Amy mimics me, "There you have it. Straight from the mouth of Bud. It was the biggest mistake of his life."

Bud hoists himself up, and wipes his hands on the Grateful Dead T-shirt stretched tightly over his beer belly. "Well, I can't sit and gab all day. Got work to do around here." He pokes a fat finger into my shoulder and says, "You listen to your friend here. She knows what's what. That Nicky is a good kid. Always pays his tab, drinks American beer -- good tipper, too. You hang onto this one, Michelle." He winks and ambles off to the bar.

Amy looks smug as she lights her final cigarette and crushes the empty package in her fist. "So," she says, blowing a thin stream of smoke towards me. "Now that the Nicky Question is settled, let's talk about me."

As glad as I am to be done with the subject, it's late and I'm starting to wilt. My eyes sting from the smoke, and the assorted cocktails I've had are becoming restless in my gut. I'm only half hearing Amy's monologue. It's one I've heard countless times lately, the main points of it being: baby Cameron is perfect, her job is so fabulous she has reenlisted for a second tour of duty with the Maxwells, and of course the ever-popular broken record called, 'Gunter is great, Gunter is good, Gunter is a musical genius.'

The sound of her voice droning on and on makes my head pound and the bile rise up in my throat. My mouth begins to taste suspiciously like the Kamikaze I drank earlier. All of my senses feel under attack. Amy's voice, the smell of smoke and flat beer, the sticky clutter of the table top, and the nauseating thrashings of my stomach hit me all at once like a tidal wave. I grab my head between my hands and close my eyes. Under ordinary circumstances I would probably quip 'Calgon, take me away!' but this is serious.

"Sorry," I mumble. "I can't take another minute of this."

"Of what?" Amy asks. Unconcerned, she continues smoking.

"This, this!" I gesture to the bar and the world at large. "And *that*!" Reaching across the table, I pluck the cigarette from between her red-painted lips and drop it into her beer where it hisses, and goes out. Amy rests her chin on her hand and gazes down dreamily at the beer-soaked butt.

"What is wrong?" she asks quietly.

"I don't know!" I answer. I meant to lower my voice, but it comes out harsh and defensive. "I just get sick of hearing about Gunter. It's not enough for you to spend all your time with him, but even when you're with *me*, it's like you're really still with him. I feel like a third wheel even when there's just the two of us."

"Why don't you and Nicky hang out with me and Gunter? Then there'll be four wheels."

"Why do we have to have them around anyway? I can't *talk* to you with Gunter there."

"What do you mean when *Gunter* is there? When did this become Gunter's fault? You know, you're being very immature about this whole thing, and it's very unbecoming."

"*Unbecoming*?" I say, astounded. "This from a girl with a ring through her nose? Excuse the hell out of me, Amy. Next time I'll consult my etiquette book before troubling you with my immature, unbecoming self." I stand up to leave. I get to the door before realizing my feet are bare. "Where the fuck are my fucking shoes!" I yell up at the lazily circling ceiling fan.

"They're right here, stupid-shit," Amy says, throwing them at me. I collect them from the floor, and stalk off without putting them on.

I walk quickly towards the West Village. I keep meaning to stop and put my shoes on, but don't want to upset my momentum. The streets are empty but I hear sirens coming from the direction of NYU -- the only evidence that the world still exists. Walking quickly, my eyes on the sidewalk, I silently curse Amy, Nicky, Jeffrey, New York and The Rail. I hate everything tonight. If I were a cartoon, I'd have thick black lines of anger spiraling up from my head.

Once inside the house, the quiet darkness immediately soothes me. Everything is wonderfully familiar: the black and white checked tile beneath my feet, the smell of wood polish, and the ghostly breathing of the furnace. This is home.

This house on Bank Street feels more like home than any of the houses I've occupied either before or since my parents called it quits. I belong to this house in a way the Goldmans never will. Sure, they own it on paper, and live within its walls, but they're not the sort of people that can be possessed by places and objects the way I am.

Before the Goldmans bought this house, it was owned by an elderly couple named Millbrook. Over the course of forty years their neighborhood had changed, and the houses on either side of theirs were portioned off into small apartments. When Mr. Millbrook died, everyone assumed his widow would sell the house and move someplace that was easier to keep up. But she had stayed among her memories until she died six months later.

We still occasionally receive mail addressed to Mrs. Millbrook; Jeffrey writes 'deceased' in firm black letters and leaves it outside for the postman. I sometimes fantasize that I will be discovered to be a distant relation of the Millbrooks, and will inherit the house. I'd stay here for the rest of my life, and even after death, I'd return to float up and down the staircases.

I pause a moment outside my bedroom. Something isn't right. I go back to the front door and reassure myself that both locks, the chain, and the deadbolt are firmly in place. I sniff the air for traces of gas or smoke. Nothing. Still, something is strange. Following an intuition like a salmon swimming upstream, I cross the hall quickly and quietly. Someone is in the kitchen.

I know right away it isn't anyone who's supposed to be there -- anyone in this household would have called out when they heard me come in the door. Standing just outside the kitchen door, I will myself to blend into the shadows. If it weren't for my knocking heart and the threat of peeing my pants, I'd feel like James Bond.

"Hello?" I say. It comes out a dry croak, so I try again. "Hello? Anybody in here?" My voice is a frightened whisper as I turn the corner into the kitchen. The room could be filled with all forty thieves and I wouldn't see them, it is so dark. Widening my eyes trying to see something, I slide my feet noiselessly over the tile towards the telephone. Reaching for the phone without looking, I am frightened by the sudden blare of the dial tone, and clumsily replace the receiver.

Just as I am thinking this is all my imagination, I notice a tiny red light glowing from the direction of the table. I inch towards the light and begin to hear a static hum. Someone has left the baby monitor on, the volume so low, all it picks up is the hum of electricity. I turn the volume up, expecting to hear the familiar nursery sounds of Miranda's breathing.

Instead, I hear something very different. For a second I think that it must be on the wrong frequency and we're picking up a neighbor's monitor. Then I remember that this afternoon Miranda napped in the master bedroom, because there isn't an air conditioner in the nursery. What I'm hearing is the Goldmans -- specifically, Debra and Jeffrey.

Of course I'd *known* he still slept with her, but the knowledge was filed away with other insignificant facts about Jeffrey. For example: he visits the dentist twice a year, and has his oil changed every few thousand miles. This sounds like he's getting a lot more than his teeth cleaned. I reach over and turn the monitor off. I turn it on again. Who wouldn't? All along I've tried to dismiss the fact that he and Debra have a history together. They've got their private jokes, and shared experiences, vacation memories and wedding pictures -- not to mention the children. Now I am confronted with audio proof that their sex life is still alive and kicking.

I hear Jeffrey's unmistakable moan, and feel myself blushing in the darkness. I wonder what she's doing to him? I hate to admit it, or even contemplate it, but she's probably a lot better than I am. Let's face it, novelty only counts for so much, and then you've got to back it up with something. Maybe if I'd done everything he wanted, or if I'd been a little more aggressive and adventurous, I wouldn't be hearing this right now. He'd be in *my* bed, and she would be miles away.

This time I turn it off, and leave it off. I feel vaguely sick -- probably just the kamikaze again. Back in my room, I undress and climb into bed, feeling worse every second. Laying down and pulling the comforter up to my chin, I feel like I need to die. Somewhere I'm angry, and have no right to be. She's his *wife*, after all. Mostly I just feel sad, and alone.

I close my eyes and breath slowly.

I turn over onto my stomach and press my face into the pillows.

Resting on my side I try counting backwards from a million.

Lying perfectly straight on my back like a toppled statue, I try to remember a relaxation exercise from eighth grade health class. Soon, though, my mind seizes once again onto what I heard in the kitchen. I wonder if they're done yet.

I watch the green numbers on my clock radio go by for a while, and at six I bag the whole project and head for the shower. It's the only place I can cut loose and cry with impunity. Turning the hot water on full pressure, I sit on the floor of the shower and hug my knees, letting the water run over me.

*   *   *   *

"I'm really sorry about last night, Amy. I don't know what's wrong with me lately. Maybe I should switch to decaffeinated."

Okay, good. Straightforward, humble, with a touch of humor. That's exactly what I'll say. The kids are both napping upstairs and I have one hand on the phone. I've never been good at apologies, but I need Amy as my friend. She's the best friend I've got now. I never see Fiona anymore, Molly's been gone for months, and Susan could be leaving anytime now.

Even Joanne and I are drifting apart. I talk to her maybe two or three times a month. She tells me what's going on at school and I try to sound like I still care. Then I tell her what's going on with Jeffrey, and she tries to sound like she approves. In fact, that is Joanne's main function for me now. As the one person who knows about Jeffrey and I, she is my only confidant. We talk about her coming to visit now that school is out, but I doubt it will happen. We'll just have to see.

Anyway, Amy has taken up the slack left by the distance and defections of my other friends. Besides, I *am* sorry about last night. I was feeling sick and cranky and took it out on Amy. I was dead serious when I told her I feel like a third wheel, but I guess it's not nice to bawl out your friends for falling in love. You're supposed to be happy for them, right? I wonder if anyone really is.

The whole thing makes me nervous. I feel this enormous pressure from Amy, Nicky and Gunter to inhabit this exclusive circle they've created. And I *do* like Nicky. I really do. I only wish I'd met him earlier. It's a case of bad timing -- bad timing and guilt. I seem to be experiencing two different brands of guilt: guilt that Nicky doesn't know about Jeffrey, and guilt about cheating on Jeffrey with Nicky. I know it's stupid to call it cheating because, of course, he's got Debra, but I still feel uncomfortable -- even after hearing what I heard last night.

Maybe I'll tell Amy about Jeffrey. If she knew the whole story maybe she wouldn't push me so hard at Nicky. She could throw one more pertinent fact into the mix, and come up with an objective idea. Maybe she could see a perfectly simple solution that I've overlooked. I think I trust her judgment. She wouldn't try to steer me wrong.

Yes, I think that's the answer. Tell Amy everything and let her decide what to do. I try to imagine the words I'd use to describe Jeffrey and I. Where would I start? Should I ease into it slowly, to spare her the shock, or come right out with it? Phrases and sentence fragments float across my mind. I close my eyes and watch them pass. Red and blue letters, both print and cursive, the ink bleeding at the edges to form a sort of halo, glowing faintly.

The phone wakes me. Damn, I bet it's Amy. There goes my right of first apology. I consider letting it ring its course then calling back saying we were outside, but I don't want the noise to disturb the kids. I pick it up, saying "Hi."

"Hi yourself."

"Jeffrey," I say, surprised. "I thought you were Amy."

"People often make that mistake. The way to tell us apart is she's the one with the pierced nose." I laugh. "So what's up?" he asks, settling in for a lengthy chat. I imagine him putting his feet up on his desk.

"Well, both kids are napping and I'm expecting a call from Amy." I hope he takes the hint.

"You got both kids down at the same time?"

"Yeah, I lucked out."

"Luck has nothing to do with it, sweetheart. You've got the magic touch."

His compliment doesn't register, I'm so busy trying to remember if he calls *her* sweetheart.

"How'd you sleep last night?" I ask.

"What?"

"I *said*, how did you sleep last night?"

"Oh. Fine. You know me, I'm asleep as soon as my head hits the pillow."

"Uh-huh," I say while thinking *liar*. "Remember back when you couldn't stop thinking about me long enough to sleep?"

"Yeah..." he sounds wary.

"I remember it, too." I pause, leaving him an opening to make any kind of declaration. After I've waited too long I say: "Well, I should go. I've got to pick up your dry-cleaning." I hang up.

I sit for a minute thinking of all he didn't say when he had the chance -- what he's *never* said. Maybe I'm sitting around waiting to hear something that he can't tell me, cause it wouldn't be true. He won't tell me something he doesn't feel, right?

No, I don't think I'll tell Amy. But I *am* going to apologize for last night. And maybe I'll even suggest that we all go out tonight and celebrate the band's return.

Amy's number is busy for ten minutes or so. I hate being kept waiting. Finally it starts ringing. And ringing. It must ring six or seven times before someone picks it up. The voice is so strange that I ask: "Amy, is that you?"

"Yeah, it's me."

"You sound weird." Maybe she's madder than I thought.

"I *am* weird," she says.

I laugh uncomfortably, unsure if she means to be funny. "Amy, is something wrong?" I ask the question, but I know the answer. Something is very wrong. My heart is pounding, and my suddenly damp palms are in danger of dropping the phone. Amy mumbles something that is so unbelievable I say "WHAT?"

She tells me again in the same dull monotone, as if she'd been repeating it all day. "Cameron died last night."

"WHY?! I mean HOW?! What *happened?*" There is a long pause, which gives me time to wish I'd been more calm and reasonable -- not so accusatory. "Amy? Are you still there?"

"He just.... just.... I found him this morning... Oh, Michelle!" She bursts into tears, and I find them coming to my own eyes, if not for Cameron -- I don't have the full story yet, and it still feels like a rumor -- for Amy. It breaks my heart to hear my tough, wise-ass friend reduced to tears.

She's sobbing and I don't know what to do. The things that work with Jake -- tickling, weird voices, and chocolate milk -- would probably be inappropriate, so I sit and feel useless until she stops. After a while she starts winding down and sniffing away the last tears.

"Do you want me to come over?" I ask.

"No," she says, her voice congested. "It's been a madhouse over here. The police, the coroner..."

"That's it. I'm coming over. Give me a minute to wake up the kids."

"Please don't," Amy says. "I've got enough to deal with without having to worry about you, too. I'm sorry, that was bitchy, but I'm just so *tired*. I feel like this day will never be over."

"Do you want to talk about it?" I hope she doesn't think I'm prying.

"I don't know. I've told it so many times, to the Maxwells, the police, the guys at the hospital--"

"The hospital? So he was sick?"

"I don't know. Nobody knows. They're doing an autopsy tomorrow, but the best guess they have now is that it was crib death."

"Oh, God," I breathe. Talk about your worst nightmare coming true.

"When the Maxwells left for work this morning, they said the baby wasn't awake yet. So I got the twins ready for school, and fed them breakfast. I figured I'd let the baby sleep as long as possible before we had to leave." Her voice breaks.

"It's okay," I tell her, knowing it isn't.

"So, when it was almost time to go, I mixed a bottle and got the carriage ready. All I had left to do was get Cameron up and changed. I went in there -- in his room I mean. I got some clothes out of the dresser. I remember thinking I needed to buy him some cute little summer outfits. So then I.... looked in the crib, and just the way he was lying there was weird, but I go 'Cameron, time to wake up' and then I lay my hand on his little back..." The last few words quavered and then she stopped talking altogether.

"It's all right, Amy. You don't have to say any more."

"He was cold. So... cold."

"Shhhh.... Don't think about it."

"He'd been dead for *hours* they said. Hours and hours, all alone...and cold."

"Amy, is there anyone there with you now?" I get no response. "Amy? Where are the Maxwells?   And the twins, where are they?"

"Dr. Maxwell and Chris are still at the hospital. The girls are with their grandma. Look, Michelle, one of these medic guys gave me a tranquilizer or something. I guess I was hysterical or something..." She chuckles weakly. "Anyway, I need to lie down somewhere, okay?"

"Okay, but I'm going to call you later to see how you're doing. Okay? Amy?"

"'Kay, bye 'shell."   I hear the receiver bump around a bit before she hangs it up.

I stare at the phone for a minute, my mind a complete blank, before it all comes back. Then I try to convince myself. Over and over in my head I think 'Cameron is dead, Cameron is dead.' I imagine his cold, stiff little body laying in the crib. I think of that word 'autopsy' and what it means before pushing that thought away violently.

I run up three flights of stairs into the nursery. Without thinking I gather Miranda up into my arms. She's warm and sleepy, rubbing at her eyes with her fist. There are sleep lines on her face, and tufts of hair sticking up in crazy directions. Suddenly my heart feels like it's going to burst open, it's so full. I hold Miranda in my arms, kissing her face and saying "I love you, I love you, little baby." I can feel hot tears coursing down my face, and I'm crying for Cameron and Amy, for the twins and their mother, and for all the lost babies alone in the cold.

*   *   *   *

When they get home Jeffrey and Debra have already heard. The neighborhood is buzzing about what happened at the Maxwells. They both give me a big, cheesy hug -- like I got a bad haircut or flunked a math test. At dinner they have me tell them everything I've heard from Amy. They say things like 'really? oh dear' as they chew their food. They give me the rest of the night off, but when I ask for Monday afternoon off to go to the funeral, Debra gives me a funny look.

"Why would you want to do that?" She genuinely wants to know.

"Because. It's *Cameron.* Besides, Amy's my friend." When pressed for the reason I want to go to a funeral, I'm stumped. It's not something you *want* to do, it's just something you *do.* Doesn't she know anything?

"Well, I don't see why you should go. It's not like you're a *relative.* And you're not religious anyway."

"Debra!" Jeffrey says. "Let her go if she wants to. Maybe it will give her a sense of closure. I think it will be good for her." He winks at me like: *There, I fixed it.*

"Fine," Debra says, engrossed in wiping up the last of the pasta sauce with her bread. "But you'll have to stay home with the kids."

"Why me?"

"I have a screening with the mouthwash people." He obviously is supposed to know what this means.

"Well *I* have a presentation at NBC."

She shrugs.

He shrugs back, then looks at me and says: "Sorry, kiddo." *My hero.*

I walk to my room, feeling like I'm surrounded by a thick soap bubble, separating and insulating me from the rest of the world. Everything seems to move in slow motion, and voices sound muffled. I'm afraid to call Amy -- she's probably still asleep anyway -- besides, I wouldn't know what to say if one of the Maxwells answered the phone. I could call Joanne, but I don't feel like talking, so I lie on my bed watching the fading light of the sun moving across the walls and ceiling. I get a sudden mental flashcard of a medical examiner's scalpel, and Cameron's lifeless face, and push it away, squeezing my eyes shut.

*   *   *   *

Hearing a strange sound, I turn over and open my eyes. My eyelids feel thick and heavy. It's light outside and I wonder what time it is. The clock reads 7:30, but I'm not sure if that's AM or PM.

There's the sound again, coming from the window. As I'm raising the blind, a shower of gravel pelts the window pane and then Nicky's grinning face appears. "Hi," he mouths, waggling his fingers.

I'm happy to see him, and open the window. "Come in," I say.

"No, you come out. It's warm, and we can sit on the stoop."

I'm going to protest that I'm not dressed for it, but looking down at myself, I see that I certainly am dressed. I've even got shoes on. "Nicky? Is it morning or night?"

"It's night, hon. I just got back from Asbury Park."

"Okay, I'm coming out."

As I let myself out of the house to join Nicky on the stoop I get this feeling that I'm forgetting something. I do that all the time -- just when I'm enjoying myself, I stop and think: hey, isn't there something I'm supposed to be worrying about? This time I know it's something important, but I can't think what.

It all comes rushing back to me when Nicky, after throwing his arm protectively around my shoulders, says, "Weird about the baby, huh?"

My face feels frozen for an instant, while I process the information. Then the whole thing hits me again, but harder. I go limp in Nicky's arms. He isn't repelled by my emotional display -- he holds me as tight as he can, supporting both of us. He isn't flustered and fumbling for something to say; everything he does is right. He strokes my hair, his long cool fingertips just brushing my forehead. He rocks slightly and croons my name. I love the way he says my name. Most people slur it lazily, and it sounds like Muh-shell. Nicky says it quietly, but carefully -- I can definitely hear the 'i.'

"You know what else?" I say, with my face still buried in the folds of his shirt.

"What, Michelle?"

"I can't even go to his funeral! They say they can't take time off from work!" I raise my head and look him in the face. Am I imagining things, or do I detect a moistness in his eyes?

"They're jerks," Nicky says, straightening up. "Real assholes."

"Nicky...."

"Yeah, I know. I know you like them and everything, but that is one of the most insensitive things I've ever heard." He shakes his head angrily, and I see his shoulders tightening under his shirt.

"They can't help it if they have to work. Besides, I don't really want to go to the funeral anyway." I pause, noticing some kids playing across the street. "I don't know if I could watch them lowering a tiny little coffin and then covering him over with dirt." I feel strangely numb. I don't feel like crying anymore. I feel guilty for it, like Cameron didn't mean enough to me.

"Do you want me to talk to them for you?" Nicky asks.

"Talk to who, about what?"

"The Goldmans about letting you go to the funeral."

"No -- thanks anyway, but no." I feel like laughing, it is so unexpected that he would even think of doing something like that. Of course I don't want him to 'talk' to them, but the fact that he offered is so.... cute. "You're a very nice boy, Nicky," I say, absolutely sincere.

He looks at me as if I've insulted him. Using both hands to plunge an imaginary dagger into his chest, he groans and keels over into my lap.

"What is *that* all about?" I ask.

"Talk about the kiss of death," he says, grinning up from my lap. "What'll you tell me next -- that you really like me 'as a friend?'" He readies his second 'dagger' for the plunge. I stop it mid-stab.

"No, I'm not going to tell you that."

"You love me like a brother?" he says, teasing me.

"Not at all like a brother," I say, smiling. "Unless we're talking about the Egyptian royal family."

"Oh...," he says. "So, in other words, if we were cousins and this was Mississippi...."

"Exactly," I tell him.

The people across the street, if they cared to look, would see nothing unseemly. Simply a young nanny sitting on her front stoop, with a clean-cut bass player lying across her lap. Very tame, very uninteresting. But the people across the street don't know that the air between us is alive and crackling with a current of electrified pheromones. It's all I can do to keep from pouncing on him here and now.

I lower my face down to his. Little flags of worry pop up that read: Cameron, Amy, and Jeffrey. Nicky must see the indecision flickering in my eyes, because he meets me halfway, and pulls me down. Then the worry-flags and neighborhood kids are insubstantial shades of background. All that is real and tangible is his mouth on mine. When I start to feel like I'm falling into a well so deep that I may never be able to find my way back out, I struggle to the top of my consciousness and disengage from Nicky's face.

"What, what's wrong?" he says, looking dazed.

I feel confused, and angry for some reason. Like I have been made the butt of a joke, or the victim of a slick con. I back away from Nicky, trying to get a good look at him. "Who *are* you?" I say, almost to myself.

"Look closely," he says, as if this were a perfectly standard line of questioning.

"Who's in there?" I muse, inspecting his face.

"Just me," he says. "Only Nicholas Edward Ware. What you see is what you get."

"Really?" I say, ready to believe whatever he tells me.

"Yes, really," he says firmly. "No games, no hidden agenda. Just Nicky."

"Just Nicky," I repeat.

"...and Michelle?" he raises his eyebrows, the question all over his face.

I'm too afraid to say anything, so I smile apologetically, despising myself for being so weak. I look up at the house behind me, and notice a curtain moving in an open window upstairs. A furtive hand pulls the curtain shut; Jeffrey's left hand -- the one with the ring.

*　　　*　　　*　　　*

The kids and I are in Washington Square Park. The playground here is one of the busiest most of the year, but now that school is out, and everyone has migrated out of the city, it's nearly deserted. The city has become hot and still. When the sun comes up it's already eighty degrees and the temperature keeps climbing from there. By lunch time it's over ninety, and you can smell the stench rising up from the streets like steam. In New York, that's when you know it's really summer; you can smell the piss on the sidewalks. Fiona and the Bouchets have left for the Hamptons, and Summer spends every other weekend on Fire Island.

Time seems to drag on and on. I feel like I'm waiting for something to happen, but I can't guess what -- maybe leaving the city and getting out to Fire Island. We were supposed to leave a week ago, but Jeffrey and Debra keep coming up with reasons to stay 'just one more day.' I feel strange -- restless, but lethargic. I feel like I should be jittery, but my body refuses to go through the motions. I'm like a Mexican jumping bean trapped in a vat of maple syrup. Ever since Cameron died I've felt like one of those hot, hot days right before a storm. The air gets thick and heavy, then just when you think you can't stand it a minute longer you hear the first rumblings of thunder, and know that relief is on the way. For me, the thunder is still a long way off, and all I can do is wait.

I push Jake in the swing, where even *his* enthusiasm has been sucked dry by the blazing sun. He sits in the swing idly, no expression on his face. Miranda is playing in the sand at my feet. I have to be extra vigilant now that she can get around so well. She is dressed in a sleeveless sundress and a white bonnet. I have slathered a thick coat of sunscreen on both kids, which in turn has attracted a layer of playground dust.

"Hey, 'shell!" Jake says, his face animated for the first time today. "Look! Riley!" He points towards the big arch. I squint in that direction, the sun so bright it even penetrates my dark glasses.

"Where?" I ask. I don't see anything but an ice-cream vendor, who looks like he'd like to climb into his freezer. There is also a small boy about Riley's age, but he's with a dark-haired woman.

Jake leaps off the swing and runs away, sand kicking out behind his feet. Miranda, seeing her big brother take off without her, starts wailing. Picking her up in one arm and collecting the diaper bag and sand toys with the other, I chase after Jake, calling "Wait! That's not Riley! Jake!"

But he runs on ahead of us, straight for the kid he thinks is Riley. I follow, huffing, puffing and leaving a trail of plastic shovels and juice boxes. When Jake reaches the two people, who have been simultaneously moving towards us, he runs up and embraces the child. Putting on an extra burst of speed, and wondering how to explain this to the brunette, I run up to them and swallow my apology when I see that the child is indeed Riley. Even more surprising is the fact that the mystery woman with stringy brown hair is none other than Montana Sue!

"Hi!" I say, catching my breath. "I didn't recognize you!"

Susan smiles and self-consciously fingers her hair, but doesn't offer any explanations. We walk back to the playground, and Jake runs off toward the climbing thing with Riley in tow. Finding a shady bench, we sit down and Susan takes Miranda onto her lap.

"She's getting so big," she says smiling uneasily, aware that I'm staring at her and her new hair.

But it's not the hair that gets my attention. I am struck by how terrible Susan looks -- like she's got consumption or some other Victorian wasting disease. Her face is drawn and pale, with deep purple crescents beneath her eyes. She is dressed in dark, severe clothing that hangs down from her scrawny shoulders.

Her hands are trembling. The fingernails have been chewed off, along with her ragged, scabby cuticles. The most disturbing change is the one that has come over her eyes. When I met her, her eyes were so brightly blue, alive and sparkling. It's not the color or the eyes themselves that have changed so much, but the expression in them -- a hunted, frightened look. No one meeting her today would believe that she'd been beautiful once.

"What did you do to your *hair*?" I say. So much for tact.

"Oh, I got a crazy idea in the middle of the night, went out to a drug store and bought a bottle of 'chestnut brown.'" She laughs nervously. "It looks awful, doesn't it?"

"It looks fine," I fib, "but your hair was so pretty before. Most people would *kill* for hair like that."

"That's what I was afraid of," she says, picking long brown hairs off her gray T-shirt.

"What do you mean?"

"Blonde hair is a handicap here. I stick out like a sore thumb, as Granddad would say. I thought with brown hair I'd blend in, and bad things would stop happening to me."

"Oh," I say. "Is it working?" Somehow I doubt it. She still looks like a victim, only now she's a *homely* victim.

"Not really," she admits. She sighs and changes the subject. "Have you heard from Amy lately?" After Cameron's funeral, Amy took a leave of absence. She's been in San Francisco with her parents for several days now.

"I left a message yesterday," I say. "She hasn't called back yet."

"Yeah, I've left two messages. I wonder if her parents are even *giving* her the messages? I know her dad was never gung-ho on her living in New York. Maybe he's trying to keep her from coming back."

"Nah," I say, "Amy's too smart to fall for that. She knows we called. She probably doesn't feel like talking yet."

"Yeah, maybe you're right. I hope she's okay. I hope she *does* come back."

"I know, I've been thinking the same thing -- trying to imagine what I would do in her place. I don't think I'd come back. I mean, Dr. Maxwell and Chris and the twins have got to stay here and deal with it all. They've got to empty out his room and answer all the condolence cards. Amy doesn't have to. She can just walk away from the whole mess and put it out of her mind."

"*Try* to put it out of her mind," Susan says. "Still, I hope she comes back."

"Me too." I say. Out of the corner of my eye I see Jake running towards us, crying and rubbing his eyes.

"Riley frew sand in my eyes!" he says. I pull his hands away so I can see.

Susan has gone to retrieve Riley, who was trying to make a quick getaway. She hauls him back by bodily force, and when they get close enough, Jake punches him in the arm.

"No frowing sand!" Jake scolds him, "Bad boy!"

Of course this sets off a brand new round of tantrums, which Miranda finds hilarious. The more they scream and cry, the harder she laughs. Susan and I calm them down, giving each one juice and a cracker, and sitting them on opposite ends of the bench.

As the kids munch away, I ask Susan what's going on with the Connollys and their divorce. She tells me that Ed has moved into the country house in Connecticut with his 'friend.' Jane is still living in the Gramercy Park apartment, which Ed is trying to sell out from under her. For the moment they have joint custody of Riley, which means he spends three and a half days a week with each parent. And where Riley goes, Susan goes.

"What a pain in the ass." I say.

"You can't even imagine," she says. "I'm spending all my time driving between Connecticut and New York."

"At least they let you use the car. You could be taking the train."

"I wish we were. Then *I* wouldn't have to drive -- I hate it. They make me drive this big black Mercedes that I'm terrified I'm going to wreck. They would just *kill* me!" She takes a sip of juice and continues. "But the worst part is being up there with Ed and *Ralph*. I'm trying to be open-minded about it -- I think 'what would Michelle or Amy do?' -- but I'm sorry, I wasn't raised that way. Where I come from we don't think two men should be... *together*."

"I would think it'd be much worse being in the city with Jane. I know *I* couldn't stand it."

"Oh, she's never around, she's out with a different guy every night. I haven't had time off in six weeks or something."

"Susan! You can't let them do that to you! They signed a contract saying you get two nights off a week. You should call Barbara at the agency. She could get you a new job." I consider her pale skin, trembling hands, and the constant look of fear in her eyes. Laying a hand on her shoulder I suggest, "Maybe you'd rather go home?"

Her lower lip trembles like a kid's before she starts to cry. "Oh, Michelle, I want to go home so badly! I keep thinking that I could be riding my horse, or fishing with my brothers. Sometimes on the freeway, I think about pointing the car west and driving all day and night 'til I get home."

"Go home then, Sue. No offense, but you need to get out of this -- you look awful."

She smiles at the understatement. "I know. It would be so easy to quit. I wish I could, but I can't leave Riley. He's too little, he doesn't know what's going on."

"Kids are tougher than you think. They bounce back," I say, but I don't believe it.

"Not Riley." she says.

Hearing his name, Riley holds out his arms to her and says, "Up."

She pulls him onto her lap kissing his plump cheeks, then lowers her voice to confess: "He calls me 'Mama.'"

"Kids do that sometimes. At this age they get confused. Miranda called the dog next door 'Dada'." This does not elicit the hoped-for laugh.

"I'm serious," she says. "Jane doesn't spend time with him at all. The only reason she wants custody is to get back at Ed." Lowering her voice even more, and putting her mouth inches from my left ear she says, "She wants me to lie for her. So she'll get sole custody."

"What does she want you to say?"

"*Gross* things. That, Ed like... *molests* Riley." She looks as though she's tasting something sour.

"Jeez, that is bad. What are you going to do?"

"I don't know, but I'm not saying *that*. Not only is it sick, but it's also.... What do you call that thing when you lie in court?"

"Perjury?"

"Yeah, that. I could go to jail or something."

I don't quite know what to say to her. The only advice I have is to go home. That's what I would do. But she really thinks that she can't leave Riley. She may even have some delusion that the court will award *her* custody and they'll ride off into the Montana sunset. Knowing that I can neither comfort nor advise her, and given the fact that the sun is merciless today, I suggest we go get ice cream.

The world looks more appealing from an air-conditioned diner booth. The kids are greedily slurping up their sundaes. Susan and I have both ordered huge ice cream concoctions heaped with every variety of syrup, sprinkle, nut and topping. Jake laughs at the whipped cream on our faces, so I reach over and dab some on the tip of his nose. Of course, all three kids think this is a scream, and proceed to coat themselves, the table, and most of Susan and I in various sticky substances.

When we're cleaned up, thanks to Miranda's supply of baby-wipes, we continue to sit in the diner, watching poor, hot, suffering souls walk past the window. The boys have full bellies and are content to play with the supply of straws and paper napkins. Miranda has fallen asleep in my arms.

"So, Michelle, what've you been up to? Seen Nicky lately?"

I feel a goofy grin creep onto my face, uninvited. "Yeah, now that Jake's out of school, we've got a lot of time to kill and Nicky's been showing us around the city."

"Showing you around? You must have seen everything by now -- you've been here longer than I have."

"I've seen a lot, it's true, but I haven't been to the big, touristy things. Nicky's taken us to the Empire State Building, Statue of Liberty, the Children's Museum..... Hmm... where else?"

"Tony Island!" Jake says.

"Oh yeah. *Coney* Island. Jake and Nicky ate their weight in hot-dogs, then rode the roller coaster three times in a row! I was willing to bet that at least one of them would barf and most likely both, but they were okay."

"I was brave," Jake says. "Nicky said so."

"You like Nicky, don't you?" Susan asks him, smiling.

Jake nods.

"Does *Michelle* like him?"

"I dunno..." Jake looks at me shyly. "'shell?"

"Yep. I like him, too."

Jake grins and turns back to his straws.

"So what's going on with you two? Anything I should know about?"

"I don't know. I mean, I really, really like this guy. He's smart, and funny, and he's an awesome musician. But--"

"But what? He sounds perfect."

"I don't know what it is." I shrug. "Something's just not right. There's something missing."

"You mean like *chemistry*?" she asks, wrinkling her nose.

"No, there's plenty of that, believe me. In fact, it's reaching dangerous levels, it's been building up for so long."

"You mean you haven't....?"

"Nope." I wouldn't admit this to anyone else.

Susan looks relieved. Then she says, "If Summer were here, she'd say *that's* what's missing!"

"Yeah, she would say that. But I think it's something else. I don't know how to explain. See, when I'm with Nicky I just don't feel all weak and desperate and miserable." *The way I feel with Jeffrey,* I don't say.

"And you *want* to feel like that?" Susan asks, perplexed.

"Isn't that the way it's *supposed* to be?"

"No."

"Oh." What does she know, anyway?

*   *   *   *

When Debra and Jeffrey get home from work, I walk over to Nicky's by way of Saint Mark's Place. I pass by some young professionals dining al fresco on tofu and bean sprouts while ten feet away a street vender is doing a brisk business selling T-shirts that read: 'Die, Yuppie Scum.' Nicky and I wander around Little Italy then pick up some take-out to eat up on the roof of his building. By standing in a certain spot, and leaning down, you can see a little silvery patch of the East River. From this distance it even looks like normal water.

After polishing off the risotto and tortellini, we lie back and watch the evening steal up over our heads. When the sky is the darkest blue that it can get without being black, there is an oddly familiar motion to the air, a stirring and rustling.

"Do you feel that?" Nicky says.

"I feel *something*. My God, it's a breeze!"

We leap to our feet and run to stand at the very edge of the roof, stretching out our arms and legs to get the maximum cooling effect. I close my eyes, for a moment forgetting where I am, and swaying dangerously over the edge. Nicky doesn't call 'watch out' or startle me by pulling suddenly on my arm, but somehow I am safely in his arms, and it seems I've been there all along.

Downstairs again, we open the windows to welcome in the breeze.. His apartment is a tiny studio, not more than twelve feet by fifteen. His double bed is the most prominent -- the only -- piece of furniture. The walls are lined with homemade bookshelves crammed with magazines, CDs, college textbooks, and paperback novels. He keeps the stereo on the kitchen counter, and his bass guitar in the corner. Tacked up on the bathroom door are all the flyers and promos for his band.

Nicky is examining these when I come out of the kitchen, two bottles of beer in my hand. "What are you doing?" I ask, handing him a beer.

"Thanks," he says, and takes a drink. "I was just looking at these old things."

"There sure are a lot of them."

"Yeah. We've been together for almost three years."

"Wow. Don't you get sick of the other guys?"

"Mm... not really. The guys are cool. The only thing is, the band's just not *going* anywhere, you know?"

"Yeah, I know. Have you ever thought of quitting? I mean, you're way better than the rest of those guys, you could hook up with a really great band, or get studio work. My dad did that for a while."

"Actually, it's funny you should say that. As a matter of fact, just last night I got an offer from another band."

"Really?!"

"Yeah. Their bass player is in rehab for the fifth time, and they're sick of waiting for him."

"This is great! Are they good? Have I heard of them?"

I doubt you've heard of them, but yeah, they are good. A lot of guys have been busting their ass to audition for them."

"But *they* came to *you*?"

"Yeah." He says, absently.

"This is so cool! How come you're not bouncing off the walls?"

"Well, there's sort of a catch."

"*Sort of* a catch? Does it involve your signature in blood?"

"No, no -- nothing like that." He laughs. "They're going to be touring this summer to promote the new album."

"They have an album out?" I'm having visions of saying I'm with the band.

"It's just a small, independent label, but supposedly the big record companies are keeping a close eye on this tour."

"This is going to be so great! I'm so happy for you!" I kiss him on the cheek.

"Wait a sec, Michelle. Nothing's settled yet. Nothing's for sure."

"Well why not?" I ask. "If they want you, and you want them, what's the holdup?"

"I told them I had to think about it first. I wanted to know what *you* think."

"I think it's the best thing in the world. Did you think I wouldn't be happy for you?"

"No," he says, picking at the label of his empty bottle, "-- but I thought you might object to my being gone for so long."

Aha, so that's what this is all about. "Well, of course I'll *miss* you, dummy. But this is the chance of a lifetime -- this is your future. You can't let *me* decide."

"Why can't I?" He sits down on the edge of the bed.

"It's too important."

"Some things are more important."

"But what'll you do if you *don't* go? Stay with the Intensers until you all end up rockin' in the nursing home?" I can't even get a smile out of him.

"There are a million bands in the world," he says petulantly.

I sit beside him and reach for his hand. "There are a million *girls* in the world."

"Not for me," he says, snatching his hand away. "Will you just think about it, Michelle? Will you do that for me?"

"I guess so," I say, a bit confused. "So what exactly are you saying? That you'll waste your big chance on me? How could I ask you to do that?"

"All I'm saying is, if you want me to, I'll stay. If you want *me*, I'll stay. Okay?"

"Okay." I say, miserably.

"Just one thing--"

"What?"

"I hate to do this to you -- I know it's a lot of pressure -- but I need to give them an answer by the weekend."

We fall silent, and it feels like we've been quarreling, though technically we haven't. We settle in for the evening with a six-pack of beer, and a bunch of oldies on the CD player. I lie on the bed flipping through magazines while he sits on the floor re-stringing his bass.

Elvis sings from the kitchen stereo. I turn the pages of a magazine, but I'm not reading. I'm not even glancing at the pictures. I am staring at the back of Nicky's neck. Usually it's covered up by his hair, but his blonde head is bent forward as he works over the strings, giving me a perfect view of the smooth, tan skin, and the two slender tendons that run the length of his neck up into his hair. There is something so sweet and trusting about that neck, it makes me want to stay nearby so nothing can hurt him.

The circumstances are right. The planets are aligned, Elvis is singing 'Surrender,' and a breeze drifts in to whisper through our hair and cool our faces. There is some sort of convulsion taking place in my chest, and I realize that I could love him.

My finger reaches out for the little valley between the tendons in his neck. I watch it moving, honing in on its target, but I have no control. When my finger makes contact, Nicky stops what he is doing, but doesn't speak, doesn't move.

"Nicky," I say, not sure what I'll say next.

He doesn't answer, but I hear the slow exhalation of his breath. He's waiting, afraid the slightest noise or movement will disturb the universe.

I move forward on the bed, my lips now centimeters from the nape of his neck. He must feel my warm breath -- little goose bumps rise up on his skin.

"Nicholas," I whisper.

Elvis is winding things down, making one last plea for surrender. I don't want the song to end. For a moment the street outside is free of sirens, breaking glass and honking horns. There is only the breeze and Elvis; Nicky and me.

What do I want? Do I want him to go and get famous, or do I want him to stay where he is? I would like God and the Fates to press *pause*, please, and let me think.

The song ends, and in the second of silence that follows, my mouth forms the words: "I want you to stay."

*   *   *   *

Jeffrey doesn't notice me in the doorway. He sits at the barren kitchen table huddled over a long-cold cup of coffee. To my new eyes, he looks almost pathetic sitting there waiting for me; pathetic but for the blue flannel shirt he wears. I don't know why, but I love that shabby garment of his. It's soft and worn, thinning at the elbows. It is in this shirt that Jeffrey appears -- to me -- the most himself. When picturing Jeffrey in my mind he is always wearing it -- he is unguarded and sweetly human.

Among its other charms, the shirt has an exotic aroma. For some reason it smells like East Indian spices -- curry and cumin, to be precise. Jeffrey is altogether unaware of the power his shirt holds; I asked him once to will it to me, and he thought I was kidding. I was very serious. If there is one thing that could bring Jeffrey back to me from the dead, it would be a whiff of that old flannel shirt.

"I was worried." He speaks up suddenly.

"What? Oh, hi. I just got home."

"So I see."

"You're up early, aren't you?"

"Actually I'm up late. I wanted to see you when you came in." He is so serious, he is bordering on grim.

"You want to see me? Take a long, hard look," I say, holding my skirt in a curtsey, and turning slowly around.

This, at last, gets a smile. "Very nice, very cute -- but then you're always cute."

Making a face, I wave away his compliment.

"Well you are," he says; and then: "I miss you."

"Miss me?" My throat begins to tighten. "How could you possibly miss me? I *live* here!" I force a laugh.

"True, but I never see you anymore. If I didn't know better, I'd think you were avoiding me."

"No!" I nearly shout. He can't really think that, can he? That makes it all so much worse.

"Of course, you've been busy running around with that Nicky character -- you're not serious about this guy, are you?"

I should blast and blaze in anger, coming to Nicky's defense. But I betray him with a simple gesture: I shrug, and turn away.

Jeffrey draws nearer, toying with the straps on my dress. "Remember when I bought this for you? I thought it was red, but you insisted that it was -- What was it?"

"Raspberry," a part of me answers. I'd forgotten he gave it to me. I'd been thinking of it only as the dress I met Nicky in.

"That's right," he says, "raspberry." His mouth moves over my shoulder where he's pulled the strap aside. I can feel it coming. The lightening has shattered the air with electricity, and it's only a matter of time before the thunder hits. Prayers and immolation are useless at this point, 'cause here it comes again -- the tragically desperate stomach-plunge, slinking back like a bedraggled and battle-weary tomcat. *You thought I was gone, didn't you?* sneers the cat, *I've got news for you, kiddo: I'm back, and I'm better than ever.*

I start to back away -- to retreat from this taunting cat. My mind gains distance first, then my body follows, reluctantly. I imagine I see a flash of panic in his eyes, but it is gone so quickly that it's difficult to know if it was ever there at all.

"Michelle," Jeffrey says, the game in motion once again, "there's something I've neglected to tell you, and I think you should hear it."

I allow my eyes to look at him, but curb the tendency to hope for too much.

"I've really come to value my relationship with you -- such as it is. You're like my girlfriend or something -- you *are* my girlfriend!" He is amused by the -- to him -- archaic term.

Something imbedded very deeply in the molten core of my self is plucked at, tugged, and finally reeled in, and I recognize that it was folly to think I was anyone's but his.

"Jeffrey," I say, loving the taste of his name on my tongue, "I told Nicky --"

"Sh-sh-sh-" he exhales in swift staccato. "Don't say anything. It'll be fine. We'll be all right, sweetheart, I promise."

*   *   *   *

"Hurry up!" Jake hollers down the stairs. "I wanna *go*!"

"Just a sec. I need to make a quick call." I sit in the playroom armchair, waiting for my chance.

"Oh, no," Jake wails, "We'll *never* get to leave."

Debra's laugh comes from the kitchen. "Honey, Michelle knows we're leaving in five minutes with or without her, right Michelle?" She pokes her head around the corner and winks.

The playroom and hallway are piled with luggage, toys, strollers, bikes, beach chairs and tennis rackets. Today we are going to Fire Island. I've been packed and ready to go for a week, and now it's finally happening. This morning at breakfast Debra said she didn't feel like going into the office and Jeffrey had looked up from the Wall Street Journal and said, "Fuck it then, let's go!" When Jeffrey gets fired up about something it is impossible to resist his contagious enthusiasm. We all got up from our breakfast and scattered in various directions to get ready. Two hours later we are ready to go. I just have one small piece of unfinished business.

Jeffrey strides into the house wearing shorts and a pink polo shirt. He claps his hands. "Okay, team, if we're going to make the 11:30 ferry we've got to get moving." He picks up a load of luggage and heads back out to the car, which he's taken out of the garage a few blocks away and driven up to the curb out front.

Miranda is having a grand old time climbing on top of suitcases, and unpacking everything she can lay her fat little fingers on. Making a trip out to the car, Debra scoops up the baby and takes her outside to strap her into her car seat. Miranda hates being confined, and I can hear her howls from here.

Jake comes down the stairs wearing sunglasses and my old U of W baseball cap, which is much too big. Once in the cluttered hallway, Jake does a quick survey of the area, his hands on his hips, then takes it upon himself to carry a bag of diapers and a Frisbee. "I'm strong," he says, to no one in particular.

I am alone for just a moment. Soon they'll all be back for another load, and I'll be expected to do my share. Hopefully a moment is all I'll need.

My heart starts thumping as I dial, and comes to a full stop at the first ring. It is picked up almost immediately by the answering machine. This really is my lucky day. I tune out the message, and hold the phone away from my ear, mindful of the long, deafening 'beep.' Then I leave this message: "Hi, it's me. We're leaving for the beach today. About last night -- I changed my mind. You should go. Good luck, and, well, good-bye."

SEVEN

"God, I hate those things," I mutter, ducking my head as a seagull swoops past. Joanne and I stand at the railing on the upper deck of the ferry on our way to Fire Island. I borrowed Jeffrey's car to pick Joanne up at the airport, then left it in the parking lot in Bay Shore to catch the ferry out to the island.

Joanne is disappointed that we won't be in the city, but what can I do? I have to work. She didn't consult me on her plans. Last Monday I'd received a four AM phone call, in which Joanne informed me in a drunken slur that she would be arriving on Friday at one, and to pick her up from the airport.

I'd warily approached the Goldmans, afraid they'd think I was overstepping my bounds by inviting a friend to stay in their house. They hadn't been angry, but they weren't completely happy. Some of the nannies before me had kept up such a constant stream of visitors that Debra said it started to feel like she was living in a sorority house.

Jeffrey offered no objections at the time, but later confessed that he was a bit uncomfortable with the fact that Joanne knew about us. He worried that she'd slip up and spill the beans. He also wasn't thrilled at the prospect of having our nightly 'visitations' interrupted. It was tougher out at the beach house anyway. We usually had to slip out to the beach late at night, or else meet back at the house when everyone else out.

Even so, as the months went by, we were becoming bolder and less discreet. Just two days ago, I had been in the outdoor shower enclosed by weathered wooden walls on the back deck, washing the salt and sand off while the kids napped inside. Debra was lounging on a beach chair on the front porch, and I could hear her talking on the cordless phone. The wooden door had opened slightly, and Jeffrey had stepped into the shower, grinning wickedly.

I had long ago given up feeble protestations. This was the whole point now -- the danger. When we were completely safe and alone the whole project cooled down considerably. The best times were the dangerous, foolhardy ones: the basement during a dinner party, the backyard at midnight. Once, when Jeffrey's parents were visiting from Florida, Jeffrey and his father stayed up late in the kitchen playing cards and drinking scotch. Jeffrey excused himself for some reason, and came into my room. Silently he'd taken the book from my hand, yanked the crotch of my panties aside, unzipped his fly, and nailed me just like that. He returned to the card game without ever speaking a word.

I love that. It makes me feel as potent as a force of nature. When he is so desperate for me that his eyes glaze over and he risks everything to connect with me I feel plugged into a primal strength as old as the earth itself, a power that draws him into my orbit against his free will and better judgment. At times like that I feel like a goddess.

So when Jeffrey had joined me in the outdoor shower that afternoon, my smile had matched his as I handed him the soap. He soaped me down until my body was so slick with lather that I nearly slipped through his arms.

There were light footsteps on the deck outside, and Jake's small voice calling: "Daddy?" Jeffrey's attention strayed momentarily toward the sound of his voice. Recapturing his attention, I pulled him into a kiss that snatched the breath from his lungs and left him wobbly on his feet.

Now Debra had joined in the search. She circled the deck calling: "Jeffrey? Telephone!" I heard her stop outside the shower door. Jeffrey stood stock still, holding his breath.

"Michelle? Do you know where Jeffrey is?"

"Nope," I said evenly, my fingers crossed.

"Hmm," she said, as her footsteps receded.

I took the soap from Jeffrey's hand and lathered his shoulders, then his chest, working my way down. As he braced himself against the wooden walls of the shower I snapped back the waistband of his swim trunks and took him in my mouth.

Afterwards he shampooed my hair, his strong, knowing fingers kneading the suds through my curls. I lifted my face to the faultless blue sky, breathing in the salty air. Bubbles cascaded down my back and I thought: *This is the way life could be.*

By this time the ferry has come to dock in the town of Saltaire. Joanne and I keep our place at the railing, surveying the island before us, as the other passengers grapple for their things, herding kids and dogs onto the dock. As the upper deck begins to clear, Joanne turns to me and says: "It's really good to see you, Michelle. I've felt weird lately, like we're losing touch."

"I know," I tell her, relieved to hear that she shares my concern for the fate of our friendship. "I was sort of worried we wouldn't get along."

"Don't be an ass," she tells me. "That will never happen to us." She gives me a long hug, and I hold back a tear or two, realizing how important she is to me, and how I've allowed us to drift apart. "I can't wait to meet Jeffrey," she says. "I can't really picture him. He's good-looking, right?"

"Well *I* think so, but it's not like he's a Greek god, or the football type that you like."

"But he's so *old.* I can't imagine it." She shakes her head in distaste.

"Maybe so," I say, smiling, "but believe me, everything still works."

"I would hope so." We start to gather up Joanne's bags, and head for the stairs when I see Summer standing on the dock waving at us. I wave back.

"Who's that tall girl?" Joanne asks.

"That's Summer Avery. She's the one from Seattle. Remember, she went to UW? I told you about her."

Joanne looks unsure, but says, "Oh yeah. Summer."

We start down the stairs when I think of something. I grab the back of Joanne's tank top, stopping her. "Jo, remember, you're the only one who knows about Jeffrey. Don't say *anything* around Summer."

"I won't," she assures me.

As we step off the ferry and onto the dock, Summer rushes up to us. I've barely made the introductions when Summer says: "I ran into Fiona in Southampton last week. She just got a letter from Molly, and guess what -- she's pregnant!"

"Really," I say, trying to imagine Molly pregnant. I picture her in a rustic cottage surrounded by the green fields of Ireland. She stands at the blackened stove, stirring a pot of something, a beatific smile on her face. A simple flowered dress swells out over her belly. I smile. In no way does this image gel with the hard-drinkin', head-bangin' Molly O'Doyle that I used to know. "She's happy," I say.

"I guess so," Summer shrugs. " She'd better be -- where she is, she's got no choice."

"She's *married*, Summer. They're probably really excited: decorating the nursery, picking out names..."

"Puking up breakfast, discovering the joys of stretch marks... c'mon, Michelle, this is *Molly* we're talking about. They've only been married a couple of months. They're probably living in some Dublin shit-hole, saving up their pennies to invest in a coat-hanger."

"That's a terrible thing to say!"

Joanne and Summer laugh. Summer always manages to make me feel like a prissy old school marm. I point in the direction of the Goldmans' beach house, and lead the way. Joanne and Summer follow a few steps behind, telling dead-baby jokes. We stroll along the wooden walkway that seems to hover above the grass and sand. There are no roads or cars on Fire Island, only these walkways which cover the island, shooting off into thinner branches, each leading to its own house. Kids with shovels and buckets run past, bumping us. Summer nearly falls off the walkway and yells after the kids: "Excuse you! Brats."

"Speaking of brats," I say, attempting to weasel my way back into the conversation, "where's Ben?"

"They're all in Lisbon for the week. Thank God."

"So what are you doing out here?"

"I came out to par-tay. It's the Leibowitzes' weekend for the house, so I thought I'd come out here and enjoy it while they're gone. Besides, I met some guys -- tax lawyers -- that are having a huge party in Kismet tonight."

"Lawyers? Tax lawyers? Sounds like the death." I don't want to go to a party tonight. I want Joanne all to myself. Besides, I don't want to have to go through the charade that I'm interested in picking up every moronic boy that Summer foists in my direction.

"They're rich, Michelle." she says, trying to tempt me. "C'mon. It'll be wild. These guys are *loaded*. They have a fully stocked bar, and you can drink rum-and-Coke to your heart's desire."

"Cool!" Joanne pipes in. She looks up at Summer in that admiring way she gets when she meets someone she thinks is really bad-ass. She does everything she can to keep up with them, mimicking their slang, complimenting them -- generally trying to ingratiate herself in any way she can. Pretty much the same way I looked up to Joanne last year at school. It's pretty sickening to see someone you once modeled your whole personality after kow-towing to someone else. Especially Summer. Summer and I had never really connected. I don't think she likes me much, and it pisses me off, especially since I "saved" her from that first horrible job with the Eagans.

"Do you want to go, Jo? Or are you too tired?"

"No, not at all. It's three hours earlier for me, remember? Yeah, I wanna go. Sounds pretty cool. Uh, if you want to go." There is an unmistakable look of excitement in her face. Her eyebrows are raised expectantly, a sheepish smile on her mouth.

"So," Summer says, "are you bitches coming or not?"

"Definitely," I tell her. Joanne's face breaks into a full smile. "What time? I've got the kids until seven."

"Well, we're going to tap the keg at three, and fire up the barbie at five."

"We probably won't be there until eight," I tell her.

"Joanne, what about you? Is there some reason you have to stay with Michelle while she wipes asses?"

Joanne giggles. "I don't know," she says.

"Well why don't you come along with me, then? We can hang out at my house or go to the beach and catch the last of the prime rays."

Joanne is nodding her head, excited by the prospects of her first wild evening in New York. I know I've lost her. To try to discourage this would make me a jerk and a stick-in-the-mud.

"Yeah, Jo," I say. "Go with Summer. You're on vacation here, you should have a good time. You can meet the Goldmans tomorrow."

We were at the place in the walkway where our paths diverged. The Goldmans' house was just over the next dune, and the Leibowitzes' a hundred yards further down. I took Joanne's bag, intending to put it in the guest room at the house for when she came back later tonight after the party.

"Wait! I need that!" she says, taking it back. I have to get ready for the party. Summer, will you help me pick out something to wear?"

"Sure, or you can always borrow something of mine. You should bring your stuff anyway. That way you can just crash at my place if you get too hammered, or if you meet somebody."

'Well, see you guys around eight, then?" I say.

"Yeah, the house is in Kismet. A big modern place with tons of windows. It's called Sandpiper."

"Okay, see you then," I call, but they are already walking away from me.

*   *   *   *

When Debra and Jeffrey come home, the kids and I are sitting at the kitchen table. I'm cutting dinosaurs and dump trucks out of colored paper which Jake glues onto a large poster board. Miranda sits in her highchair, scribbling with a fat yellow crayon.

Jeffrey heads immediately for the back bedroom to strip off his suit and take a shower. Debra stands and admires our artwork for a while before she follows Jeffrey.

I don't leave the house until after 8:30. I haven't heard a word from Summer and Joanne inquiring as to my whereabouts. They must be having a good time.

When Debra takes over the kids, I take a hurried shower, slip into shorts, tank top and sandals, and giving myself the once-over in the hall mirror conclude that I look awful enough to scare away even the drunkest of tax lawyers. Then, in an after thought, I run back to the bathroom and cover myself in a liberal spritzing of bug spray. That should do it.

I step out onto the front porch, the screen door squealing painfully before banging shut. I waggle my fingers at Jake through the screen. His face glows with blue television light as he watches a cartoon. Debra is on the phone making plans to visit an old girlfriend in California who is getting married in a couple of weeks.

It's thoroughly dark now, though a full, yellow moon hangs just over the roof of the house next door. Hearing a thud and a muttered curse, I turn toward the side of the house to see Jeffrey coming out of the toolshed struggling with something.

"What are you doing?" I call softly, walking towards him.

"What I'm *trying* to do is get this fucking bicycle out -- there we go." He wheels out a ridiculous-looking old bike -- a grandmother type -- with a wire basket attached to the handlebars, and a cracked and faded blue vinyl seat. There is a considerable amount of creaking as he walks it toward the wooden pathway, and the back tire looks as if it's been patched more than a few times.

"What's all this about?" I ask, suppressing a laugh.

"I'm meeting Ted and Richard at the Out in Kismet. I was supposed to be there fifteen minutes ago."

"And you think that contraption is going to get you there faster than walking? Who are you, Greg LeMans?"

Jeffrey ignores this, and throws one leg over the bike. "Hop on," he says, "I'll give you a ride into Kismet."

"On *that* thing? No way."

"It's perfectly safe, Michelle. Get on."

"Well where do I sit? I'm *not* riding in the basket." I fold my arms over my chest and look at him skeptically.

"Here," he pats the seat. "You sit here, I'll stand up and pedal."

I climb aboard and Jeffrey steps down hard on the top pedal, launching us forward. The old bike shudders under the weight of us and the unaccustomed movement. A yelp escapes me as I am thrown off balance and have to grab the sides of the bike seat. As we wobble along the wood planks, I hold my legs straight out at the sides, like a tightrope walker's balancing pole.

It's terrifying at first and I scream and laugh when we turn sharply around a corner nearly landing in the underbrush.

Jeffrey laughs and calls over his shoulder: "Don't worry sweetheart, I've got it under control!"

Yes, he does have it under control, I think. *Everything is in his control, and I , as usual am off-balance and unsure, trusting him completely yet wondering if I should.*

We fly through the night, leaves and small branches catching at my clothes and stinging my outstretched legs. There are only the sounds of the persistent thud of wooden planks under the tires and the hum and chirp of night insects. Off in the trees and beyond the dunes are spots of light and distant laughter. As we approach the house called Sandpiper the frogs and crickets are drowned out by the thumping of a stereo. There is loud, raucous laughter, a shriek here and there, and the startling sound of breaking glass. The party is well under way. As we round the final corner on the bicycle, I wish the ride would never end.

"Can't I come with you to the Out?" I say, leaning forward to Jeffrey's ear.

"Honey, you know that's not possible. These are guys I work with. How would it look if I showed up with the hired help?"

I shoot a death-ray from my eyes to the back of his skull for that one.

He stops the bike at the front of the house where Joanne is talking to a guy on the front porch. I climb off the back and motion her over. Joanne's face is flushed with alcohol and she just smiles when Jeffrey shakes her hand and says: "I've heard a lot about you -- though you've no doubt heard much more about me."

I nudge him with my elbow, and he laughs. Summer suddenly appears, galloping across the yard, her hand already outstretched for Jeffrey's. "Hi, I'm Summer. I work for the Leibowitzes."

Jeffrey's brow furrows as he thinks about this.

"You know," she prompts, "Jake and Ben play together."

"Oh *right*. Hi, how are you."

They shake hands again, and I notice that Summer is maybe three or four inches taller than he is.

"Well, I've got to roll. I'm meeting some people." Jeffrey climbs back on the bike and takes off, calling: "Nice meeting you, girls!" I watch him go, until he disappears into the darkness.

"So, Michelle..." Summer says. I turn slowly, hesitant to take my eyes from the place where I lost sight of Jeffrey. Summer has that smug, vaguely threatening flicker in her eyes.

"What?" I ask, leery of that familiar look on her face.

"How long have you been fucking Jeffrey?"

Joanne bursts out laughing, then claps a hand over her mouth and looks from me to Summer and back again, her eyes wide.

I glare at her, as close to assault and battery as I've ever come.

"I swear to God, Michelle, I didn't say *anything*!"

"She didn't have to say anything," Summer says, still with that same smug look. "It's totally *obvious*. I could tell just by looking at the two of you. Shit, I could almost *smell* it!"

Joanne allows herself a small chuckle. I hate them both for a second or two, and then my face relaxes and I laugh with them. I feel strangely relieved.

"Let's go inside and get a drink," Summer says, placing her arm around my shoulders and steering me towards the house. "I want to hear all about this. Every last detail."

Joanne trots along behind us, calling: "She told me when it first happened! I've known about it all along!" Suddenly, I'm the star of the evening.

I spill my guts.

In an attempt to catch up with Joanne and Summer who have been drinking for five hours already, I do three quick shots of vodka before moving on to my customary rum and Coke. The kind of drunk I have acquired tonight is smooth and pensive, where everything seems to slow down. The sort of drunk where you speak slowly and carefully about important matters while slouching back in a chair and gazing at the world through droopy, bloodshot eyes -- an amused, tolerant smile playing on your lips.

Summer, Joanne and I sit around a low coffee table, one end of which is being used for a rowdy game of quarters. A coterie of tax lawyers and CPAs hover on the periphery of our little group stepping forward to refill Summer's drinks and light her cigarettes. They most likely think that if they attend to her every wish and anticipate her every desire they'll get laid tonight. Actually, they probably will.

Summer and Joanne listen attentively as I tell them the whole story. They are especially intrigued by the close calls -- they laugh and shake their heads in amazement.

"And Debra really has no idea?"

"Nope."

"I don't believe that," Summer says. "She couldn't be that stupid. I'll bet she knows but is putting up with it because she knows it won't last."

"No," Joanne shakes her head. "How could she stand to have Michelle in the house if she had the slightest clue about what's going on?"

Summer shrugs. "I guess you're right. But maybe she's so into keeping up the appearance of a happy family that she doesn't want to go through the whole divorce thing. Or maybe it's just a little vice that she overlooks. He's probably done this with all the nannies and she figures it's better for him to be boffing the au pair in the kitchen than out buying it on the streets."

"Yeah, I bet that's it!" Joanne claps her hands, sloshing her drink down the front of her blouse. "Debra doesn't worry about him getting attached to any of them because they only stay for a year."

At this point, listening to my friends discuss my life like it's a plot twist in some mindless soap opera kicks my pleasant buzz into a belligerent drunk. How dare these bitches make these insane conjectures?

"Jeffrey hasn't touched another nanny!" I tell them. "He has never even thought of them that way!"

"Not a single impure thought?" Summer smirks.

Joanne laughs. "Yeah, how do you know? 'Cause he *said* so?"

"He told me, and I believe him." I can't look at them. "He loves me," I say quietly.

Joanne perks up. "He said that?"

"Well, not exactly..."

Summer bursts out laughing. "I knew it. He's fucked every other nanny and told them all the same things. Michelle," She pokes a finger in my chest. "You are a chump."

Joanne nods, her face serious.

"If I'm such a chump, then why do they want me to stay for another year?"

"But you're not going to, right?" Joanne says.

"I'm thinking about it."

"Michelle," says Summer, "don't be an idiot. What are you going to do, hang around playing the other woman for the rest of your life? Get a grip."

"Maybe he'll leave his wife," Joanne pipes in. "Maybe he'll marry Michelle and they'll get custody of the kids."

Summer throws her head back and laughs viciously. "That will never happen. Not if she waits a lifetime."

"Maybe Debra will get in a plane crash or something," Joanne suggests.

Summer crushes out her cigarette on the table, flicking the butt onto the carpet. "That wouldn't be too bad," she admits.

"I don't want her to *die*," I say. "I like her -- kinda. I thought if she met someone else and ran off to Tahiti. That'd be good."

"Don't hold your breath," Summer says, accepting a fresh drink from one of her admirers. "Seriously Michelle, you need to get out of this situation. You're going to end up getting hurt. Come back to school with us. Get your degree. Drink beer, play with boys your own age -- have a real life."

"I like my life." No one believes me.

Summer scoots forward to the edge of her chair. "Look -- you, me and Joanne will rent a little house by Greenlake. It'll be great. We'll throw parties, be wild, study when we have to..." She waves her hand dismissively.

I think about that. Summer, Joanne and I sharing a little house. Fighting over the bathroom, and sharing clothes. We'd do each other's hair, counsel each other on various boyfriends, record a cute, clever message on the answering machine... We'd be the three musketeers. It would be one long slumber party!

"That might be fun..." I say, surprising myself.

"Fun!? It will be fan-fucking-tastic, girl!"

"Yeah, Michelle, come back with us. You don't need Jeffrey. He's too old for you anyway," Joanne says, growing visibly excited by the prospect of getting her roommate back.

"Not to mention the fact that he's losing his hair," Summer says.

"Actually, I found a *gray* hair last night," I admit.

"You see what I mean? He's going straight downhill. First will be a beer belly, then hairy ears. The next thing you know he won't be able to get it up at all! Who needs that?"

"Not me," I say, growing convinced. "Maybe you guys are right."

"Sure!" Summer says, handing me a lit cigarette. "You deserve better than some aging yuppie. You're young, cute, smart -- about most things. You should find yourself a hot young dude with a sports car."

I laugh, choking on the cigarette smoke.

"I wish I'd met Nicky," Joanne says.

"I only met him once," Summer says. "In fact, one night Amy and I had done a bit of coke and I actually *propositioned* him." She laughs.

Joanne looks at me, expecting some wild reaction but I flick the ashes from my cigarette and smile. Nicky'd told me this already.

"Well what happened?" Joanne asks. "You didn't...?"

"Oh no. He generally said thanks but no thanks. He was quite a gentleman about the whole thing, but he only had eyes for Michelle." Summer bats her eyes facetiously.

I stand up abruptly. "I need a drink -- or two." I head for the bar, then smile back over my shoulder: "Well, are you coming or not?"

Joanne and Summer exchange a look and hurry towards me.

An hour or two later we are all dancing in one writhing mass to an old Duran Duran song. It plays over and over -- someone must have pressed continuous repeat on the stereo. Some anonymous soul gropes me from behind and I laugh wildly, never bothering to look back and see who it is.

The carpet is sticky with beer and burnt in several places. Someone has punched a hole in the wall and another sad sack is puking in the kitchen sink.

In a fit of ecstatic release I leap up onto the coffee table and fling my arms out. "I'm going back to school," I scream. Joanne and Summer give me the double thumbs up. "Good-bye Jeffrey, hello frat boys!" I yell. Grabbing the nearest male, I plant a big sloppy kiss on his astonished mouth. My friends howl like wolves as I shove the guy aside and say "Next..."

*   *   *   *

I don't know where I am. All I know is that I need to lie down, and can't find my house. I trot along the wooden paths looking for my house through bleary, half-closed eyes. I giggle to myself every now and then. I'm happy. I have my friends back and my future is accounted for. As a once and future co-ed, I have many nights like this to look forward to.

Well damn, this was funny for a while, but it's getting old fast. I need to lie down. I don't know what happened to Joanne. I assume she's crashing at Summer's. My last clear memory of her is someone putting Bruce Springsteen on the stereo whereupon Joanne and I began to shriek and weep for joy.

I'm thinking that it would be nice to lie down on the smooth wooden planks beneath my feet and mosquitoes be damned, when I spy a familiar-looking structure three houses ahead. Can I make it that far? Stomach, don't fail me now.

I creep along the periphery of the house, still unsure if it's the right one. There's an old blue bicycle leaning against the porch rail and some toys that look like Jake's, but you never can be too sure about these things. That bug zapper looks just like the Goldman's, but then again everyone out here has one.

Just what I need is to wander into the wrong house and set off some alarm system. The police show up -- does Fire Island even *have* a police force? -- and haul me away, busting me for breaking and entering as well as walking while intoxicated.

As I'm pondering these things a wave of nausea and fatigue swells up and crashes over my head and I sink down onto the nearest lounge chair. Who could fault me for resting here a minute? What kind of people would refuse shelter to a weary traveler?

I watch the bug zapper do its thing as my eyes slowly close. The gnats and mosquitoes don't bother me a bit, but the moths with their furry little bodies make me sort of sick when they hit the electric blue cylinder. They're almost like animals -- like tiny, winged kittens or something. I close my eyes when the moths come close, but watch the others with an evil fascination. *Zap!* No more diapers. *Zap!* No more whining. *Zap!* No more 'hired help.' *Zap! Zap!* Play group and bratty kids. *Zap!* Debra. *Zap!* Jeffrey. *Zappity-zap!* New York, filth, crime and attitude. I'm going home.

*   *   *   *

I dream of a cemetery. Green lawns with gentle swellings here and there. Off in the distance, rows of poplar trees blot out any evidence of civilization. Despite the modern, well-tended landscaping the stones are all of the old style. Sturdy and upright, with carved angels and flowers. The names are inscribed, not followed by mere dates of birth and death, but by poetry and words of those left behind.

I wander through the legions of tombstones, looking for something. I'm wearing my old prom dress. It's long and made of white taffeta -- my senior year attempt at Scarlett O'Hara. The puffed sleeves keep falling off my shoulders and the full skirt drags on the ground. My feet are bare and dirty.

I'm supposed to be somewhere but I don't know where. All I know is that I'm late. I begin to run through the rows of graves trying not to let the sickly sweet odor of moldering flowers overtake me. Hot tears make their way down my face and into the bodice of my dress.

Stumbling upon a marble fountain complete with dolphins and cherubim, I realize I have a terrible thirst. My mouth is so dry that my tongue sticks to the roof of my mouth and my lips stick to my gums. I have to drink. Kneeling at the side of the fountain, I cup my hands, bringing the cold clear water to my mouth. The water looks clear and refreshing, but when I drink, the water tastes just the way the old flowers smell. I spit it out and run on, wiping my mouth with the back of my hand.

I'm sprinting now, my breath hard in my chest, the tombstones just a blur. I break through the line of poplars and come upon a funeral scene. Clusters of black-clad people surround a flower-wreathed coffin. The fresh grave waits close by, the earth yawning patiently to accept another offering.

Running up, I stop abruptly when I see Debra in a veiled hat standing with two children. The boy is about six, standing very straight and handsome in his dark suit and tie. The little girl -- surely Miranda -- clings to her mother's skirt. I hear her cry "Oh, Daddy!" before she covers her eyes and gives herself over to crying.

Debra looks beautiful, I note with interest. She looks very Audrey Hepburn in her little hat and slim, black dress. A single tear, hard and shiny as a diamond glistens on her cheek.

I recognize only a few other faces in the crowd. The Zherings are here, and Jeffrey's parents. Mrs. Maxwell is here too, holding a smiling, two-year-old Cameron, the picture of health.

I shove my way through the crowd to get a better look at the grave site. No one sees me or can hear my muttered apologies. As I move through the forest of mourners there is only the swish of black silk as I pass.

On the other side of the coffin I see Amy and Summer passing a joint back and forth and giggling. I wave, but they don't see me either. The only person who seems to notice me is Molly Doyle, who rubs her belly maternally and smiles. I could swear I saw her wink.

Suddenly Debra breaks her silence by dropping to her knees in the grass and wailing. Jake stares straight ahead, oblivious to everything but the sight of his father being slowly lowered into the earth.

This is real, I think. *They're taking Jeffrey away from me!*

"Noooooooooo!" I scream, running toward the grave. But they don't stop. No one can hear me. I don't exist. The coffin has hit the bottom with a piney thud, the dirt has been sprinkled. Debra throws a single rose and is led away. Everyone is leaving.

"Don't leave him there!" I scream again. "He's *mine*!" Still running, tripping over my dress I take a flying leap into the open grave. I expect to hit the coffin lid with a painful jolt, but it doesn't happen. I keep falling. Falling and falling through the dark. I hear unintelligible whispers, and a baby's laughter.

The dark gets closer, and I can smell the dirt and decay. The awful flower scent is getting stronger, filling my head and making my eyes water. Cobwebs brush my face and stick to my flailing arms. When I think I'm going to pass out from the smell and the fear I land gently on my feet, graceful as the ballerina I'd always wanted to be. It's lighter here at the bottom, though not by any source that I can see. Looking around and picking the cobwebs from my hair I spot the coffin. *Jeffrey.*

I lift the lid, expecting him to come straight into my arms. The lid is heavy, and it crashes shut once before I roll up the white sleeves of my dress and try again. This time I get it open, and catch sight of his dark gray suit.

"Jeffrey," I say. "I'm here." I lower my face to his and find nothing but a skull, the empty eye sockets staring, mocking me. "Oh, God!" I wail. Sobbing I lift the bone-filled suit from the coffin and hold it in my arms. "Come back to me," I cry, rocking what used to be Jeffrey. "Please come back. I need you."

Even as I'm trying to love the skeleton back to life, it dissolves at my touch, and drifts through my fingers. Jeffrey's dust clings to my dress and my skin. It's in my hair and my eyelashes. I try to brush it off, but can't do it. The dust mixes with my tears, forming an ashen mud on my face.

I wake up brushing myself off. The sky is pink and the birds are singing. I can smell coffee brewing in the kitchen and hear Jeffrey's hum from the shower. I could never leave him.

Christa Charter

152

EIGHT

Sitting at the kitchen table, I leaf through a magazine, one eye on the clock. Everyone is asleep and has been for hours, yet every little creak makes me jump. I nibble at some peanuts, trying not to look at the clock. It can't be time yet. My head swivels on its own and the clock reads 3:14. Two more minutes. God, it's taking forever. They call this fast?

I wish Joanne were still here. She would come up with something funny to make me laugh and forget myself. But she would also take the whole thing seriously, and would be just as concerned as if it were herself. It makes me sad to think of her. Since she left I've had the feeling that nothing will be the same between us again. Of course, that's what I feared the first time I ruined her plans. Having backed out for the second time I doubt she will ever trust me again.

Oh well, she and Summer are best buddies now anyway. They took no pains to disguise their contempt when I told them I'd changed my mind and had signed up for another year as the Goldmans' nanny. It seems like I've been saying that an awful lot lately - sorry, I changed my mind. The question is, do I ever really make up my mind in the first place?

3:15. I wish I could say that all is well. I guess in another minute I'll find out, won't I? I lay my head down on the table. Just what in the fuck is wrong with me, anyway? Why can't I make decisions? Why do I find it so impossible to simply decide what sort of Michelle I'm going to be and go with it?

I came so close to going back with Joanne. I guess a part of me really misses college life and hanging out with people my own age. But if I shacked up with the two of them I wouldn't be anyone special. I would be just like them, except less so. I would be the diluted Summer Avery -- Michelle, the quiet one who can't seem to make up her mind. I don't want to live in anyone's shadow.

They're right, I do deserve better than being the other woman, and I may very well end up getting hurt. In fact, I don't imagine I'll get through this without a broken heart. If not broken, then severely mangled. But maybe it would be good for me -- snap me out of this ridiculous torpor in which I've festered my life away. Whatever happens, I am determined to see this Jeffrey thing through. Win, lose, or draw, this is one thing I'm not running away from.

It's time. 3:16 AM. Standing up slowly, I'm surprised at how weak I feel. My hands quiver as I set my soda glass in the sink and plod slowly toward the bathroom. Please God, don't let anyone wake up and have to pee just now. How on earth would I explain all this? The bathroom door squeaks on its hinges, and I cringe, holding still and silent until I assure myself that I haven't woken anyone.

In the bathroom I flick the light on, frightened for a moment by a long-legged crane fly sputtering near the mirror. I turn the water on to a silent trickle and wash my hands. It couldn't hurt to wait a few more seconds, I think. Finally I can't stand it any longer. Bracing myself for the worst, I turn and look at what has been cooking on the lid of the toilet tank.

I take a breath. The stick is blue.

Catching sight of myself in the mirror, I am surprised and bewildered to find that I am smiling.

*　　　*　　　*　　　*

Debra is spending the week in California. Her friend is getting married -- her third husband -- and then she's going to be doing some work in LA. I can't say that I miss her. In fact, I'm enjoying myself tremendously. It's a relief not to have to have her looking over my shoulder all the time, suggesting that I take less than perfect care of her children. It's wonderful to have the freedom to do what I want. Whatever I decide to make for dinner -- that's what we're having. I can relax, take things easy, and not adhere to any special schedule she's laid out, or feel that angry bolt of resentment when she gives me a list of chores for the day.

Best of all, Jeffrey has taken the week off from work, so instead of taking the ferry in every couple of days, or else only coming out for the weekend, he is spending the week playing house with me. He says on more than one occasion that it's fun to have a 'teenage wife'. I love that he calls me that. I look at it as a sort of personal triumph that the thought not only crosses his mind, but he actually goes so far as to verbalize it.   When we go out, people assume that we are married and the kids are ours. I love that. Jeffrey seems to get a kick out of it, too.   At the grocery store in Ocean Beach a woman was complementing Miranda's strangely dark eyes -- just like Jeffrey's -- and said to Jeffrey: "And this is the mother?" nodding towards me. Jeffrey said, "Yes," and elbowed me to play along.

We get up fairly early, and while Jeffrey makes a run to the store for bagels and the paper, I get the kids up and dressed. We have a nice, leisurely breakfast together, then adjourn to the living room to read the paper and lounge around. The whole week is like one long Sunday afternoon, without the threat of Monday.

The afternoons we spend at the beach, soaking up the sun and leaping the foam as the waves roll in. We stroll along the sand holding hands until Jeffrey spots someone he thinks he knows and whisks his hand away like I'm on fire. But even that can't spoil this week for me. I have Jeffrey all to myself -- a preview of what our life together could be. Although he doesn't say so, I know he's thinking the same thing. He often sighs heavily, and when I ask what's wrong, he looks at me, smiles and says "Nothing's wrong. I'm just happy." He describes it as a "bittersweet sort of happiness," and I guess by that he means that Debra will be home soon, and then we'll have a long, long wait until were really and truly together.

At night I sleep beside him in his and Debra's queen-sized bed. He strokes my face and smiles in a goofy way and says he's happy when he's with me. Then he holds me as tight as he can, so tight that I find it hard to breath.   And then he kisses me with everything he can muster and, as if he's said something, asks: "Do you know what I mean? Am I making myself clear?" His eyes are like mine when I'm trying to telepathically transmit to him how much I love him.

'Fucking' doesn't seem to be an appropriate term anymore. I won't say we 'make love', only because I despise that phrase so much. It's what old people do when the sex has gotten lame. We don't fuck, and we don't do that other thing. It's somewhere in between. Although it's completely intense, and he's as incredible as ever, there's something else behind it now. Some extra level of meaning. Sometimes he looks at me as if he can see right through me, and knows exactly what I'm thinking and feeling. Then I'm tempted to tell him. But he strokes my still-flat belly in a purely lascivious manner, unaware of our little child blooming beneath his hand, and I keep quiet.

When he falls asleep, I lie awake listening to him breathe. I match my breaths with his, until we're in sync like two halves of the same soul. I watch his eyelids quiver and know that he's dreaming. Every once in a while I drift off for a few minutes myself, and when I wake to see Jeffrey sleeping beside me, I feel peaceful, and safer than I have since I was a little girl. I feel his body heat rising up, infused with his own intoxicating odor of pheromones and a little soap. Knowing that I could just reach out and he would be mine makes me feel like I could pass out. Sometimes I lie there in bed and just cry for loving him so much. No one told me love would feel like this. It's completely mind-altering. I can't even remember who I used to be. What did I care about before I met him? What did I think about? What on earth did I want?

That is how I know that I was made for him. The Fates or whatever made a slight scheduling error -- what with his marriage and the age difference -- but now we've found each other, and for the first time in my life everything is crystal clear.

*   *   *   *

Debra is back and has brought her obnoxious friend Trish with her. She is only staying the weekend, but it's Friday afternoon, and I already hate the sound of her voice. It's not just that she was there the night of the dumbwaiter incident, but that she is continually annoying. Since she is still single, she thinks that the two of us 'girls' should spend a lot of time talking about how rotten men are. She doesn't seem to see humor in the fact that while she rambles on and on about the evils of men, she is also trying to pick them up. A reasonably cute specimen walks by, and Trish sits up and swells out her chest, points her toes, and lifts one knee at a slight angle in a *Sports Illustrated* pose. She wears tiny, high-cut bikinis in wild animal prints, and bakes herself to a dark, leathery brown. Maybe she thinks that will cancel out the fact that her tits are saggy and the backs of her thighs look like cottage cheese.

The worst thing is when she tries to give me pointers on how to meet men. "Michelle," she'll say, "Why don't you go walk up and down the beach? Get out there and be seen, that's the first step. That's exactly what I would do if I had a cute little nineteen-year-old hiney like yours." I'm sure she would. She's just the type that would parade herself up and down the waterline, swaying her ass back and forth as bait. I bet she used to practice that walk in the mirror.

Anyway, as long as Trish is here, I'm spending every spare moment out of the house. I volunteer to work overtime so that the Goldmans can take her out to dinner, and I scrounge for playdates with anybody I can dig up. I even take Jake all the way to Cherry Grove to play with the little artificial-insemination child of two 'married' lesbians.

The only person I even know anymore is Summer, and she acts like she'd prefer a herpes outbreak to a day in my company. She's leaving pretty soon, anyway. She's all registered for fall quarter, and she has Joanne out house-hunting for the two of them. I try to tell myself that they deserve each other and that I'm going to have a much better, more adult life, but I still feel left out and hurt. Still, in my desperation to escape Trish I arrange to meet her on the beach on Saturday afternoon. The kids are off spending 'quality time' with their parents, so this is purely a social visit.

It's strange to lie back and do nothing except apply tanning oil and read. I keep thinking there's something I should be doing, and have to remind myself that the kids are perfectly safe and that it is my day off. Summer digs her toes into the sand and proceeds to tell me all about her's and Joanne's plans for the fall. She's obviously excited, but I can't help thinking that it's partially meant to make me jealous and perhaps reconsider.

"So are you all packed to go?" I ask, trying to act interested.

"Oh no way. I've acquired so much shit while I've been here. I need to ship some stuff UPS. I meant to save money this year, but when they hand me a big wad of cash every Friday, I feel compelled to go out and spend it. And I'm usually broke by Tuesday at the latest."

"Yeah, I do the same thing. What do you spend your money on? Besides alcohol." I ask, chuckling a bit so she doesn't think I'm condemning her.

"Clothes, mostly. That and CDs." She shakes her head. "I definitely wish I'd saved some. When I get back to school I'm going to have to get some shitty part-time job delivering pizza or something." She grimaces.

"I thought your parents were paying for school."

"Tuition, rent and books. If I want to eat, drink and most of all be merry, I've got to foot the bill myself." She sits up and peeks under the edges of her bikini to see how her tan is progressing. "What about you? Did you save any money? I guess you don't have to worry about paying for school and stuff if you're really staying another year."

"Nope, I didn't save a dime. I spent it all on books, mostly. I have a sort of addiction to books. Someday I'm going to have a big old house with a library. There'll be a fireplace and a big leather chair, and the walls will be floor-to-ceiling books. I could spend the rest of my life in a room like that."

"Weird. I like to read, but I also like to get out in the world. If I read too much I start feeling like I'm living by proxy, y'know. Not actually experiencing things, but reading about other people's experiences." Summer shrugs, and smiles.

I think we're actually having a conversation. I think we might be getting along, and am very anxious to stay on her good side. "There's a part of me that would really like to go back to school," I admit. "But I just can't afford it. I blew my chances when I left. Now my parents are saving up to send my brother for a year."

"You could apply for financial aid."

"I tried once. I followed my dad around for a month with the forms, but he would never fill them out, and we missed the deadline." I frown. "I guess I'm still pissed off about that."

"I would be, too," she says. "Hey! Time to rotate."

Groaning, we both turn over onto our stomachs, to roast our backsides. Resting our heads on folded arms, it seems cozy and intimate suddenly, like a slumber party. I was always the last one asleep at those things. The two or three of us who made it until the sun came up would always cluster in a circle eating stale potato chips and whispering about which boys we liked and if we'd ever kissed anyone. I wonder why it is that the middle of the night seems to inspire us to bare our soul?

Today, though the sun is bright, I suddenly feel like confiding in Summer. Part of it may be that I want to purchase her friendship with a juicy secret, or maybe I want to punish Joanne by not telling her first. Mostly, though, I think I can't keep it to myself any longer.

"Summer," I say, all ready to just come out and say it.

"Hmm?" She turns and looks me in the eye.

I chicken out. "Uh... I talked to Montana Sue last night. I called her at the place in Connecticut."

"Oh, really? How is she, anyway? God, I haven't talked to her all summer."

"She doesn't sound good at all. I could barely understand what she was saying. She kept whispering, and her words were all garbled. She seemed to be trying to tell me something, but couldn't. She was sort of hinting that her phone was tapped."

"A little paranoid, huh? Poor Susan, she was never cut out for this."

"Yeah. I asked her when she was going home and she said "Any time now." Isn't that sort of weird? I guess she hasn't told the Connollys that she's leaving yet. Poor little thing."

"Did she say anything about the divorce and all that?"

"Well, she said that both Ed and Jane have tried to bribe her into spying on the other one. Ed even wanted her to plant a video camera in Jane's bedroom so that he could prove she's an unfit mother.... And... Oh yeah! This is *really* nuts," I continue. "Jane accused Susan of trying to steal her boyfriends!"

"No way! Susan?"

"Yeah, Sue is just taking care of Riley and when Jane's dates come to pick her up, of course they're going to give Susan the eye. Even looking like shit the way she does now, she's a lot better looking than Jane."

"How's Riley holding up?" Summer asks.

"Not well. Susan says that he's stopped talking except for a few words, and that he wakes up crying several times a night. So Sue's not getting any sleep either."

Summer shakes her head and takes a long drink of water from her sports bottle, then offers it to me. "God, I hope she gets out of there soon. Poor Riley. They better set up a trust fund to pay for all the therapy that kid is going to need."

"Yeah, really." We sort of chuckle, but it's too sad to be very funny. I clear my throat. "Have you heard anything about Molly?" I ask, tip-toeing nearer the subject.

"No, I haven't talked to Fiona, either. I assume she's still pregnant."

"Yeah, she probably is." I clear my throat again, panic rising up. "Um, I am too."

I freeze, waiting for her reaction.

"'Am too?' You what? What are you trying to say?!" She sits up, looking sort of mean and confused.

"I... um..." I giggle weakly. "I'm... *you know*." The word pregnant refused to cross my lips.

Her mouth opens, and her eyebrows shoot up. She looks at me, a question on her face.

I nod by way of an answer.

"Michelle West! You fucking idiot! What the hell were you thinking?"

"Well, I...."

"You complete dumb-ass! Where were you in eighth grade health class? Didn't your mother ever teach you anything -- not that mine did, but still...!"

"I know how it works, Summer. But nothing is 100 percent. I guess I fucked up."

"You sure did! Christ, how could you be so stupid?"

"Shut up," I say, blinking furiously to keep from crying. I don't know which would give me more pleasure, crying my eyes out, or scratching hers out. "Don't yell at me, you stupid bitch!"

I have no idea where that came from. Summer looks just as surprised as I feel. "Oh God, Summer, I'm sorry. I'm not thinking straight. You're my only friend left here, and now you hate me." Now I really do start crying. What a mess I've made of everything. She's right, I am a complete fucking dumb-ass idiot.

"Oh jeez, Michelle, don't do that. Come on." Summer is thoroughly uncomfortable with my emotional display. She lifts her arms awkwardly several times before putting them around me.

I throw myself into her embrace and simply let loose. I cry so hard and so long I'm afraid I won't be able to stop. I try to speak, to tell her that it's not her fault I'm so stupid, and to reassure her that I'm not hysterical, but I end by just blubbering.

Summer gives me little pats on the back and says "It's okay," innumerable times. When my crying starts to let up a bit she seems relieved. She draws back, and holding me by the shoulders tells me: "It's going to be fine. I'll even go with you if you want, okay?"

I wipe my nose on my arm, which leaves a sandy residue on my upper lip. "Go with me?" I ask. "Where? What do you mean?"

She looks astonished at my ignorance. "To get the abortion of course. Unless you think it would be better to make Jeffrey go with you. That would serve him right, the bastard."

Seeing the look on my face, she adds: "It *is* Jeffrey's isn't it?"

"Yes! What do you think?" I can't believe she could be so dumb. "Besides, who says I'm getting an abortion?"

"Michelle, you can't be considering keeping it!"

"Why not? It's mine." I'm offended.

"You haven't told him yet, have you?" she asks knowingly.

"No, not yet."

"Michelle, I hate to be the one to break this to you, but if you think he's going to divorce his wife and marry you simply because you're pregnant..."

"I never said that!" I blurt.

"Listen, the minute he knows, he's going to march you down to the doctor and make you get an abortion. I can guarantee it."

"No! You don't know him at all, Summer! He loves his kids, and he's a wonderful father. Sure, he'll be a bit annoyed at first. I mean, I didn't exactly plan it this way either, but he'll get used to it. There's no way he would want to get rid of our baby."

Summer starts gathering up her stuff. "Well," she says, "At least it won't be such a big of a shock since you've heard it once from me." Standing ready to go she tells me: "Look, I'm sorry I went off on you about being stupid. It could happen to anyone, and frequently does. I really hate this cheesy douche-commercial kind of lingo, but if it all hits the fan, you know where to find me." She stands a minute more, then walks away.

Back home again I find Jeffrey, Debra and Trish sitting around trying to decide what to do for dinner. I offer to baby-sit, so they can go out, but they say they're tired and want to do something here. Debra and Jeffrey make a run to the store for groceries, leaving me with Trish. She pours herself a glass of white wine and settles beside me on the couch. "Well," she smiles, "now we have a chance for a little girl-talk."

Inwardly I groan, hoping that one of the kids will wake up and need me. Anything but 'girl-talk.' I've had all I can stand of that today. I listen to her for twenty minutes or so, telling me about her various boyfriends. How one was a painter and another one was the executive vice-president of something. I've given up trying to keep them all straight, and am surreptitiously doing a crossword puzzle in my lap. Then she says something that gets my attention. Something having to do with Jeffrey. I wasn't aware that we had changed subjects.

"Huh?" I say, breaking in rudely. "What does Jeffrey have to do with anything?"

"I just said that back before he and Debra got married I had a little fling with him."

"No way," I say, knowing she's lying.

"What, you don't believe me, ask Jeffrey. He won't deny it. Debra knows all about it. They patched things up years ago."

"I don't know, Trish. I think you're making it up. Jeffrey's not that kind of guy." *Is he?*

"I know he seems like a boring old family man now, but he's had his share -- maybe more than his share -- of extra-curricular activities. And from what I've heard, it didn't stop when he got married."

"Well, what about you? You're supposed to be Debra's friend." I really can't take all this in right now. I'm starting to feel my first urge to puke.

"Oh, it was no big deal. We weren't in love or anything. We just had a couple of tussles in the coat room at a party."

"How can Debra stand it?" I say, almost to myself.

"Look, she's got a nice life with Jeffrey. He makes a good living, they have two beautiful children. She can afford to be forgiving." Trish shrugs, and tosses her hair back.

Jeffrey and Debra come home soon afterward and we're all busy getting dinner together. We concoct a Mexican feast. I volunteer to make margaritas, which gives me the opportunity to make mine virgins without being noticed.

When the kids are in bed, we continue to drink margaritas long into the night, and, as I had anticipated, Trish brings up the topic of our earlier discussion.

"I told Michelle what a pussy-hound Jeffrey used to be, and she didn't believe me."

Debra almost screams with laughter. "Oh, honey, he was the *worst!*"

Jeffrey blows on his fingernails and polishes them on his shirt, smiling.

I have to ask. They're so drunk they won't think anything of it. "If he was so bad, then why did you marry him?" My face feels hot, and I'm getting a headache.

Debra leans forward and says in a stage whisper: "He's great in bed."

Trish raises her hand and says: "I can attest to that!"

All three of them laugh it up. I make some excuse which no one even hears, and leave the room. As I'm closing the door I hear Debra say: "Isn't that cute? She's jealous!"

I don't let Jeffrey come near me for the next week. I can't even stand to be in the same room with him. He tries to act cool about it, but I can tell he's worried. I look at him and feel like I don't know him at all. This whole situation, lifestyle, even my job, feel unnatural somehow. It's as if I've stepped in as an understudy for someone else.

But even that doesn't last. Starting nearly from scratch, Jeffrey flirts and charms, flatters and cajoles, and by the next weekend, has won me over again. When I finally relent to his kiss, he trembles in my arms, and I feel a flash of the old goddess-power once again.

Mostly I just feel weak, though. I don't have what you could call typical morning sickness. It would be heavenly to wake up, puke, and get on with things. Instead, I've got *all day* sickness. I wake up feeling like shit. All day long I feel as if I'm just on the verge of barfing, but I never do. The thought or smell of food sends me scurrying to the bathroom, only to stare into the toilet bowl.

I thought for sure that Jeffrey would notice right away. After all, he's been through two pregnancies with Debra, you'd think he'd be acquainted with all the subtle little signs. It's just as well, though. I'm still not completely over the Trish thing, and I've been thinking quite a bit about what Summer said. Maybe in her blunt, unfeeling sort of way she knows Jeffrey better than I do. She may see what I can't, blinded by love as I am.

*   *   *   *

Lying on my bed, on top of the covers, it occurs to me that I've never been this miserable in my life. There had been a cooling ocean breeze this afternoon, but tonight the air is hot and stagnant. I'm hot, pregnant, confused and disillusioned. Although everything seems nearly normal as far as Jeffrey and I are concerned, there is something missing. Maybe I've lost just a smidge of respect for him. It's silly that I would disrespect him for sleeping around -- considering -- but I can't help it. Even though I probably would have guessed that he had never been completely faithful, I didn't think it was that extreme. I thought I was the exception. I had it romanticized in my head, where a fine upstanding family man reluctantly breaks his marriage vows because he falls so deeply in love with another woman. I guess that's all just bullshit.

Summer could be absolutely right. I could be the latest in a long string of nannies. I think that would be worse than anything. Knowing that it's just a matter of convenience and proximity -- or else a nanny fetish. It wouldn't have anything to do with *me*. And if I allow myself to hypothesize that far, then why don't I admit that he probably doesn't love me at all. I'm just a warm body in a nanny outfit. I may as well be a blow-up doll. Hell, that's pretty much how he treats me. I sit around waiting for him to have a few minutes to spend with me. He takes me out of the box when he feels the need, and when he's done, deflates me, folds me away, and trots back to sleep next to his wife.

God, sometimes I hate him.

I'm getting more and more upset and angry as I lie here thinking these thoughts. I even have a brief fantasy of stealing off into the night, leaving them to scramble for their new inflatable hired help. Man, I'm so pissed right now I know I'll never get to sleep. I can't remember the last full night's sleep I had. It hasn't been since we came out to Fire Island, I know that. It's too quiet here, for one thing. I'd grown used to listening to the crime and punishment going on outside my window in the city, and I really miss that. The crickets just don't do it for me. They remind me of camp, which brings back unpleasant memories of being afraid of the dark, bugs, snakes, bears, the older girls, and most of the counselors. I never did learn to whittle.

This can't be good for the baby, this not sleeping. Just my luck, I'll be awake through the whole pregnancy and end up with some deformed, retarded kid that I'll hate. I can't think about a baby right now. It's too unreal. I don't feel particularly maternal, and I'm sure as hell not glowing. All this little blob of cells has done thus far is make me cranky, weepy, and nauseous. And I'm only --what?-- six weeks along? Oh the joys of motherhood. This is like Super Killer PMS from Hell, and I suppose I've got seven months more of it to look forward to. I'm not sure I want to do this.

"Michelle?"

I jump. "Huh? What?" I squint toward the doorway. Of course it's Jeffrey. Who the hell else would be creeping into my room at this hour? God, I'm cranky.

"Can't sleep, huh?" he says conversationally, sitting on the edge of my bed.

"Too fucking hot to sleep. It's too hot to do anything but lie here and suffer." I sigh, not looking at him, and angrily snap: "Why don't you do something about this heat? Get some air conditioning for God's sake!"

"How 'bout this?" he says, and starts blowing on me.

I wave him away. "Get out of here," I say, but I'm smiling. I do love him, the asshole.

He laughs. Leaning over, he kisses me lightly. "It's too hot to fuck," he says regretfully. "Want to go for a walk? There's supposed to be a big storm coming in."

I'm up in a flash, slipping my shoes on.

There is no moon tonight, and I can't see a thing. All I can hear is the roar of the surf. It's so disorienting, walking in the uneven sand, listening to the power of the ocean, and not being able to see a thing. It's a bit like standing on top of a fatal cliff, and not knowing exactly where the edge is. I grasp Jeffrey's hand tightly, and he pulls it away.

"But I can't *see*," I protest.

"Neither can I. It doesn't do you any good to hang onto me."

We walk along in silence for a while. I feel more hurt and rejected than I'd like to admit. If Jeffrey wasn't here with me, a big wave could knock me down and drag me away, and no one would ever know what happened. But somehow, having him here makes me more afraid. Especially since he's so oblivious to, and uncaring of my fears. It suddenly occurs to me in a flash of paranoia that maybe the most dangerous element on the beach is Jeffrey himself. I thought I knew him so well, but obviously I don't. He could be some sort of psycho, and has lured me here to a dark and deserted beach to chop me up into little chunks and hand-feed me to the seagulls. What really happened to all the nannies before me? Did my agency thoroughly investigate the Goldmans?

Stop it. I'm being ridiculous. I sound like Montana Sue. She goes crazy in the big city, and apparently I get a little schitzo myself when out in the country.

"When's the storm supposed to get here?" I ask, just to being saying something relatively normal.

"Anytime now," Jeffrey's voice comes out of the dark. "Let's sit down for a minute. I think there's that big piece of driftwood around here -- yep, have a seat my dear."

I sit down on the log, hoping that no bugs will bite my ass. My eyes must be adjusting to the dark a bit. I can actually see Jeffrey's profile. He is taking something out of his pocket.

"Brought a little something..." he says. He holds a small flask, and tips his head back. He hands it to me. "Cheers," he says.

I take a whiff, and it blows my head back on my neck. "Whew! What is *that*?"

"Jack Daniels."

"Oh. Yummy." I hope he can't tell I'm just pretending to drink. I even give a dramatic little shiver and wipe my mouth on my arm. I think it's a nice touch.

"So," he says, after taking another drink. "Have you heard anything from your old pal Nicky?"

I look at him, amazed that he would mention his name. "No, why?"

"Just curious. Truthfully though, I've been feeling a little guilty about stealing you away from him. I had no right to do that."

"What do you mean?" I'm getting nervous. This is sounding suspiciously similar to a dismissal.

"I just mean that I should have bowed out and let you go. You should be with guys your own age."

"I don't like guys my own age -- I never have."

"Well, there is an imbalance in this relationship. I'm so much older, I have money -- I'm *married*." He whispers this last word. "You deserve somebody that's totally in love with you. And I can't allow myself to do that." He takes another hurried drink.

"Not even a little bit?" I ask. What the hell, go for broke. I think I'm being dumped here.

Jeffrey turns to face me full-on. "Oh, I'm more than a little bit in love with you -- but you knew that."

I can't speak for a moment and then I say: "How could I know that?"

"All those times that I would almost smother you, and ask if I was making myself clear, if you knew what I meant?"

"I didn't know! I figured if you did, you'd say so!" I'm thinking of all the wasted months.

"I wanted to tell you. I've wanted to tell you for the longest time."

"Well, why didn't you?!" I think I'm actually mad. I feel gypped.

"Because...." he searches for the words. "I feel that if you tell someone you love them, it's a commitment in itself. You should be prepared to give that person everything, and obviously I'm not in a position to give you anything right now."

I sit there listening to the waves. A tiny bit of wind has come up, but it's so slight that I can smell it, rather than feel it. Still, it's a good sign.

"I've only said that to one other person in my life -- and I married her. It's not something I bandy about."

"You're weird, you know that? You and your stupid rules." I lean back, my hands behind my head.

"You don't think much of my rule, huh?"

"Nope." I'm already thinking about telling all this to Joanne.

"Michelle?"

"Hmm?"

"I love you."

I am in total shock. My throat closes up and tears just start falling indiscriminately.

"Am I the first guy to ever tell you that?"

I nod, then amend: "The first who's ever meant it."

He pulls me into his arms. "Then I'm proud to be the first." He holds me for the longest time and then he whispers, his hot, hot breath in my ear: "I love you I love you I love you."

I try to take stock of every detail, every emotion passing through my heart, so that I can remember this moment for the rest of my life. My face is buried in his T-shirt, and I can feel his heartbeat on my cheekbone. I just want to devour him. I want to crawl inside him and walk around in his skin, looking through his eyes and feeling with his hands. I want to inject him into my veins and *become* him by osmosis.

"The question is," he says, pulling away slightly so he can look at my face, "Do you love me?"

"I always have."

"Say it. Tell me you love me."

"I love you." My voice is small and squeaky.

"Louder," he says.

"I love you!" I holler.

The wind has come up, and is frolicking in my hair, teasing it, making it stand out in wild directions. I hear the faint rumble of distant thunder, and the old fear resurfaces. But I don't want to go in yet. I have one more thing I need to tell him, one more thing to make the evening complete. I'm not afraid anymore. I know that Summer and Trish and everyone was wrong about him. Whatever he used to be, he's mine now, and he loves me.

A crackling of lightening illuminates the beach, making the sand look like drifts of snow. Almost immediately afterward, thunder rolls directly overhead, and it starts to rain. Jeffrey pulls my hand, and we run back towards the house.

NINE

I try to find the right moment to tell him. When the right moment pops up, I can't get started. Finally I slip a little note into his briefcase, then sit by the phone waiting for him to find it.

The phone rings around ten. In anticipation for his call I have installed the kids in front of the television with juice, crackers, and plenty of toys.

"Hello?" I ask, like I don't know who it is.

"Michelle."

"Hi!" I say, brightly.

"This is a joke, right?" His voice is nervous, yet gruff.

"A joke? Well...no." I'm confused. Why would I joke about a thing like this?

"You actually mean to tell me you're pregnant."

"Well, I guess so -- I mean, yes." I don't understand why he's acting so strange.

"Oh, Christ. Listen, are you sure it's mine?"

"Jeffrey!"

"Right, right. Sorry." There is a pause. "Tell me this, how long have you known?"

"Uh, I don't know, a month maybe." Why do I feel like I'm on trial here?

"A month...great. So how far along are you? Six, seven weeks?"

"Something like that."

A heavy sigh. "The sooner the better then. Jesus, what a pain. I'll make the arrangements and call you right back. Start looking for someone to watch the kids."

"Watch the kids? What are you talking about?" I feel like I need a decoder ring to understand him sometimes.

"Michelle," he says impatiently, "we've got to get this taken care of. You can't take the kids with you -- can you imagine? Debra asks what he did today and Jake says he went with Michelle to get an abortion?" He laughs weakly.

"I... I..." I can't think how to express my disappointment and shock.

"What? What's the matter?"

"I don't want to," I say, my voice sounding more like a six-year-old's than my own.

"What do you mean you don't want to? Don't want to take the kids with you, or don't want to get an abortion?" He doesn't understand me, can't comprehend why I don't just bend to his will and do as he says.

"I want to keep the baby. I'll be a good mother, don't you think?"

"You'll be a wonderful mother *someday*, but not now. Michelle, you don't know what you're saying. This is just your hormones talking." A sort of panic is creeping into his voice.

"No, I'm serious. I've thought about it a lot, and I think we'll be happy."

"Wait wait wait wait. You are *not* having this kid, Michelle. You're a smart girl, don't ruin your life because of one mistake -- and for God's sake don't take me down with you!"

I can't believe I'm hearing this.

"Michelle, sweetheart," he continues. "You can have all the babies you want later on. But now is not the time. It's not fair to the kid, or any of us. Just get the fucking abortion, okay?"

"I don't *want* to!"

An exasperated sigh. "I know how you feel about doctors. It sounds much scarier than it is. It's not bad at all, I promise. It's like having a tooth pulled -- not something you'd want done every day, but it doesn't kill you. And when it's all over you can go back to college."

"Go back to college?" What was he saying? I just signed a contract for another year! He told me he loves me! "What *about* college? You know I'm staying here."

"Oh... right. Of course. I'm getting senile in my old age. I just meant that you'll go back to school *someday*. You're too smart not to finish college."

"But I thought..." *Just say it. Make a fool of yourself. Better to find out now than walk around with your head up your ass.* "I thought we were going to be together."

There is a lengthy silence. Then Jeffrey begins carefully, "Well, yes.... we will be together -- sweetheart. But this isn't the way to do it. We need to start off with a clean slate. It's going to take a while, you know. It can be a long, ugly process."

"I don't care how long it takes. I just want to be with you." I don't even want to get custody of Jake and Miranda anymore. I want out of here, away from Debra and the past. I do wish we could have this little baby though. "Are you sure we can't keep the baby? We could hide it until your divorce is final."

"Absolutely not. Honey, it's the only way, really. Trust me. Just do this for me and I promise I'll make it up to you."

"Well...can I have another one right away? As soon as we're married?"

"...married? Oh! Yes, of course. You can have one right away. We'll have lots of babies. Listen, I've got a meeting downtown in a few minutes. I've just got time to get a taxi and make it down there --"

"Our babies will be cute, won't they?"

"Just like their mother. Honey, I really do have to run. We'll talk about this when I get home. Deal?"

"Okay. Jeffrey?"

"What?"

"I love you."

"Oh... me too, sweetie. Bye."

"Bye."

I hang up the phone and brush my hand lightly over my belly, trying to detect some presence of life. "I'm sorry, baby," I whisper. "Your daddy says not this time."

*   *   *   *

As he promised, Jeffrey makes all the arrangements. He has come up with a wonderfully convoluted set of excuses and alibis to allow the two of us to be in the city for the weekend, while Debra stays at the beach with the kids. I don't understand all the various nuances of it, but as far as I know, he's supposed to be working, and I'm entertaining a visiting cousin.

So the next Friday, after Debra gets home from work, I hand off the kids, and catch the next ferry back to Long Island. From there I take the train, and meet Jeffrey back at the house on Bank Street. Walking up the stoop and through the front doors feels like greeting an old friend. I feel like I've been away forever. It smells a bit musty, and I walk through the house opening windows, reacquainting myself with the rooms. I don't see any sign of Jeffrey. I guess he's still working.

Even though the purpose of this weekend is unpleasant to say the least, I'm still looking forward to spending time alone with Jeffrey. I make a mental note to myself to get all I can out of Jeffrey tonight, because after Saturday, I guess I won't be able to do it for awhile. But I don't want to think about that.

I guess one good thing about this is that I can feel free to drink with impunity now. Jeffrey and I can get shit-faced if we want to, and have wild, rollicking sex on every surface in the house. That doesn't sound like a bad idea at all. I wonder if I should attempt to cook something and have a cozy little dinner *a deux*, or if I should make him take me out. It might be fun to get dressed up and check out some of the clubs I've heard about. Oh, but Jeffrey can't go anywhere he might be recognized. I suppose that's something I'll have to deal with for a little while longer.

I start to unpack my weekend bag, putting things into my dresser, when I remember that I won't be sleeping here tonight. I'll be upstairs in the big bed with Jeffrey. Throwing the bag over my shoulder, I trudge up two flights of stairs to the master bedroom. Passing the nursery, I feel a little pang of guilt remembering how pink and helpless Miranda first looked in that big, ruffled crib. The first time I held her in my arms I couldn't get over how such a tiny, fragile package could hold so powerful a life force. It was as if I could feel the growth and potential coming through her pores. She struck me as a little fireball containing the secrets of life wrapped in a helpless, squeaky doll.

I find that I don't have anywhere to stash my clothes. I'm certainly not putting anything in Debra's drawers, and I'm afraid if I borrow one of Jeffrey's I'll forget something and blow the whole thing. I can just see Debra happening upon a pair of frilly panties among Jeffrey's boxers. Of course, she would probably just think it was some momento of his checkered past -- oh, but I wasn't going to think about that, either.

The phone rings, and I pick it up. It's Jeffrey tells me that he's going to be later than he thought -- in fact he probably won't be home until ten or eleven. Despite my violent protestations, he insists on staying late to get some work done. It crosses my mind that he could be lying, and could in fact be doing something he shouldn't, but I shake that thought away, and attempt to deal with the prospect of spending the whole evening alone in the house. As much as I love this old place, I've never been crazy about being alone in it at night. I mean, people *have* died here.

I try calling Summer, and then Susan, but get no answer at either number. I don't even have a book to read. I didn't think I'd need one. I remember seeing some dusty old books in the basement, but there's no way in hell I'm venturing down there by myself.

I lie down on the master bed and pull the bedside phone onto my lap. I make quite a few attempts at contact, but no one is home on this Friday night. Both parents, my brother, and Joanne are out, and I can't even rustle up any of my former dorm-mates that I haven't talked to since my going-away party. I flip on the television for a minute or two, briefly intrigued by a commercial for a party line. When I find myself picking up the phone and dialing 1-900, I am shocked into sensibility.

"Fuck this noise!" I say, in a truly Jeffrey-esque manner. "I'm going out!"

I walk quickly towards the Rail, anticipating a cold beer and some conversation with Bud. Bud'll be there, he's always there. We make jokes that he sleeps in his supply room, using crates of beer for a make-shift bed. When I step in the door, I feel even more at home than I did on Bank Street. I've really missed this dump.

The place is packed. "Son of a Preacher Man" is blaring on the jukebox, and a bunch of bearded, biker-looking guys are playing darts toward the back. Every table is full, and I make my way through the crowd to the bar. I think I see a girl who looks like Amy, but on second glance I see that it's more like Amy's strung-out evil twin lurking in the far corner there.

"Well, I'll be damned!" Bud cries, when he catches sight of me. "Where the hell have you been?"

"Oh, I've been working. You know how it is..." I smile at him. It's good to be back. This is something I can understand. This bar and this man are two things that will never change. "So, how about a Bud, Bud?" I say, repeating the oldest joke in the bar's history.

"I might be able to fix you up with one," he says, reaching for the bottle. He starts to hand me the beer, then stops, and holds my chin in his hand, turning my head from side to side, examining my face from all angles. "Huh!" he says, and whisks the beer back under the bar.

"Hey! What about my drink?" I protest.

"None for you -- mommy."

"Mommy?! What's that supposed to mean?" I can feel myself blushing.

"You think I don't know a pregnant woman when I see one? You must think ol' Bud is pretty dim if you thought you could come in here and slide that past me." He shakes his big, grizzled head.

"But Bud, even if I was, you think I'd keep it? How dumb do you think I am?" My voice begins to falter.

"So you're getting rid of it?" Bud says, his hands on his ample hips.

"Yep. Uh, *if* I were pregnant, that's what I would do."

"Unh-unh. Summer or Amy, sure. Maybe even Susan. But not you. Not a chance."

"So I don't get a beer, is that it?"

Bud folds his arms across his chest. "I reserve the right to refuse service. I'll give you club soda, cola, plain orange juice -- I've probably even got some milk around here somewhere. But as for the other stuff, no dice."

"Bud!" I can't believe this is happening.

He shrugs his big shoulders. "Hey; my place, my rules. You don't like it you can take a hike."

"Well I guess I'll have to!" I stand still a minute, waiting for the punch line, but he looks at me expectantly, not wavering. Slowly, I turn and face the door, shaking my head.

"Hey!"

I turn around, ready to smile at his joke.

"Better say hello to your friend before you go." He jerks a meaty thumb toward the back.

I walk off, intending to leave, but my curiosity gets the better of me, and I make my way towards the pool tables in back. The air is thick with smoke, and the odor of smelly bikers and stale beer makes me nearly nauseous. I swivel my head back and forth, scanning the room for my so-called 'friend,' but it's so crowded that I can only see the few people directly in front of me. I hear a somewhat familiar-sounding voice saying "Excuse me, let me through," and wonder if Bud meant Annie, one of his barmaids. I certainly wouldn't call her a close personal friend of mine, and am a bit annoyed, but while I'm here I may as well say hello.

That's when she bumps into me, dropping the tray she'd been holding above her head. Lucky for me, it held only empties, and fell the other direction. It is the girl I thought looked a little bit like Amy. Only she has long dred-locked hair, and a gaunt, sickly face.

"Mick?" she says.

"Amy? Is that you?" My mouth has dropped open, and I close it again with effort. "What are you doing here? When did you get back?"

She looks uncomfortable. "I've been back a few weeks, I guess."

"Why didn't you tell me you were back? I've been worried about you. I haven't seen you since the night Cameron..."

"Hey," she says, cutting me off, "Let me see if I can get Bud to let me take my break now."

"You work here now?" But she is already headed to the bar. Of course she works here, I'm sure she's not clearing tables for the sheer joy of it.

Looking around at the crowd, I know Bud won't spare her, but he lets her go, and she leads me outside to the sidewalk, where she immediately lights a cigarette. She closes her eyes as she inhales, then looks at me.

"Pretty pissed off at me, huh?"

"No, I'm just confused. I thought you were in San Francisco. I tried to call..."

She looks at the pavement, rubbing at a petrified piece of gum with the toe of her boot. "I know, I'm sorry. I was really out of it."

I'm silent for a bit, thinking about Cameron, which leads me to think of the baby inside me -- but no, I won't think of that.

"Why didn't you call when you came back? I thought we were friends."

"We were -- we are. I kept meaning to call, but I was looking for a job, and then we didn't have a phone..." She sighs. "I am sorry. I should have called."

"Yeah, you should have." I swallow my hurt, and try to find out what's going on with her. "Where are you staying?"

"We have a place on Avenue A."

"'We?'"

"Me and Gunter." She can't help smiling at his name.

"How's he doing?" I ask, though I don't give a damn.

"Pretty good, I guess." She shrugs.

"How's the band?"

"Oh, they broke up. After Nicky left, they sort of fell apart. Perry -- you remember him, the drummer? -- he hooked up with another band, and..."

"So what's Gunter doing now?"

"Oh, he's looking at several options. Trying to get a new band together. Sometimes he works as a messenger in midtown." She pauses. "I should probably get back inside. I can't afford to lose my job."

She starts to stand up, to brush the sidewalk dust off her backside. I feel a sort of panic that I'll lose touch with her again if I let her go now.

"Amy, wait. Just a couple more minutes. Bud would never fire you, you were always his favorite."

She laughs. "Not anymore." But she sits down.

Having convinced her to stay, I am at a loss for conversation. "I like your hair," I tell her, remembering that those were her first words to me. Seems like a million years ago.

"Thanks," she says. "Extensions. Four hundred bucks. That was when I still had money."

I'm feeling very uncomfortable suddenly. I want to end this conversation and go home to Jeffrey. I'll sit on his lap with his warm arms around me, and I'll know who I am again. "Well, Ame," It feels phony and insincere to call her that now. "We'll have to get together sometime. We should go shopping or something. We have a lot of catching up to do." This time it's me who starts to stand.

Amy drops her head down and laughs, her long, ratty hair forming a curtain of black over her knees. "Oh Michelle. You never change. You're still the same nieve girl you were a year ago." Her head comes up again, and she looks me up and down with a critical eye. "We won't be getting together, Micky. I don't mean to be insulting, but it's the truth. We're totally different now. I live in a different world, and you couldn't handle it."

Instead of being mad, I sit back down. "Amy, what's going on? Are you all right?" I have a strong feeling that something is very wrong, that she's trying to scare me away.

"Take a good look at me. Do I look all right?"

"No, you look like shit. You look like you haven't slept in weeks, you must have lost ten pounds. You look like some kind of drug addict."

This elicits a sharp peal of laughter. I know I've hit on it.

"What is it, Ame?"

"'What is it, Ame'" she mimics. "Little miss goody-two shoes..." It's weird to hear such a prissy, old-fashioned word come out of her mouth.

"Come on, Ame, 'goody two-shoes?' I seem to recall many drunken nights we've spent. Not to mention the numerous times we got stoned together."

She laughs again, a hollow, unamused sound. "That doesn't count, it's not a real drug. You don't know what you're talking about."

"Coke?" I ask, remembering Summer's story about the night she put the moves on Nicky.

"On *my* salary?"

"What is it then? Tell me." I try to check her arms for track-marks without knowing exactly what to look for. All I see is Amy's pale, translucent skin unblemished except for a bruise the size of a man's fist. I never did like Gunter.

Amy just sits there, shaking her head, and smiling vacantly.

"Come on, are you smoking crack or something?" I mean it as a joke, but the look on her face says it all. "Amy!" I say, totally shocked. At least heroin is sort of glamorous in a seedy, rock-and-roll sort of way. Crack is so, well, *low-class.*

"Is there anything I can do?" I offer, knowing how stupid I sound.

Amy looks at me and snorts. "What? Are you going to take me to Betty Ford?"

"No, I just want to help. We used to be so close."

"Yeah, well, shit happens." She flips her hair out of her eyes and looks up at the sky.

This time I do stand to leave. I can't do anything for her. I don't even know her anymore.

"Wait, Michelle."

I turn around, expecting an apology.

"There is something.... Could you loan me some money?"

I raise my eyebrows.

"Not for that, I swear," she vows, holding up two fingers, like a boy scout. "The rent is late, and I'm afraid we'll get evicted. You don't want me to end up living on the subway, do you?" She attempts to smile.

"No, I don't want that," I say, pulling bills from my back pocket. I never carry a purse anymore.

"Here," I say. "Do me a favor and get some groceries, will you?"

She nods as I hand the money over. It's all the money I have. Two hundred dollars that Debra gave me before I left. So much for payday.

Amy takes the money and counts it surreptitiously while slipping it into the top of her boot. I know I'll never see that money again, and for that matter will probably never see Amy again. I am also aware that my money won't be paying any rent, but what can I do about that? She was my friend once, a million years ago.

On an impulse, I throw my arms around her, hugging her. It's like holding a bag of bones. I can tell she wants me to stop, so I let her go reluctantly. Then I turn and walk back to Bank Street.

$*$ $*$ $*$ $*$

My appointment is for eleven. Jeffrey and I sit in the waiting room reading and glancing at the clock. I had been afraid we'd be late because we brought the car, and had a terrible time parking. The doctor's office is on the Upper East Side, not far from Flemings, the Irish bar I used to visit with Molly. The building is a tall, gray number, distinguished and anonymous. The office is on the ground floor, maybe because the women leaving this particular establishment are not in any shape to use the stairs.

I had remained discreetly silent while Jeffrey checked in with the nurse at the desk, and pulled out that Platinum card. He obviously can't put this on his insurance. I hesitated a moment with my pen poised over the release form. I felt Jeffrey's strong hand on my shoulder, took a deep breath, and signed on the line.

I look over at him in the chair next to me. He has his ankle crossed over his knee, as he reads the paper calmly, his mouth turned down at the corners, and his eyes crinkled slightly as he squints at the page before him. He'll be needing glasses soon.

There is one other occupant of the small, spare room. It is a middle-aged woman with stringy hair and glasses. Her clothes are a year or two out of fashion, and she has lipstick on her teeth. I wonder if she's here for the same thing I am, or if they have more than one item on the menu. She looks up, catching my glance, and I look hurriedly away, and begin to examine my cuticles with mock fascination. They are bloody and ragged from my chewing and pulling at them. I hold them out away from my face to see how noticeable they are from a distance. My hands are trembling.

I get up and go to the water cooler, returning to my seat with a cup. As I sit down I spill a little on the front of my shirt. I am wearing a Mets T-shirt and jeans. I didn't know what one wears to an abortion. My face is bare of make-up, and I haven't even bothered to brush my hair.

Jeffrey makes a great racket in the silent room when he clears his throat and turns his newspaper, folding it over and smoothing the crease. This is exactly what he's like at home. This is just like any other day for him.

"Jeffrey?" I whisper.

"Hmm?" he says, still reading.

"I'm scared. I hate pain. I hate doctors."

He looks at me, a touch of annoyance in his eyes. His eyes are so black in this windowless room. They look as flat and dead as newspaper ink. "Michelle," he says, "It's not that big a deal. Like I've told you, it's like having a tooth pulled."

"I know you've told me that, but how do you know? You've never had one."

"No, I haven't. But I've been on the periphery of quite a few, and I'm telling you..." He stops when he sees the look on my face. "They weren't all mine." he says.

"How many?" I ask. "How many were yours?"

He suddenly becomes very tender and loving, holding my hand and putting his arm around me, stroking my hair. "You'll be fine, sweetheart. When it's all over we'll go have a nice lunch somewhere... Hey, you want to see the Russian Tea Room? I'll take you there."

"Miss West?" A heavy-set nurse stands with a clipboard at the door to the inner sanctum.

I stand up and notice Jeffrey is still sitting there. "Aren't you coming in with me?"

"You'll be fine," he says, turning back to his paper.

I follow the nurse through a hallway and into a small room. It looks just like a regular examination room. I had imagined something more like a torture chamber. The nurse hands me a paper gown and tells me the doctor is running a little late, but will be in shortly. As she closes the door I can't help wondering what she thinks of me and what I'm doing. I guess she wouldn't work here if it bothered her.

Following the nurse's instructions I undress and pile my clothes on a chair. I slip into the paper gown and hoist myself up onto the table. The thing about these tables is that you have to get into a comfortable position the first time, or else you've got to unstick your ass from the roll of white paper and reposition yourself. Of course by that time the paper is all wrinkled up and impossible to work with.

I sit leaning back on my arms. I haven't allowed myself to think about this moment, but now there seems little else to do. It's about to happen. At any minute the door will open, the doctor will come in, and there won't be any chance to think. Maybe they have that gas the dentist uses.

I sit and I wait. There is nothing to read, nothing to look at. Nothing at all except me and my furiously spinning mind. My thoughts are so fast-paced and jumbled together that they are more like dream-like than lucid. I lie back on the paper and close my eyes, wondering how long it's been since I slept. Last night I didn't even bother to try. After Jeffrey fell asleep I went down to the kitchen and made some toast. That seems to be the only thing I can eat lately. I took the toast into my room and turned on the little TV. There was this old Barbara Stanwick movie on about an unwed mother who gets in a train wreck. After that was over I took some time to catch up on my journal which I've been neglecting all summer. I don't like to keep it out at the beach house because there's less privacy and someone is likely to stumble upon it.

I hear footsteps approach the door and sit up, bracing myself for the doctor. But they go on down the hall. I sat up too quickly, and my head is swimming. Why do they always overheat these offices? They think just because your clothes are off you need it to be 95 degrees. I breathe long and deep, but all my lungs can get is this hot, dry air. I hop down off the table and cross the few steps to the window. It opens onto a little courtyard, green with trees. Opening the window I am overcome by the cool freshness of the air that rushes in to fill my lungs. I lean out, inhaling deeply. It is drizzling a little bit, the kind of half-hearted rain we get in Seattle. It's wonderful, and clears my head immediately. There is nothing like the smell of damp earth. When it first begins to rain, the ground is just teeming with texture and life. The smell always reminds me of the playground at elementary school. I remember skipping rope, playing kickball, twirling on the bars and running away from the boys and their 'boy germs.'

My whole childhood comes back to me with that smell. The good times, before my parents divorced and I had to grow up. I feel a sudden awful pain inside me as I realize that I can't reconcile the life I have now with the child I once was. The two don't mix. For a moment I'd give anything to be a child again.

I look at my watch. It's 11:29. Something suddenly occurs to me, and I almost laugh to think I was so blind to it. But I've got to hurry, the doctor really could be here any minute. With my heart racing, I pull my shirt on over the gown, and then squeeze into my jeans. They're getting a bit snug. I wad up my panties and socks, shoving them into my pockets. I cram my bare feet into my shoes and stand with one ear to the door.

I open it slowly, and seeing no one, I walk quickly the opposite direction from the waiting room where Jeffrey is. I make my way through a maze of corridors, growing more and more terrified every minute. They're probably looking for me right now. Just as I'm thinking I'll have to backtrack and try to sneak out past Jeffrey and his newspaper I spot an exit sign.

I shove the door with all my might, realizing too late that it is for emergencies only. I run through the drizzle, away from the shriek of the alarm. Now that I am safely outside a rush of exhilaration floods my senses, and I start to laugh as I run through the streets.

I go ten blocks before remembering the rest of my plan -- the escape was the most important part. I duck into a little bodega and ask where the nearest phone booth is. I guess I look pretty shaken-up, because the little Korean woman leads me into a back room and lets me use her own phone. I dial Summer's number in the city, and pray that she's home.

"Hello?"

"Summer, it's Michelle. Look, I need your help." It all comes out in a breathless rush, and I'm afraid I'll have to repeat myself, but she asks what's wrong. I give her the short version.

"Jesus, Michelle," is her only comment.

"You were right about him not wanting the baby. You're probably right about everything else, too."

"Yeah, well, I'm sorry anyway. I'm sorry you ever got mixed up with that guy. What can I do to help?"

"I've got to get out of here. I'm just all fucked up right now. Can you meet me back at Bank Street?"

"Sure thing. Not to detract from your dramatic moment Michelle, but I've kind of got some news of my own."

Oh no. What now? "What is it?" I ask, looking over my shoulder to see if I'm being pursued yet.

"The Leibowitzes just fired me."

"Really? Why?"

"Something about my attitude. It's pretty funny since I was leaving in a couple weeks. Anyway, I've got a 2:30 non-stop to Seattle. Why don't you come with me?"

I hesitate for only a moment before agreeing. She says she'll pick me up at my house and we'll share a cab to the airport.

"Thank you, Summer," I say, hoping she knows I mean it.

"No problem, kid."

After thanking the lady with the phone, I find myself out on the sidewalk again, still exhilarated, but disoriented. I start walking downtown, keeping my eyes open for a subway entrance. I find one a few blocks away, and head down into the darkness.

At the token booth, I realize I don't have a dime. I forgot I'd given all my money to Amy last night. I turn my pockets inside out searching for spare change, and even scan the dirty floor for a dropped token. Nothing.

There's no way that I can make it home on foot before Jeffrey gets there. He's got the car. I can hear a downtown train coming down the track, and in a moment of desperation, I leap the turnstile. I can hear the token guy hollering at me from his booth, and pray that no transit cops are about. This is no way for a mother to behave.

Hurling myself into the train, I sink down into a vacant seat as the doors slide shut. Safe.

*   *   *   *

Standing in my room, I look at all the stuff I've collected over the past year. There is no way I can pack this up before either Jeffrey or Summer gets here. I'm just going to have to leave most of it here. I drag my battered suitcase up from the basement and proceed to toss in the items that I can't live without. I'm glad I have my journal with me. I've also got a ton of stuff out at the beach house, but there's nothing I can do about it now. Maybe Debra will send my stuff out to me later. If all else fails I'll ask Barb from the agency. Wouldn't she be surprised to know all that my job entails? There's no mention of this in the nanny handbook -- not even in the back pages.

Well, that's about all I can cram into my suitcase. I have to sit on the lid to get the latches shut. I wish I had time to fill up another little bag as a carry-on, but Summer will be here anytime now. I set the suitcase down in the entryway, and stand for a minute, to let my mind catch up.

My biggest hope, of course, is that I am safely out of here before Jeffrey gets back. But my second wish would be to say good-bye to the kids. They are really going to feel abandoned. I love those little twerps as much as a person can love someone else's kids. I decide to run upstairs and take a last look at their rooms. It won't be the same as kissing them good-bye, but it's as close as I can come right now.

On the fourth floor I sit on Jake's bed and think of all the stories I've told him, and all the songs we've sung together. For some reason I remember the time I took him to the movies. At the concession stand he told me to ask the man not to put 'seeds' in his popcorn. I forget what the movie was, but there was a gorilla involved, which Jake referred to as the 'bad monkey.' He got so scared that we had to leave, and he had bad dreams for a couple of nights after.

The worst thing is remembering his nightly warning not to go away. The day has finally come when I would have to tell him that I'm leaving, and he's not here to tell. I hope it doesn't screw him up and make it impossible for him to trust people. I hope his next nanny is patient and understanding. It hurts to think of being replaced, but I just hope the new girl loves them half as much as I do.

I give each one of his stuffed animals and dolls a pat on the head, straighten up a few toys, and smooth the cover on his bed. I whisper good-bye as I shut the door behind me.

I'm heading down to the nursery on the third floor when I hear the door slam, and Jeffrey holler "Michelle!" up the stairs. I resist the impulse to hide in Miranda's closet. My heart begins to thump as his footsteps ascend the stairs.

A jolt of true terror grabs hold of me as I see him round the corner on the second floor. He starts to yell as he climbs.

"I'm not doing it!" I shout, surprised at the force of my voice.

"Oh yes you are," he says, his eyes threatening.

"I won't do it," I say, more quietly this time. He is almost at the top. "I've made up my mind, and there's nothing you can say to make me change it."

He sneers. "Michelle, you change your mind every five minutes. Cut the crap, and let's go back and get it over with."

"I said *no*." I am beginning to feel calm. I am stronger than I thought.

He has reached the top of the stairs, and stands facing me. His face is red, his lips twisted in barely controlled rage. "Get in the car. Now."

"Don't talk to me like that. I said I'm not doing it, and I mean it. You're not my boss anymore. I quit." I spread my hands to show that there is nothing left for him to say. I make a move toward the stairs.

"Where are you going?"

"Home," I say. "Excuse me, but I've got a plane to catch."

"What are you going to do, show up on your father's doorstep? 'Hi Pop, I'm knocked up'? That's ludicrous."

I turn to face him. "Look, I'm having this baby no matter what you say. I'm going home to Seattle, and you'll never have to deal with me again. Just pretend the baby isn't yours. That's what I intend to do."

"Pretend it's not mine?" His voice is getting higher and more frantic by the minute. "I'll have some illegitimate kid on the other side of the country, and I'm supposed to just pretend it doesn't exist?!"

"Do whatever you feel is necessary." I say, feeling the ice creep into my voice. I'm beginning to hate him.

"You can't do this!" His voice is as high as mine, and his eyes are wide with fear. I've never seen him like this, never could have imagined it. "You think you can just trot off to Seattle and have this baby? You don't have any idea what this is going to do to me! You'll *ruin* me!"

I roll my eyes.

"Don't do this Michelle! Don't do this to my family. You're killing me with this, you know that? *Killing* me. Things like this don't stay a secret. Everything will come out and my whole life will be ruined!"

He grips my shoulders so hard I know they'll be bruised tomorrow. When I see that he's crying, I find I really do hate him.

"Take your hands off me, Jeffrey. I'm leaving."

"No! Don't do this to me! Michelle, don't do this to Jake!"

My foot is poised over the edge of the top step, ready to descend the staircase. At his unfair invocation of Jake's name, I turn and send back over my shoulder these words: "You never should have fucked me."

That's when he pushes me down the stairs.

The shock comes first, before the pain. Then the liquid warmth between my legs. Ignoring the pain, I pull myself up to see. The warmth is spreading slowly outward, the crotch of my jeans a Rorschach inkblot in red.

My vision begins to cloud and blur, darkness advancing from the outside in, like the end of a cartoon. The last thing I see before it goes completely dark, is Summer standing over me.

Christa Charter

TEN

The hospital sheets are stiff and scratchy. Even with the pills they give me, I still can't sleep. I can't get comfortable for one thing. I can't roll over because of my cracked rib. Besides, the bed is so narrow, that I'd probably roll right out. I guess whoever designs these things figures that if you're sick, you may as well be uncomfortable.

What's surprising is the way Summer has reacted to all of this. Right after it happened she got me to St. Vincent's right away, and has rarely left my side since then. I've only been here a day and a half, but it feels like forever. I want to go home -- wherever that is.

Summer sits in the yellow vinyl armchair all day long. I really believe she would curl up and spend the night there if the nurses didn't kick her out. She sits next to me, silent for the most part, but sometimes she reads me the newspaper. She refills my water glass, fluffs up my pillows, she even smuggled a Big Mac in for my dinner last night. Despite her motherly ministrations, she is the same bitchy, sarcastic Summer, butting heads with the nursing staff and making snide comments about the room's two other occupants.

A huge, gaudy floral arrangement arrived this morning, which Summer immediately dumped in the trash. She is still very upset that I wouldn't let her call the police, and she is not about to let me accept a peace offering from "the bastard who did this to you."

I simply lie in the bed, staring at the television on the wall. It is the only spot of color in the white, antiseptic room. When the nurses send Summer on her way -- I don't even know where she's spending her nights since the Leibowitzes kicked her out -- they bring me "something to help you sleep" and turn out the lights. Closing my eyes, I feel the sedative working its way through my veins, attempting to pull me down into unconsciousness, but it never takes complete hold. I'm not aware of fighting it off, but something in me still feels so threatened, that I have to stay awake. The dream state is too vulnerable.

The nurses all love me here. I don't complain, and I accept their medicinal offerings with smiling thanks. When they come to check on me, I dutifully pretend to be asleep. I don't want them to think they're not doing their job.

The pain isn't very bad, as long as I keep still. And frankly I don't feel like ever moving from this spot. I know that they will be releasing me fairly soon as I am healing nicely. But I can't bear to think of rising up from this bed and leaving the safe white cocoon of the hospital. It hurts to think of stepping out into the bright, noisy world with all it's dangers and disappointments.

My ribs don't hurt half so bad as my heart. I should say the place it used to occupy. There is a vast emptiness in my chest. It's numb and cold with the wind rushing through. It's not as if my heart has been 'broken,' or 'ripped out', it feels more like it was never there at all.

I don't think about him. I don't think about much of anything. My mind is like a polished sphere of cold concrete within my skull, but I'm not a complete vegetable. I listen and talk. I make the proper responses. But the Michelle part of me is gone. Utterly wiped out. I send feelers out, searching for where she might be hiding. Maybe she's made herself very small, and is waiting until it's safe to come out. But my searching proves fruitless, and I don't have the will to try very hard.

Summer is reading to me from the Weekly World News. Something about an eight-year-old albino giving birth to Elvis reincarnated. She laughs and holds the picture up for me to see. I smile, and chuckle obligingly. Then I turn my eyes back to the I Love Lucy rerun. The sound is all the way down, but I've seen this episode more times than I can count. It's the one with the chocolates on the conveyer belt.

The door, which is always partly open, swings wide and Jeffrey walks in. Summer stands up, looking more than willing to beat the crap out of him. I keep my eyes glued to the television.

"What are you doing here, asshole? You'd better get the fuck out of here before I call the police." Summer leans over him, her fists clenched at her sides.

Jeffrey's face reddens, and he actually looks scared. "I just want to talk to Michelle."

"Get out. She doesn't want to talk to you."

"Michelle? Is that true?" His eyes are pleading.

I shrug.

"Just give me two minutes. Then I'll leave, I promise." Jeffrey asks for Summer's permission.

Summer looks at me, and I nod. She gives me a dirty look for my defection, but tells me: "I'm going to be right outside this door." She turns her back and stalks out of the room.

Jeffrey stands there for a minute before attempting to sit on the edge of my bed. The look I give him stops him cold. He compromises by standing right next to my head, his hands resting on the bed rail.

"How are you feeling?" he starts, his voice husky.

I shrug, and look up at Lucy.

"The nurse at the desk says you cracked a rib."

I pull the sheet down to let him feast his eyes on my bandages. I still won't look at him. He reaches a finger out to the wrappings, but thinks better of it.

"I...I guess we lost the baby, huh?"

I turn and glare at him.

"I'm sorry about that, sweetheart. I'm sorry it happened like that, but it's better this way, believe me."

He suddenly makes a gasping noise, trying to catch his breath, and I can hear him crying. I hate him for crying. I'm the one who should cry, but I can't do that any more than I can sleep.

"Oh, God, Michelle, I'm so sorry. I didn't mean to, I'm not a violent person. I -- something just came over me, I was so afraid. I wasn't myself."

Lucy and Desi embrace, the Mertzes clustered around them. I see Lucy's mouth say "Oh, Ricky!"

"Please Michelle, please forgive me. I'd do anything to make it up to you. Just tell me what you want." He waits for me to make a request.

I am silent, the shed skin of my former self.

"I have something for you," he says, pulling a paper out of his pocket. He holds it in front of my face, and I wince as I catch his scent. "Jake drew it for you. Everyone is very concerned, and sends you their best." He pauses, and lowers his voice. "I told them you have food poisoning." He laughs, then his voice turns serious. "Are you going to talk to me, Michelle?"

I raise my chin, and move my gaze to the ceiling.

"I guess I'll be going then. I want to give you something first, something to make up for... and not telling. Your discretion means a lot to me, you can't know how much. Anyway, I thought maybe you could go down to the islands for awhile, relax, get some sun. You'll feel much better, and then when you come back, we'll start fresh."

I open my mouth, and he leans forward to catch my words. I only yawn.

"If you decide to come back. I guess I'd understand if you didn't." He drops his head, like the bad little boy who got caught in the cookie jar. What a performance.

"Well, I have to go. Try to forget about all this, huh? I think once you've thought about it, you'll realize that I was right, and understand why I had to do what I did."

He reaches into his pocket again, pulling out a thick, business envelope which he drops on my bed. He turns, and giving a little backward wave of his hand he leaves the room. I listen to his footsteps fade away.

Summer comes back in, and I tell her everything Jeffrey said. Handing her the envelope, I watch as she counts out fifty thousand dollars.

*   *   *   *

Summer and I are among the last to board the plane. We find our seats and set about making ourselves as comfortable as possible for the six hour flight. Summer grumbles about the lack of leg room, but I feel fine. As the plane makes its way to the runway I open the newspaper that I bought in the airport. Summer offers me a stick of gum, and I chomp away happily, scanning the paper for an interesting article.

The plane picks up speed, and as we lift off the ground I cry: "Oh my God! Summer, listen to this!"

"What?" she says, leaning to read over my shoulder.

"Police are baffled by the disappearance of a toddler and his live-in caretaker. Little Riley Connolly was last seen in the company of his nanny, nineteen-year-old Susan Thomas of Butte, Montana. They were en route to Connecticut to see the boy's father, Edward Connolly, a professor of philosophy at Columbia University. The boy is the subject of a bitter custody battle between his father and his mother, Jane Harrison Connolly.

"Both parents have made accusations that the other has hidden Riley away. Mrs. Connolly has gone so far as to suggest that Mr. Connolly has sold the child to a homosexual cult in Vermont, an accusation which Mr. Connolly adamantly denies. Nevertheless, Child Protection authorities are investigating.

"The last person to see the missing pair seems to be Mr. Duane Peterson, owner-operator of the Pit Stop gas station in Rockland County. Peterson claims to have seen the little boy and his nanny at three 'o clock Friday afternoon. He says that Riley and Thomas drove up in a black 1987 Mercedes sedan, purchased twenty-one dollars worth of gasoline and a map of the United States.

"Riley Connolly was last seen wearing a red and yellow Gymboree playsuit, and Barney hi-top sneakers. He has blue eyes, blonde hair, and stands 32 inches tall. Susan Thomas is five foot three, and approximately one hundred pounds. She has dark brown hair and blue eyes. Anyone having information on the missing child or his nanny is urged to notify the Connecticut State Police."

Summer and I stare at each other.

"Holy shit," she says "She really did it."

"She must be completely mental! Does she think she can just take him back home to Butte? They're not going to stop looking for him. Sooner or later they'll hit on the idea of kidnapping."

"Kidnapping," Summer repeats. "I can't believe one of my friends is a kidnapper."

I fold the paper and drop it on the floor. "Well," I say, "They won't be able to do anything to her. She's obviously lost her mind."

"Poor Susan."

"Yeah. This city really fucked her up good." I stare out the window at the receding skyline. "This is no place for a kid."

When a flight attendant comes by with the beverage cart, Summer buys a little bottle of gin, while I order milk. I'm actually acquiring a taste for the stuff. I sip my milk slowly, watching the ground pass by beneath me. When I look over, Summer has finished her drink and is asleep.

I think about the money, and the freedom it will bring me. I can go back to school now. Joanne has rented a four-bedroom house near campus, and will be there to pick us up at the airport when we arrive.

I set down my empty cup, and lean the seat all the way back. I feel drowsy and content. Passing my hand over my belly I whisper: "Everything's all right now, baby. We'll be home soon." I've got my freedom, a future, and my baby. Having everything I want, I fall into a sweet, dreamless sleep.

EPILOGUE

I've just gotten the baby to sleep when Joanne comes into the room to tell me that my mother is here. The three of us are going out tonight, and Mom is baby-sitting. This is my first time leaving the baby since I had her two months ago.

I'm what you could call a nervous mother. It probably has a lot to do with what happened to Cameron, but I'm still driving everyone crazy. I can't go more than twenty minutes without checking on her. I creep into her room and lay my hand on her little back, feeling for the rise and fall of her breathing. In my own bed at night I turn the baby monitor up all the way so I can hear every little breath. I love it when she snores because it's easier to hear when I wake up in a panic, grabbing the monitor and holding it to my ear.

I still don't feel comfortable leaving my little Chloe -- even with her grandma, but Summer and Joanne were absolutely relentless in their campaign to go out on the town with them. I don't feel quite ready to face the outside world yet. For me the universe still revolves around Chloe. Besides, I argued that I won't be able to drink, since I am nursing, but they insisted, and I guess I owe it to them. After all, they put up with Chloe's crying at all hours, and most importantly, they were right there with me through the whole pregnancy -- telling me I was glowing when I felt like shit, making jokes about hemorrhoids, shopping for baby clothes and furniture. Summer single-handedly assembled the entire nursery. I would get up in the night for a snack, and find her sitting on the floor of what was to become the baby's room, poring over instructions, a screwdriver in one hand.

Joanne had actually gone to the extent of learning to crochet. The finished product was lopsided, and full of imperfections, but I love it more than any other gift, and Chloe seems to know that it was made by her 'auntie' Jo.

A month before my due date, the two of them had thrown the wildest, rockin'-est baby shower in recorded history. Instead of the typical shower, consisting of a room full of pastel-clad women playing silly games, it was an all-out beer blast. I, of course had to drink non-alcoholic brew, but got drunk on excitement.

And when it came to the crucial hour -- when my water broke at four AM, they were both right there with me. I stood at the door, shaking with nervousness while the two of them scrambled around for my suitcase and the car keys. In the delivery room Joanne rubbed my back and fed me ice chips while Summer stomped up and down the halls of the maternity ward looking for the anesthesiologist. When Chloe Joanna Summer West emerged into this world her two 'aunties' cried harder than I did. The nurse took a picture of us that hangs on the wall in the kitchen. I am in the bed, with Chloe bundled up in my arms, a little hat on her head. Joanne and Summer stand on either side of me, one arm around my shoulders and the other on the baby. It seems impossible, but they look as proud and exhausted as I do. In the house, we have gotten in the habit of referring to Chloe as "our baby."

I credit Summer with saving Chloe. In a way, I feel she is as responsible for Chloe's life as Jeffrey and I are. She had taken me in a taxi straight to the emergency room at St. Vincent's. In the cab she held me in her arms and remained perfectly calm while all I could do was scream "My baby!" The bleeding seemed to have stopped when we pulled up to the hospital, and I wasn't feeling any cramping, which would have indicated that a miscarriage was imminent.

The doctors gave me an injection of something to calm me down, and Summer stayed right there holding my hand while they examined me. It was touch-and-go for a while. The placenta had been slightly damaged in the fall, which caused the bleeding. Fortunately, the entire placenta had not separated and enough remained to sustain Chloe. All the tests showed that she was still alive and thriving. I hadn't known how badly I wanted her until I almost lost her.

The doctors were very kind, and didn't ask too many questions about what had precipitated my tumble down the stairs. They gave me the name of an obstetrician in Seattle before I left the hospital.

I'd planned on going to school through winter quarter, but Dr. Reddy put me on six weeks bed-rest to ensure that the placenta had time to heal. And, as it turned out, everything was all right.

I'll be starting school in the fall. Joanne, Summer and I have arranged our class schedules so that one of us can be home with the baby at all times. I don't know what I'd do without them. In fact, everything is so perfect now that I worry about one of them getting married, or else taking a job somewhere far away when they graduate.

Summer has two quarters to go to get her teaching certificate, but jobs are scarce in the Seattle area. We're afraid she may have to look in a more rural area.

Joanne plans to get her Ph.D. in Comparative Literature, and then teach at the college level. But she has a boyfriend that she seems quite serious about. I know it's selfish, but I don't want to lose either of them.

My mother comes into the room, with Summer close on her heels. I've barely said hi to Mom, before Summer is spinning around, modeling her outfit for me.

"How does this look?" she asks, tugging at the skirt of her tight, mini-dress.

"You look spectacular," I admit. "I wish I didn't feel so fat."

"Oh come on. You just had a baby, for God's sake. Cut yourself some slack. Besides, you've only got five pounds to go, right?"

"More like ten," I say. "I don't have anything comfortable that doesn't look like a big, fat, preggo outfit."

"Wear something black," she suggests. "It works wonders. Besides, it'll be less noticeable if your tits start leaking."

Joanne starts laughing. "Yeah, remember that night we took Chloe to '101 Dalmatians?' Michelle had those two wet patches the size of Texas."

"Good thing it was dark," I say.

My mom starts laughing, and I remember that she's in the room. "Why aren't you using the nursing pads I gave you?" she asks. "They'll soak up any leaks."

"I know, Mom, but they're so thick. My boobs already feel like they're somebody else's, I don't need the extra quarter inch of cotton making matters worse."

She spreads her hands in exasperation. "Well, you'll do what you want. You always have."

"Mom..."

Sensing a family squabble, Joanne and Summer make a hasty exit. Joanne to hunt up her shoes, and Summer to see if she has anything black in her voluminous closet that would fit me. I spend the next fifteen minutes showing Mom where the diapers are kept, where to find the musical ducky that Chloe likes, and showing her how to prop her up with blankets so she'll sleep on her side.

"They always told me to put babies on their tummy," she says. "So they won't choke if they spit up."

"Well, they changed it. Now they say babies sleeping on their stomachs smother in the bedclothes. They recommend putting them on their side."

"Hmm! They'll say something else in another twenty years, no doubt. They'll want you to suspend them by their heels or some such nonsense."

"Yeah, well, just put her on her side for tonight, okay Mom?" If I come home and find her on her stomach, that's the last time she's ever baby-sitting.

Summer knocks lightly at the door, and comes in with a black garment on a hanger. "Try this one," she says. "I think it'll work."

I squirm my way into it, holding my breath while Mom zips it up. I can hear Joanne and Summer downstairs, calling for me to hurry up, so I race around showing Mom where the thermometer is, and the liquid baby aspirin, and the anti-gas drops. I thrust into her hand a list of all the phone numbers where I could possibly be reached, along with the doctor's number, police, and fire department.

When Summer hollers up the staircase that she's going to drag me out by my hair, I grab my purse, give Chloe a kiss on the head, one more on the nose for good measure, and run downstairs.

We pile into Joanne's car, and head for Pioneer Square, the oldest part of Seattle. Since Joanne refuses to pay for parking under any circumstances, we have to drive up and down the streets for nearly half an hour before Summer sees someone pulling out of a spot. Joanne spends another ten minutes trying to parallel park in a space about six inches too small. She does it, though, and we head down the sidewalk to our favorite Mexican restaurant, a wild, noisy place, where the barkeeps yell "Ariba!" as they pound tequila slammers on the bar. The food is good and spicy. I love strong flavors myself, but they tend to upset Chloe's stomach. Besides, I can't imagine taco-flavored milk would be any great taste treat.

After placing our order, we all lift our margaritas -- mine virgin, of course -- to toast my first night out. We nibble on chips and discuss our plans for the evening. We don't know exactly where we'll end up yet, we thought we'd stroll along First Avenue and see what's happening where.

The dinner is great. It's absolutely liberating to be able to eat with both hands, without a squalling infant in my lap. Summer and Joanne each drink a couple more margaritas, but it's fine. If necessary I can drive us home.

I'm chatting away about taking a road trip down to California or someplace when I notice that Joanne keeps nudging Summer, as if goading her. This goes on for quite a while before I lose my temper and demand to know what's going on.

"Joanne wants me ask if you've heard anything from Jeffrey." Summer avoids my eyes. I had long ago forbidden the mention of his name.

"Is that why you guys were so hell-bent for me to come tonight? So you could cross-examine me?"

"No!" Joanne says. "We're worried, that's all."

"I'm not worried," Summer says. "I'm pissed as hell. That asshole needs to know he has a daughter. She's his responsibility too."

"No," Joanne disagrees. "That jerk doesn't deserve Chloe. She's way too good for him."

"I still think you should tell him, Mick. Wouldn't you want to know, if you were him?"

Joanne sets her glass down hard. "He wanted to kill her, Summer! When he pushed Michelle down that flight of stairs, he gave up all right to know his child."

"Wait, you guys." I say, holding up a hand for silence. "I didn't know this was such an issue with you. I mean, I know you love Chloe, and I appreciate your concern, but this is between me and Jeffrey."

Neither of them say anything. Summer picks up her fork and starts tapping a rhythm on the salty rim of her glass.

"Having said that," I continue, "Here's what's going on: I sent a birth announcement to the Goldmans about a month ago."

They both open their mouths in surprise.

"It came back. Apparently they don't live on Bank Street anymore. So, I waited another week, and then called Jeffrey at the ad agency. He didn't return my calls. By this point I was frustrated. I thought about writing him a letter, but I knew he wouldn't read it."

"So you still haven't talked to him?" Joanne says, hopefully.

"No," I admit, "but I talked to Barb at the au pair agency. I asked if she had their new address, because I wanted to send Jake a birthday present. She told me that they didn't come to her for a replacement nanny, but she's heard that they're getting a divorce."

"A divorce!" Joanne says.

"It's just a rumor," I say.

I don't admit that when I'd heard the rumor I experienced an insane glimmer of hope that we would become the family I'd once hoped for. Every time the doorbell rings I imagine he has shown up on my doorstep, ready to claim his daughter and take us away.

Of course I still think about him. The memories come back, unbidden, and I wallow in them nostalgically before remembering his shoving hands on my back. The thing that haunts me the most is the night he rode me on the back of that old bike. That night I'd wished that the earth was flat, and we'd go flying off the edge, into the unknown, together.

I wonder if I'll ever hear from him? Even after what he did, I can't stand the thought that he hates me.

I also wonder what I'll tell Chloe when she's old enough to understand that she's missing one parent. She looks like me. She's got my curly hair and my smile. She even has my dimple in her left cheek. But her eyes are Jeffrey's. Most of the time I just think of her as Chloe, my baby. But once in a while I'll look into her sweet face and see Jeffrey looking at me, accusing me. And I hear the echo of his words: "You'll ruin me."

We sit for a while longer, each of us lost in our own thoughts. The waiter brings the check, and we head back out into the night. We walk along the sidewalks, peeping into the various bars and clubs, looking for somewhere to go. We talk about Susan a little bit. She's home now, living with her grandparents in Butte.

After she took Riley, it was only a matter of days before some genius hit on the idea that maybe the nanny had kidnapped him.

They looked for her in Montana, and there they both were. When the FBI showed up, Susan had been teaching Riley how to ride a horse. She insisted that Riley was her own son, and pulled her shirt up to show them her stretch marks. Her stomach was flat and unmarked.

Jane Connolly had wanted to press charges, but when they did a psychological evaluation and found her unfit to stand trial, the Connollys had let everything drop provided that Susan be committed to a mental institution. Susan was so far gone by that time that it would have happened even if the Connollys hadn't insisted.

She spent ten months in a private facility in Bozeman, Montana. She didn't speak for the first three months, and when she finally started, all she could do was scream that someone had stolen her baby. But she wasn't a danger, so they had to release her. Her grandparents hired a private nurse to look after her. They don't know if she'll ever be normal again.

No one has heard from Amy. I tried to get hold of her at the Rail, only to be told by Bud that he'd had to fire her, not long after I was in there the last time. He had no idea where she was living.

Molly had her baby; a boy named Diarmit, and is expecting another. It seems motherhood agrees with her.

Fiona finally got out of the nanny racket. She met and married an Irish man who owns a construction business in Westchester. So far she's holding to her resolution not to have any kids.

We come to a place where there is a line stretching around the block. People have been waiting to get in for over an hour. Summer approaches a group of guys near the front of the line and asks what's happening. He tells her that it's a hot, new band that has just signed a contract with a major record label. Haven't we seen their video on MTV? Summer tells him we don't have cable. She also manages to get him to let all three of us in line ahead of them.

As we stand there, waiting for the doors to open I begin to get a tight, full feeling in my breasts. Chloe is probably hungry right now. I've left a bottle of formula for Mom to give her. I hate the stuff, but she's got to start getting used to it, since I start classes in September. I check the front of my shirt for leakage, but don't see any. I'm trying not to think of the baby at all, because sometimes that starts the milk flowing.

When the bouncer finally lets us in, there is a mad rush for the stage, though it is as yet unoccupied. Summer goes off to get a pitcher of beer, while I look for a table. Not finding one, we stand against the side wall, waiting for the show to start. I'll have a pretty good view from where I stand.

Suddenly there is a roar, and people stand on their chairs and lift their friends onto their shoulders. What I thought was a perfect spot has now become absolutely useless. I can't see a thing. When the music starts, the crowd cheers and jumps around. Apparently this is their first big hit. I've never heard it before, but it sounds pretty good. A damn sight better than the Intensers. I wish I could see them.

As the show goes on, all three of us get caught up in the music. It's really good. It's not trendy or angry, and you can actually hear and understand the lyrics, which are thoughtful with a sort of ironic humor.

"I have got to get closer," Summer complains. "I can't see a thing. Let's go up there." She points toward the stage with her glass of beer.

"It's too crowded," I say. "You'll never get through."

She doesn't hear me. She grabs Joanne by the hand, and pulls her to the front. Halfway across the room she turns and beckons to me with a crook of her arm. I stay where I am. I'm not ready for the crowd scene yet.

I can see them moving through the mass of people, and miraculously they get pretty far. Summer leaps into the air to see over the people ahead of her. When she comes back down, I see her mouth distinctly form the words 'oh, my God.' She pulls Joanne to her side, yells something in her ear and points toward the stage. Joanne begins jumping to no avail. She's a good six inches shorter than Summer.

Then they both do something strange. They turn back, and catching my eye start making frantic gestures for me to join them up front. I shake my head, but they persist, and I finally laugh and walk towards them. The place is packed. I say 'excuse me' and 'pardon me' a few thousand times before I abandon courtesy and start shoving. My breasts feel so engorged right now, that if someone bumps into the front of me, they are going to get a big, wet surprise. Maybe I can veer off to the restroom and squeeze a little of this out. Just to take some of the pressure off.

The crowd shifts and I lose sight of Joanne and Summer. I keep shoving, moving in what I think is the right direction. Suddenly I am bang up against the stage, front row, center. The noise is deafening, and all I can see are amplifiers and Levi-clad knees. This is no place for a mother.

I turn around, my back to the band, and try to find my friends. I stand on tiptoe and crane my neck, looking for any sign of them. Everyone here looks the same. I get quite a few strange looks, as I am facing the wrong way. The song comes to an end with a burst of applause. The crowd begins shouting requests.

A voice, full of feedback, announces that this will be the last song of the show. The crowd groans. I spot Joanne standing back where we were originally, and wave. She's motioning to me frantically, mouthing something I don't quite catch. I start to make my way back to her, but I'm hemmed in too tight. I can't move at all.

"This isn't one off the new album, but something for an old friend," says the microphone. First the guitar, then the drums. The crowd looks perplexed, but I'd know that intro anywhere. Turning slowly, afraid of disappointment, I face the stage and look up.

"Michelle, my belle. These are words that go together well, my Michelle." he sings. He leans down and sings it right into my face, and it seems I've got tunnel vision. The crowd, the noise, the rest of the band filter out into the blackness and there is just Nicky and I in the whole world.

Somehow, I guess, the song ends and people disperse. The band begins packing up their equipment. Nicky stretches out a hand and pulls me up onto stage.

"Hi," he says smoothly.

"Hi." Not smooth at all.

"Long time no --"

"I have a kid," I blurt.

Surprise rises in his eyes, and then is blinked away. "Good," he says, smiling invitingly, "I like kids."

"Good."

ABOUT THE AUTHOR

Christa Charter grew up in Bellevue, Washington and has dropped out of more colleges than she cares to recall. She has been a nanny, apprentice film editor, receptionist, preschool teacher, magazine editor, copywriter, technical writer, website editor, community manager, and public relations account supervisor. She is perhaps best known as "trixie360" from Xbox LIVE. She now owns a community and social media company called Trixieland Consulting. She has three clever children, one sexy Marine husband, and lives in Redmond, Washington.

10527378R00118

Made in the USA
Charleston, SC
11 December 2011